DEATH OF A UNICORN

I put the box on the Embankment wall, opened the lid and took out a handful of pieces, but before I could throw them someone gripped my wrist and forced it back over the jigsaw.

It was a man, not one of the pair I'd talked to in B's flat but another of the same sort, only younger. He let me spill the pieces back in the box and took it from me . . .

'Please,' I said.

He handed it back to me and watched while I took the pieces and threw them in handfuls on to the river. They seemed to vanish as they touched the surface. The water was their colour, dark green or cardboard. The few white bits of unicorn might have been flecks of foam.

DEATH OF A
UNICORN

Peter Dickinson

Hamlyn Paperbacks

A Hamlyn Paperback

Published by Arrow Books Limited
17-21 Conway Street, London W1P 6JD

A division of the Hutchinson Publishing Group

London Melbourne Sydney Auckland
Johannesburg and agencies throughout
the world

First published in Great Britain
by The Bodley Head 1984
Hamlyn Paperbacks edition 1985

Printed and bound in Great Britain by
Anchor Brendon Limited, Tiptree, Essex

ISBN 0 09 939240 2

My dear Fiona,

I do not yet know whether I shall leave this manuscript for
you to find, or whether it will be you I shall leave it for. We
are a long-lived family, and a lot may yet happen in both
our lives. But assuming I do, and it is you, I think you may
find it easier to understand if I tell you how it came into
existence.

It was written in two stages, the first almost thirty years
before the second. In the summer of 1953 I had an absolute
need to get the events of the previous ten months out of my
system so that I could start creating some sort of a life for
myself again. So I wrote the first part of this manuscript, put
it in the bottom of a drawer, and let other unwanted papers
accumulate on top of it.

Last year, partly as a result of your coming to stay at
Cheadle, I found I needed to reconsider the details of those ten
months, so I got the old manuscript out and read it through. It
struck me, doing so, that I might show it to you to help you in
the decision I was hoping you would make, but then, as more
old history came to light, I discovered something which
meant that it would be extremely unfair on my part to use it
in an attempt to influence you. You will see why when you
read it.

What I discovered was a considerable shock, though very
different from the simple, primitive event I believed I was
coping with in 1953. Besides, I had been a simple, primitive
person then, and am no longer. But it still seemed necessary
to use the same old simple magic. Write it out. Put it in a
drawer. Bury it. Only this time for you (perhaps) to find.

I have been unable to refrain from adding a few modern
footnotes to the older part of the manuscript, for instance

5

where the gulf of time struck me most forcibly. I would not dare do this in my other books, for fear of irritating my readers, but here I have no one to please but myself.

And you. I mean this. I take great pleasure in pleasing you, so if you do read it, read it for pleasure, my dear.

Your loving aunt,
M M

PART ONE
1952–1953

I

It began with a yawn.

I knew Mummy could see me, though she was pretending to listen to Lady Fosse, so I made a meal of it. I raised my hand, white-gloved to the elbow, just far enough for the tip of my middle finger to reach my mouth and yawned like a waking cat.

'Bored already?' said a man's voice beside me.

I was standing at the bottom of the stairs in Fenella's uncle's house, waiting for Jane and Penny to emerge from the cloak-room. Penny was wearing an off-the-shoulder dress which had been made for me two years ago, when I'd had a lot of puppy-fat. It was supposed to have been altered by one of Mummy's little women, but as Penny had been taking off her coat it had suddenly become obvious that the alterations hadn't been drastic enough. Mummy had given Jane the sacred ring of safety-pins she always took to dances and told her to do something, and we would wait for them at the bottom of the stairs. So the rest of our party had to wait too. Other people I knew and half-knew—Dickies and Susans and Cordelias and Lizzies and Pauls and Tommies and Henriettas —trudged past us up the stairs and I exchanged wide-eyed glances with the girls and little smiles with the men. Signals. We be of one blood, thou and I. Our party was a bit of an obstruction, especially after Mummy had trapped Lady Fosse in order to give herself a reason for hanging around there. She was watching me because she knew I was in a bolshie mood. She'd always been good at that, totally unsympathetic but totally aware. Would I ever, I wondered, be able to look at her without a rubbery little knot suddenly tightening in my stomach?* As a king of counter-magic I produced the yawn, and the voice, summoned by my spell, spoke at my elbow. I turned.

---

* Even now, after almost thirty years, not always.

9

It was a frog prince. No, not really. In fact it was obviously somebody's father, a hideous little man, shorter than I was but broad-shouldered. Glossy brown skin, too smooth to be the remains of a ski-tan. Almost bald. A bit pop-eyed. A wide mouth like a toad's.

'Not as bored as I'm going to be,' I said.

The pop eyes looked me over. There was something chilly about him, like the cold patch on the landing which you're supposed to find in haunted houses, though I've never felt one at Cheadle. His inspection paused at my necklace and I could see he knew what it was—the real one stayed in the bank practically all the time because of the insurance. He made me feel as though I was one of those jeweller's trays on which the famous sapphires were displayed for him to inspect.

'If you had stayed at home,' he said, 'you would be doing an old jigsaw with three pieces missing.'

His voice was quiet, almost a whisper, but grainy.

'In fact I would be at my desk rewriting the third chapter of my novel,' I said.

He gave a minute nod, recognising what I was in the same way that he'd recognised what the sapphires were—the literary one of the family who'd started to try and live up to her idea of herself and was finding that the knack of writing amusing letters to aunts wasn't going to be enough.

'I'll go and buy a jigsaw tomorrow,' I said. 'I suppose you'd like me to do *The Hay-Wain*.'

The cold patch vanished. He smiled. It was like that trick where the conjuror makes dozens of gaudy umbrellas explode out of a small black box. Charm, interest, excitement, danger flooded out of him. It was difficult to understand that nobody else in the crowd had noticed the shock of change—except, perhaps, Mummy.

'Mabs!' she called. 'Do go and see why those girls are being such a time!'

I shrugged to the man, making the sapphires crawl slightly on my skin. He raised a small brown hand, letting me go. He still looked really amused, as though he understood exactly what was going on, even that Mummy was now punishing me for the yawn. She could just as easily have sent Selina, who wasn't talking to anyone, and she must have known

10

what would happen if I tried to help Jane fix Penny's dress.

It happened. I'd told myself as usual that if Jane exploded I wasn't going to react, but as usual it didn't work. Pink-cheeked, blotchy, wide-nostrilled, we hissed at each other across Penny's bare shoulders while other girls, and mothers or chaperones, went in and out and pretended not to be interested. Penny burst into tears. In the end Jane said, 'Well, it's your bloody dress, you fix it!' and threw the pins on the floor. She'd undone the ring and I had to scrabble about for them. It turned out she'd practically finished so I put a couple more pins in, told Penny to keep breathing in and re-did her face for her. She wasn't grateful. She and Selina always take Jane's side. It's only natural.

Jane was born twenty minutes after me. Identical twins. When we were small we were dressed alike and had our hair done alike and were treated almost as though we were a single person who happened to be living in two bodies. Selina came two years later and Penny a year after that. Then there was a gap. I don't imagine my parents really expected to have another child, but there was always the faint chance a boy would be born until my father was killed on the beach at Dunkirk. At that point it became certain that I was going to inherit Cheadle, and Mummy changed the rules. I became the elder sister and the other three were younger. They wore my old frocks and dresses. Later I did everything a year before Jane was allowed to—put on nail varnish, had my hair permed, went to finishing school, drank gin, came out and so on. Mummy was bringing out Selina and Penny in the same season, despite their being a year apart, to save money. But there'd been no question of that with me and Jane. She'd actually used Jane's clothing coupons to get me grown-up clothes. It was totally unfair, and I sometimes said so, or tried to, but I knew it wasn't any good. Besides, I liked being treated, outwardly at least, as a grown-up. So I ate my cake and had it still.

It was different for Jane. Once, my first season, Jane had to come up to London suddenly to see a dentist. Most of the house in Charles Street was still let and we had to share a bed. There is something about touching, about closeness. We lay awake and talked and cried and made promises and blamed

11

Mummy and I suppose it was some use. But still Mummy knew she only had to lift a finger to set us clawing away at the scar-tissue of the wound where she ripped us apart, and from time to time she made it happen on purpose. Not because she enjoyed it, oh no. It was her duty to keep reminding me that I was not like anyone else, especially not like Jane, though nobody outside the family could tell us apart. Jane was not going to inherit Cheadle.

When I'd tidied up Penny I looked at myself in the glass. I was still piggy with the after-effects of rage. The Millett family face is like that. Penny and Selina took after Mummy, but Jane and I had round plump faces and noses so snub that the nostrils face forwards. That makes us sound repellent, but actually we've got good complexions, big mouths, long-lashed brown eyes, and can look really fetching when we're not in a foul temper. I can just remember my great-great-uncle in his wheelchair, glaring at me because I wasn't a boy. He looked like a rabid little hog. I wasn't going back with that look still on my face, so I told Penny to tell them to go on up while I finished collecting the pins. Next time I looked it wasn't too bad, though I was still in a filthy mood. The necklace had fallen skewy and as I was putting it straight I had an impulse to hide it and tell Mummy I'd flushed it down the loo. Although it was only the replica it was still worth several hundred pounds.

I didn't, of course. Actually I was extremely fond of the necklace, though it meant choosing half my dresses to go with the sapphires and not with my eyes. Daddy left it to me direct, and not as part of the Trust. Mummy was furious because it meant we had to pay death duties on it. She brought this up whenever there was a money crisis. But I hadn't got much of my own to remember Daddy by, and besides, it was useful for things like keeping the conversation going with dismal partners, showing them the stone that had belonged to Mary Queen of Scots, and so on. But at the same time, in Mummy's eyes, it was a sort of price label. For sale, with wearer. Condition of sale, that the purchaser undertake to maintain Cheadle Abbey and estates in good order for a period of one generation.

*

Around midnight I was hiding from Mark Babington and trying to get squiffy. Hiding wasn't too difficult because Fenella was having her dance on the cheap and her uncle's house, just north of Hyde Park, wasn't really big enough for the crush they'd invited. Girls who were actually longing for their next partner to find them weren't having much luck. But for the same reason getting squiffy was difficult—the caterers only released fresh supplies of champagne every half-hour and you couldn't always get to where the bottles were in time for a first glass, even. Mark had insisted on checking my card to see that I'd got his dances down right, so he must have known I wasn't keen, but that didn't put him off. He was used to having his own way. He told people that he was going to make a lot of money before he was forty and then go into politics. He was the reason why Mummy had made me wear the necklace that night.

By now he had me cornered. I was in a sort of enlarged alcove off one of the sitting-out areas. Round a pillar I saw him push through a gang of that year's debs and speak to Selina. She pointed her fan towards my alcove. It was between dances, and a rumour was on that another ration of champagne was being got ready, so there were a lot of people milling to and fro between us. I was screwing myself up for a row—I could feel the blotchy look beginning to come—when I noticed a crystal door handle on one of the painted panels of the alcove. Probably locked. Probably only a cupboard anyway.

It was a magic door, a black slot for me to vanish through. Beyond it I found a dark passage leading back to the top of the stairs, but roped off that end to keep people out. I was already slipping off that way, intending to go and hide in the cloakroom for a bit—the utter last resort, really—when from behind me I heard a cork pop. Aha, I thought, they're opening the next half-dozen botts. I'll get some at source and then I can refuse to dance with Mark till I've finished it, in case someone pinches it. Saved!

A small, dark-panelled room, with bookcases. Fenella's uncle's study. Men playing bridge. The one facing me frowned as I came through the door, and the one who'd had his back to me at a side table turned and walked over, holding a bottle with froth bulging from the mouth. He was the one who'd spoken to me at the foot of the stairs.

'Dotards only, I'm afraid, Lady Margaret,' he said.

'Oh, please,' I said. 'Can I hide for a couple of minutes? And may I have a drink?'

Instantly—he didn't seem to think about it—he went to the door and closed a little brass catch above the handle, then came back and filled my glass. It was far nicer champagne than they'd been giving us outside.

'Thank you so much,' I said. 'Do go back to your bridge. I won't stay more than five minutes and I won't tell anyone else.'

He produced his terrific smile, on purpose, for my benefit.

'My partner is in six diamonds in a lay-down two-way squeeze,' he said. 'He will take an absurd time to think it out and then get it wrong. I prefer not to watch.'

'I don't play,' I said. 'Ought I to learn?'

'Have yourself taught by a professional. Or don't start. How do you occupy the daylight hours, Lady Margaret? Work on your novel?'

I thought he wanted me to be impressed by his knowing my name, but it wasn't difficult, once he'd recognised the sapphires.

'I sell lampshades.'

'For Mrs Darling in Beauchamp Place?'

'They should have made her into lampshades herself.'

He raised his eyebrows a millimetre. I thought I was getting used to him. He liked to seem to know everything, my name, the sort of shop someone like me might have a job in, and so on. And he liked to make the smallest possible gestures and still get his meaning across. It was a way of showing how powerful he was, inside. The eyebrow-raising meant that I'd got something wrong, though nobody who'd worked for Mrs Darling for five minutes could possibly have a good word to say for her. But before I could ask I heard a click and squeak from the door, then a distinct thud, then Mark's voice calling my name.

'Obstinate?' said the man.

'Pretty.'

He smiled a different smile, thinning his lips so that I half

14

expected a toad-tongue to flicker across them. He pointed to a place where a bookcase jutted from the inner wall. I slid over and tucked myself out of sight. Just like playing sardines at Cheadle. It struck me that I'd been hiding from Mark— versions of Mark—practically since I could walk, behind nursery curtains, in empty servants' rooms along the bare top corridors, in cellars and stable lofts, and now at London dances.

I heard the bolt click and the hinges whimper, and shut my eyes to strain for the voices. Mark's, angry, my name in a question. Man's flat murmur. Mark angrier still . . .

'Two down,' called a man at the table. Automatically I opened my eyes to look. One player was turned towards the door, shuffling a pack, looking smugly amused. His partner was dealing. My man's partner was leaning back in his chair, trying to frown his way through the mis-played hand. Above their heads, between the two windows, rose a narrow pier- glass, black-blotched with age but still with enough good patches for me to be able to see Mark standing in the doorway. He looked straight into my eyes above the man's bald scalp. Anger and the contrast with the black and white of his clothes made his large face seem bright scarlet. He spoke to the man, who turned, nodded to my reflection in the glass and turned back to Mark. As far as I could hear he used the same tone as before, only four or five words. Mark's face changed. He took a half-pace back, as though the man had shoved him in the chest. The man shut the door but didn't bother to close the bolt.

'Two down, Brierley,' called the bridge player again.

'One moment,' he said.

I discovered I was quivering. A mixture of excitement and fright. Nothing much had happened. At any large dance there must be at least a dozen sticky moments like that when some girl is trying to get away from a man, but I felt as though I'd got sucked into something much more important. Mr Brier- ley topped up my glass without my asking. The cold patch effect was very strong. I thought he was going to tick me off for getting him caught out lying to Mark.

'You're a writer,' he said.

'Not really. Only beginning.'

15

'You can explain that your friend interrupted me in the middle of offering you a job on my magazine.'

'Did . . . Did I accept?'

'Tomorrow afternoon, three o'clock, 83 Shoe Lane, *Night and Day* office. Ask for Mr Todd. You must make your own arrangements with Mrs Darling.'

'Jane will stand in for me. Mrs D can't tell us apart.'

'Stay here as long as you wish. Don't drink any more.'

He went back to the table, looked through his hand and when his turn came called without sorting it. It wasn't even his house—Fenella's uncle was the one with his back to the door. But here he was, telling another guest what she could and couldn't do in it. Not just because I was young, either. He would have said the same to anyone, though he wasn't even somebody's father, just here because he wanted to be, to play bridge. It was typical.*

---

* Really? I wrote that nearly thirty years ago, but even then I was looking back on an earlier self. Did I really perceive in those first few minutes what kind of person B might be? Me, twenty, far too self-absorbed to be perceptive or objective about anyone, myself included? Wasn't I, as I wrote, already reading back later knowledge? I cannot now tell, though I agree that B's behaviour had been typical, from his casual kindness to pretty girls, or to men who took his interest for other reasons, to his flabbergasting public rudeness to people who'd done even less than poor Mark to offend him. I saw that sort of thing happen again and again during the ten months I was his mistress.

II

'Saw little Penny Millett looking sweet,' I wrote, 'and big sister Mabs (knew it wasn't Jane because she was sporting the saphires) looking too too bored, poor darling.'

I hit the typewriter as hard as I could, furious and disgusted. The machine looked and felt like a spare part for a mechanical elephant. Later I used to think that I should have had it shot and hung it up somewhere as a trophy, so that I could tell people how it changed my life. The dusty, drab-yellow room smelt of nerves and unemptied ashtrays. The hem of my stupid pencil skirt caught my calves when I tucked my legs back under my chair, the way I used to, so I'd hoicked it up round my thighs and the hell with creases. I re-read what I'd written, sick with disappointment. The machine was slower than my fingers and kept typing letters on top of each other. It had only put one 'p' in 'sapphires', for instance. I rolled the carriage back to type it in and then thought, 'Why not? I don't want this job anyway.' I left the word as it was and instead I exed out 'sweet' and wrote 'delish'. A picture of Veronica Bracken came into my mind, incredibly pretty, incredibly stupid. I pulled the paper out and rewrote the paragraph about Fenella's dance in pure, illiterate debutese. The words seemed to flow straight out through my fingers without my thinking about them at all.

I tugged my skirt down and minced along with maddening nine-inch steps to Mr Todd's office. He was on the telephone and something the person at the other end had said had caused him to explode into a harsh, bellowing laugh. He took the sheet of paper from me and read it, still apparently listening to the telephone.

'The spelling mistakes are intentional,' I hissed.

He nodded and went on reading and/or listening. A big man with the look of a horse which guesses it's on its way to the knackers. Bloodshot brown eyes, skin loose over coarse bones, like a sofa whose stuffing has come adrift, huge

17

quivering hands, cigarette smouldering between yellow fingers. Office a clutter, roll-top desk, shabby leather armchairs, newspapers on floor, originals of cartoons on walls.

'Fine,' he said, interrupting the quack of the telephone. 'Get it on paper and bung it in, old boy. No, on spec, I'm afraid. I've got a new proprietor and I haven't broken him in yet. No, don't talk about it any more or it will die on you. Got a meeting now, but let's have lunch—where the hell's my diary? Bugger. You'll have to ring Miss Walsh and fix a date. It'll be good to see you.'

He put the telephone down and shook his head.

'Poor sod,' he said. 'Never be any use again.'

He picked up another telephone.

'Nellie? Fellow called Gerald Astley will ring and say I told him to fix a lunch. Fend him . . . Did I? Oh God, how awful! All right, I'll see it through this time. Somewhere not too pricey. Oh, he'll ring all right. Geralds never get the message.'

He put the telephone down, looked me in the eye and brought out that ghastly laugh. Then he tilted his chair back and re-read what I'd written, dragging at his cigarette. I felt shy and nervous. Although I'd written it to show him what I thought of the job he seemed to be going to offer me, I felt it had come out really funny. I wanted him to like it, after all. Considering how he'd dealt with the man on the telephone he seemed to be taking a surprising amount of time. Perhaps, I realised, what he was really doing was thinking of a way of getting rid of me without offending Mr Brierley. Rather slowly he heaved himself to his feet and stood, still looking down at the paper.

'All right,' he said. 'Let's see how far her ladyship's jaw drops.'

He rushed past me with a shambling Groucho stride. I hobbled behind and found him out in the corridor holding a swing door open. There was more corridor beyond, but quite different. The change was almost as sudden as the one when you went through the little door in the corner of the Banqueting Hall at Cheadle and found yourself in Wheatstone's pantry. Mr Todd's side of the swing doors had a battered, clubby, male feeling. Here there was a receptionist's desk, unoccupied except for a bowl of tulips. White telephone. Photograph of Queen Mary, signed. Lime-green carpet. My stupid skirt and high heels belonged this side, in a way they didn't on the other. Mr Todd knocked at a door with a painted porcelain handle and fingerplate, put his head into the room, said something, then held the door for me.

The same, only more so. Smell of pot-pourri, pale pink walls, thick cream carpet, silk lampshades, little gilt chairs covered in ivory watered satin, painted escritoire—you couldn't call it a desk, that would be rude—and commode. Signed photographs on every ledge and shelf. A woman rose from the escritoire and came forward to greet me. I had seen her hundreds of times, at dances and weddings and Henleys and Fourths of Junes and Ascots, but I'd never known who she was. Small and plump but ultra-stately, blue rinse, flat face heavily powdered.

'Lady Margaret,' she said, holding out her hand. 'How well I remember your parents' wedding. Such a happy occasion. How is your dear mother?'

'Firing on all cylinders,' I said. 'I had a colossal row about coming here at all.'

I don't know why I said that. It wasn't true, because actually I hadn't risked telling Mummy, though there really would have been a row if I had—I'll explain about that in a moment. Anyway, the woman looked blank and glanced at Mr Todd in a manner that told me no one had asked her whether she needed a new assistant.

'Something I want to show you,' said Mr Todd and passed her my paragraph.

She took the eye-glasses that hung on a silk cord round her neck and held them to her face. Her eyebrows went up almost an inch. She only read a couple of lines before letting the glasses fall and staring at Mr Todd.

'Oh, no,' she murmured. 'Quite impossible.'

'Nice and lively, I thought,' said Mr Todd.

She turned her stare on me, stony-blue.

'If you wouldn't mind, Lady Margaret.'

'I did a grown-up version too.'

'I like this,' said Mr Todd. 'It's a fresh note.'

He didn't sound at all sure of himself.

19

'If you don't mind, Lady Margaret,' said the woman again.

It was like being back in the nursery when Nanny and Mummy were setting up for a battle. I went scarlet and hobbled out. Mr Todd closed the door behind me. All my misery and fury came back. I leaned against the receptionist's desk and tried to will them away, but I was now quite certain I knew what was happening. Until this morning I'd hardly thought about *Night and Day*. It was just another magazine, slightly more exciting than some of them because Mummy wouldn't have it in the house. The reason she gave was that some of the cartoons were 'unsuitable' (there was usually at least one of an artist saying something to a naked model and another of a blonde saying something to an old gentleman she was in bed with), but really it was because she hated the 'Social Round' pages, which were written by somebody called Cynthia Darke. She disliked all that sort of thing, I think because she thought that what they were about was extremely important but private, and it was obscene to have it all written down for dentists' wives in Wimbledon to read. But though she disapproved of 'Jennifer' and the others she had an especial hatred for Cynthia Darke. Presumably the woman I'd just met *was* Cynthia Darke, which made what she'd said about my parents' wedding and my dear mother a bit ironic.

Anyway, when I read the magazine in the hairdresser's —naturally grabbing it first because it was banned at home —I used to glance at the grisly 'Social Round' to see if any of my friends were in it, then look at the cartoons, then read the theatre and book reviews, and then if there wasn't any other magazine handy try some of the articles and poems. I was so used to it that it had never struck me as at all odd that a magazine that was mainly like *Punch* or *Lilliput* should contain a section on what the debby-and-horsey world was up to. Now I was actually in the place and had seen and smelt the difference between the two sides of the swing door I realised that I was dealing with two almost separate kingdoms. Mr Brierley had talked about 'my magazine' and I'd heard Mr Todd saying that he'd got a new proprietor. Naturally he wasn't happy about having some chance-met girl foisted on him so he'd decided to shunt her over the border into the other kingdom. He was only pretending to like what I'd written so that he could put all the blame on Cynthia Darke for turning me down. And equally naturally Cynthia Darke wasn't going to let it happen like that. Well, if they didn't want me, I didn't want them. I pushed through the swing doors and along the corridor to the landing, where I pressed the button for the lift.

It was an age coming. In any other skirt I could have gone clattering ostentatiously down the stairs. I waited and waited, working myself into a frenzy that Mr Todd would come out and find me there. From down the stairs a tenor voice began to sing one of those Irish ballads about a prisoner turning his last gaze on the green hills of Erin before the English did something unspeakable to him. The voice enjoyed itself, enjoyed the echoing stairwell which made it sound as though it was filtering up from some dungeon deep under Shoe Lane. Another voice interrupted and the singing ended in a laugh. Footsteps tapped on the polished wooden treads. Not wanting to be caught so obviously running away from my defeat (that's what I felt, though I don't see how the men could have known) I moved away from the lift and pulled myself together a bit. When they came in sight I realised that they'd only just finished luncheon, though it was nearly four o'clock.

One was about forty, scruffily shaved, balding, stooped. Thick spectacles. Hairy tweeds. The other was a few years younger and very dapper. Pale brown suit and yellow waistcoat. Small hooky nose, cheeks flushed and pudgy, dark eyes. As they reached the top of the stairs he laid his hand on his friend's arm to draw attention to me.

'Good afternoon,' he said.

I muttered back.

'Are you here for a purpose, other than the enhancement of the scenery? A sufficient purpose in itself, mark you.'

He swayed, deliberately I thought, to show he was a bit tight and so to be excused.

'I came for an interview,' I said.

'Shorthand and typing too!'

'No shorthand. Two fingers. And I can spell "accommodation".'

21

'Do they know you're here?' said the other man. He gave the last word a funny hooting emphasis, as though the problem was that they thought I was somewhere else.

'I've been sent to wait in the corridor while Nanny has an argument with the master,' I said.

The younger man laughed vaguely. The other man moved aside so that he could peer through the open door of Mr Todd's room. He frowned.

'I'm Tom Duggan,' said the younger man. 'And Ronnie Smith here.'

'I'm Margaret Millett.'

'And your genius is about to burst upon the world through our poor pages?'

'I came to see Mr Todd about giving me a job.'

'Did you, indeed? Come and inspect the conditions of work, Miss Millett.'

He pushed at the door beside Mr Todd's and held it for me. A large, cream-coloured room with a long-used look to all its furniture. Three roll-top desks, bookshelves along the side walls and a set of high, broad tables running the full length of the inner wall. Above the tables was a long baize-covered board with a row of pages pinned to it, some blank, some roughly scribbled on, and some with type and cartoons pasted to them.

'Sit you down,' said Mr Duggan, 'and explain how Jack got hold of you. Can there be a crack beginning in the great monolith of his uxoriousness?'

The chairs were the same large, leather-covered sort as in Mr Todd's office but even more worn and sat into shape. I couldn't risk getting that low in my skirt so I perched on a creaking arm.

'Somebody called Brierley arranged it,' I said.

'Oh, God!' said Mr Smith.

He'd been fumbling with a packet of Craven A, apparently screwing himself up to offer me one. But now he swung away and retreated to a window where he lit his cigarette and stood staring at the building opposite.

'Somebody called Brierley?' said Mr Duggan. 'There is an unlikely innocence to the phrase.'

He sounded much soberer.

'It's the thin end of the wedge,' said Mr Smith, without turning round.

'I don't really know him,' I said. 'I met him at a dance.'

'Oh, God!' shouted Mr Smith. He glared at me and strode out.

'I'm terribly sorry,' I said.

Mr Duggan studied me.

'Your friend Brierley bought the magazine last week,' he said. 'No doubt he has plans for it, but we have not been told. Naturally we are somewhat on edge. Your arrival upon such credentials appears a dubious omen.'

'Don't worry. The idea seems to have been for me to help with "The Social Round". Only Mrs Darke, or is she Miss Darke . . .'

'Mrs Dorothy Clarke. Yes?'

'She doesn't seem too keen. Mr Todd asked me to write a specimen paragraph and I did a silly little bit which he said was all right but when he showed it to her . . .'

'Ronnie!' shouted Mr Duggan 'Ronnie, come and listen!'

He smiled at me, less sober again, but friendlier.

'A very English phenomenon,' he said. 'The radical ego and the conservative id. Long ago at some Bolshevik panchayet Ronnie saw an American delegate smearing treacle over his bacon and eggs. Get Ronnie on to some theme such as the capitalist conspiracy and the world-wide tentacles of the Wall Street octopus and you will hear him utter phrases winged with red lightning and impetuous rage. Ronnie! Come back! Just remember that he's thinking of the treacle. He does not appreciate any change in the superficial order of things. He is naturally deeply suspicious of a new proprietor whose first act is to attempt to introduce on to the staff a pretty girl he met at a dance.'

'I told you he needn't worry. Mr Todd tried to fob me off on Mrs Clarke and Mrs Clarke is putting her foot down. It doesn't look as if I'm going to pollute your lives either way.'

Mr Smith had come back while I was speaking and stood glowering inside the door. Neither of them seemed to notice the bitchiness of my tone. Mr Duggan explained what I'd said. Mr Smith blew out a contemptuous smoke cloud.

'Of course Brierley has told Jack what he wanted,' he said.

'Jack wouldn't take Dorothy on without his backing. She lost her majority on the board when Colonel Stackhouse's executors sold out, but she's still got thirty-eight per cent. No. Jack's persuaded Brierley that the first thing is to do something about the Round. Interesting.'

He sounded thoroughly excited. His eyes glistened behind his thick lenses and his breathy hoot of emphasis—usually on improbable syllables—had become much more marked.

'I only met him late last night,' I said.

Mr Duggan laughed.

'And were at once swept up into portentous events,' he said. 'The end of an era, to coin a phrase.'

'Did Mrs Clarke own *Night and Day*?' I said.

'She had an effective veto,' said Mr Smith. 'The paper was founded in 1936 by a gang of literary adventurers with the idea of imitating *The New Yorker* and doing *Punch* down, but it ran on to the rocks after six months. There was a libel case and other difficulties. It was then rescued by one Cyrus Clarke, a paper manufacturer with some publishing interests, in particular a society magazine called *The Social Round*, which was edited by his wife. Neither paper prospered, and shortly before the war he amalgamated them.'

'Most of the staff left in protest,' said Mr Duggan. 'That was when Jack Todd came in.'

'The point is that on Clarke's death Mrs Clarke inherited his shareholding, and with the backing of another major shareholder was able to insist on total independence. That chap died a few months ago. Next thing we hear, only last week, is that a totally unknown financier has acquired a majority shareholding. A. J. Brierley, Esquire.'

'It makes it difficult to concentrate on the nuances of humour for next week's issue,' said Mr Duggan. 'But if it means something's going to be done about the Round . . .'

'Is he really a mystery man?' I said. 'He sounds like one when you talk to him, but I've always assumed that people who talk like that are really utterly boring when you get to know them.'

'He is a man of some mystery, but not total,' said Mr Smith. 'Naturally we have asked around. He appears to have been on the Control Commission in Germany. Two years ago he acquired a number of small companies specialising in the by-products of the sugar-refining industry, reorganised them into a group and sold them at a considerable profit. He is unmarried, but . . .'

He was interrupted by a bellow from along the corridor, only slightly muffled by the swing doors.

'The laceration of laughter at what ceases to amuse,' said Mr Duggan.

He waited for the sound of footsteps and then called, 'In here, Jack, if you're looking for Miss Millett.'

Mr Todd came shambling in, holding my paragraph at arm's length in front of him, like a reprieve from the scaffold.

'Get that set, Tom,' he said. 'Type as for Round, but a couple of ems less. I want it in a box, fancy rules, so readers learn to pick it out. Give it a lead in, make it clear it's not by Cynthia Darke but is part of the Round. Right? And the girl's got to have a name. Be with you in a second, Lady Margaret.'

He flapped out.

'Stand-off,' murmured Mr Duggan.

'More like partial victory,' said Mr Smith. 'Jack has surprising resources of will. This is decidedly interesting.'

Mr Duggan had started to read my paragraph. He looked up and glanced at me.

'Decidedly,' he said.

He went on reading. My heart was thudding absurdly. Whatever had happened between Mr Todd and Mrs Clarke, I realised that he hadn't been only pretending to like what I'd written. Readers were going to learn to pick it out. That meant next week, and the week after . . . I felt I was living through one of the most crucial moments in my life. * It seemed desperately important that Mr Duggan should like it too, but he gave no sign. When he'd finished he looked up.

---

* I have just looked the paragraph up. There is nothing to it at all. Mysterious business. Once it must have been impregnated with the odour of its time, now clean gone. This is always the case. Writing my own books about the Edwardian period I have to mark each page with some pungent signal—a brand name, song, form of speech, public person or event in the news—in an attempt to bring the odour of period to life. Cheating, of course. Few people living in a period notice such things. Their real sense of their time is as unrecapturable as the momentary pose of a child.

'Did I hear right, what Jack called you?'

'I'm afraid so.'

He nodded, apparently unimpressed, which was good, then picked up a pencil and made a couple of small marks on what I'd written.

'She'd know there was a "c" in "luscious" wouldn't she?' he said. 'She'd try and get it in somewhere.'

'Oh, yes, I suppose so.'

'What about a name?'

'She's based on a girl called Veronica.'

'Libel. Ronnie, name for an illiterate young socialite. -ite, not -ist.'

'Petronella.'

'All right,' I said.

'You sound doubtful.'

'I expect I'll get used to it.'

'We go to press Monday, so you've time to change your mind unless Bruce decides to order special type for the heading.'

'What do you think? I mean, is it all right? Mr Todd seemed to like it.'

'Jack's got to keep his job,' said Mr Smith.

I didn't mind. He hadn't read it. Mr Duggan had gone back to writing on the sheet of paper. He folded it carefully and put it in a brown manilla envelope, which he weighed in his hand.

'I'll pass an opinion when you've done six of them,' he said, and tossed the envelope into a wire tray on the roll-top.

III

It was a real job. I adored it from the very beginning.

This wasn't only because it was new and interesting, though it was. But I'd had my row with Mummy, worse than I could have imagined, about taking it on, and for the first time ever I'd won. So it seemed like the beginning of freedom.

She hadn't minded me working for Mrs Darling, because that wasn't a real job; it certainly didn't pay enough for me to be able to afford to live anywhere except at Charles Street. If anyone thinks it peculiar that the heir to a vast house and estate in Leicestershire, and another house in Mayfair, should have needed to think about things like that, all I can say is that Cheadle ate almost everything*, and the rest was taken up with what Mummy thought important, such as bringing my sisters out. I had an allowance from the Trust till I was twenty-five, when I was due to inherit, but the Trustees were completely under Mummy's thumb. She could stop it whenever she wanted. In fact she threatened to when I said I was going to *Night and Day* until I explained that Mr Todd was going to pay me as much as my allowance and Mrs Darling put together. I could actually have afforded (just) to rent a tatty little room in Pimlico or somewhere and move out of Charles Street altogether. I could have got away.

Of course Mummy's argument was that the job was 'completely impossible' because of the cartoons of naked models and blondes in bed and so on, but in a funny way she made me feel as though the real reason was that she had magically known all along that this was going to happen, and that was why she'd banned the magazine—like Sleeping Beauty's

---

* This is still the case, and always has been. When Bartrand Millett built Cheadle in 1712 he effectively bankrupted all his heirs, in perpetuity. Looking through the account books I can see the same scrimping going on generation after generation. My mother and I are only the last two in a long line of cheeseparers. But I am the first, I think, ever to have put money in, not counting the heirs who did it by marrying money.

parents trying to avert her doom by banishing anything sharp from the palace. My finding the door in the alcove at Fenella's dance had been like Sleeping Beauty discovering the room at the top of the turret with the old fairy at her spinning-wheel. She gave in all of a sudden. At one moment she was saying that she was going to have me made a ward of court, and the next she was ringing up Mrs Darling and apologising for my letting the old hag down. I started work next morning.

In theory my desk was the one outside Mrs Clarke's room, but there was nothing for me to do there except answer the telephone when she was out. She had her job totally organised and didn't need or want any help with it, so in practice I spent most of my time in the middle room with Tom and Ronnie. I read the articles sent in by casual contributors and weeded out the hopeless ones; I read the rough proofs from the printers and learnt how to correct them; I sorted the books that came in for review on to the shelves behind Ronnie's desk and kept his file of publication dates in order; I scissored and glued for Tom when he and Bruce Fischer were working out which articles and cartoons were going on to which pages of next week's paper; and on Thursday mornings I lugged the mechanical elephant along to my desk and wrote another Petronella paragraph.

'It was a lot harder this time,' I said when I handed Tom my second piece with the magic letters 'OK. JT' scrawled across the top. He looked it through and nodded.

'You'll be needing to find a variation,' he said. 'Always the trouble with these jejune vocabularies. They weary the ear. You want another voice, for contrast.'

'But I've hardly got going with this one,' I said. 'There's a mass of things for her to do. Ascot and a Garden Party and Cowes and the Twelfth . . .'

'The material's there, no doubt. That's never the problem. It's the means.'

'But provided there's something new for her to rattle on about . . .'

'All matter is illusion. Only the Word—cap doubleyou —gives it reality, by allowing it to persist beyond the transient series of events which composed its apparent existence.'

'Words have got to be about something, haven't they, or they don't mean anything?'

'In this imperfect world. But I tell you, Mabs, when the trumpets sound for you and you come dripping from the river and shake the final impurities of matter out of your ears, the first sound you will hear will be the fine tenor voice of the Blessed Thomas Duggan celebrating the glory of God in a language infinitely rich in vocabulary and syntax but utterly purged of all gross content of meaning.'

'I can't wait.'

'Meanwhile, look for an answering voice, a different kind of idiocy from that of this little idiot. Something worldly wise, perhaps.'

He tucked the paragraph in an envelope and flipped it into the wire tray. That, I suppose, was the moment at which Uncle Tosh began to come into existence, utterly out of keeping. Of course I cribbed parts of him from Nancy Mitford, and parts from things that Wheatstone had told me about my great-great-uncle. And I didn't think I'd taken any notice of what Tom had said until the following Thursday when I had to think of something new in a hurry. I'd finished my paragraph but Mr Todd had a crony with him and Ronnie was interviewing a would-be reviewer in the middle room, so I was at my own desk, rejecting manuscripts, when Mrs Clarke came out.

'Have you finished, my dear?' she said. 'May I please see?'

I gave her the page. She read it and sighed.

'I do wish you liked her,' I said.

It was true. I really longed for Mrs Clarke to approve. I think it was because she reminded me more and more of Nanny Bassett, who had meant so much to me until Mummy had suddenly fired her while I was away at school. They were both people you couldn't help liking, whatever they did or said, and Nanny had the most extraordinary opinions about people and things, which nothing could persuade her out of. They both had quiet but extremely strong personalities—Nanny was one of the very few people at Cheadle who regularly stood up to Mummy. And they both, in Nanny's words, 'knew how to behave'. This wasn't the same thing as having good manners, or rather it meant having inner good manners, having standards, however dotty, and sticking to them without fuss. I felt Petronella didn't conform to Mrs Clarke's standards. She wasn't meant to, but that's not the point.

'It isn't that, my dear,' she said. 'I have agreed with Mr Todd that what you write is his concern, but I think it my duty to tell you that Mrs Brett-Carling is dying.'

'She can't be! I mean Corinna was talking last night . . .'

'Corinna does not know. Her mother is determined not to spoil her season. She's an extremely brave woman. But it is a fact.'

'That's awful!'

I looked through what I'd written, feeling sick. The dance had been held at the Dorchester, which Petronella had christened 'The Mourg', and I'd let her pretend she'd been to a funeral there. I knew Corinna wouldn't mind—she'd have given anything to be back with her horses in Worcestershire —and I'd worked in a lot of little undertakery details which I thought were funny in a bad-taste way—but not if you knew Corinna's mother was dying. She'd always looked a bit death's-doorish, beautiful, glassy-pale, dazed.

'I must ask you not to say anything to Corinna, or any of your friends,' said Mrs Clarke. 'Very few people know.'

'Of course,' I said, without thinking about it. 'Hell! What am I going to do? I went to Minna Tully's cocktail party, but I didn't make mental notes. Hell!'

'Mrs Turner is looking after Minna,' said Mrs Clarke.

'There was a crowd of arty-hearties there. I suppose Petronella . . . Do you think I could say anything about Mrs Turner taking fees for bringing people out?'

'I think it would be most unwise.'

'You mean after what happened to Veronica Bracken? But that wasn't Mrs Turner's fault. She had flu. And Veronica really was incredibly stupid. You know there was a story going round that she put her head in an oven but she didn't realise it had to be gas.'

'But it was gas,' said Mrs Clarke. 'The concièrge found her just in time. That was just after the abortion.'

'Abortion? But Veronica wouldn't know how . . .'

'Mrs Turner would.'

She didn't snap or raise her voice. She didn't need to.

'I'm sorry,' I said. 'I didn't realise.'

'Of course you didn't. Tell me, has it ever struck you, when you go to these parties and dances, what it must be like to be one of the fathers?'

'Not specially.'

'A man still in his own mind in the prime of life, having to sit and watch the girls swing past in the arms of their partners, all those clear young eyes, those bare shoulders, when his own wife . . . You understand?'

'But everyone said it was a chap in the Coldstream.'

'It was a man old enough to be your father, a director of several companies. One of those companies was a tin-mining business. During that year they opened a new seam which turned out to be unexpectedly rich, and the value of the shares went up to seven times what they'd been. Mrs Turner spends her winters in Monte Carlo. She played in the high-stake room that year, which she cannot normally afford to.'

'Golly! Are you sure?'

'I know a very great deal about the people I write about, my dear. I need to, so that I do not make mistakes. And I must tell you that you would be doing society a serious disservice if you were to write anything which might make other parents feel that Mrs Turner was a suitable person to help bring their daughters out.'

'Golly! How do you know all this?'

'I keep my ears open. I think about it. My husband was a very clever man, so I have friends in the City who tell me where the money is coming from. Nothing can be done without money. You see, my dear, though I know you and your friends probably laugh at it, I happen to believe that what I do is extremely important, so I take it seriously.'

'I know you do. They only sort of half-laugh, Mrs Clarke. They always turn there first . . . I wonder what's happened to Veronica. Modelling, I suppose, though I don't think I've seen her picture anywhere. She's really incredibly pretty.'

'That type of looks does not always wear. Didn't I see—was it that Bournemouth paper?—a Flight Lieutenant—the name will come to me—not Suarez, but something foreign-sounding . . .'

She slipped back into her room. For somebody so dignified

she had a habit of moving around very unobtrusively. You could easily imagine her picking up snippets of gossip because people didn't notice she was there. I went and stood in her doorway and watched her unlock the top drawer of her commode and begin to walk her fingers along one of the racks of filing-cards that filled it. My telephone rang. I went back to my desk and answered it in the bright-girl-on-the-make voice I was developing for the purpose.

'Cynthia Darke's suite.'

'Is she now?' said Tom's voice. 'On whom?'

'I'm terribly sorry. I'm going to have to do it again. It seems I've trodden on a sort of social land-mine. Can it wait till the next messenger?'

'I will hold the roaring presses. Doing anything for lunch, Mabs?'

'Rewriting Petronella, by the look of it.'

'You've got an hour. I was thinking you ought to see the inside of a Fleet Street wine bar. Purely as part of your training, mind.'

'Provided we go dutch.'

'I was willing the thought into your mind. Think you'll have done by one-thirty?'

'Oh, God, I hope so.'

I put the telephone down. Mrs Clarke was in the doorway, reading a filing-card with the help of her hand-held eyeglasses.

'Seago, of course,' she said. 'Flight Lieutenant Paul Seago. Not foreign at all, only Norfolk.'

The card seemed to have a hypnotic effect on her. She stared at it like a hen on a chalk-line. I thought of Veronica Bracken, the first time I'd noticed her, at Queen Charlotte's Ball three years ago. I was feeling nervous and ugly. White doesn't suit me, and Mummy had decided the occasion was important enough to get the real sapphires out of the bank, the first time I'd worn them in public. I lined up in the famous queue next door to a blonde child. She turned to me.

'Isn't this *super*!' she whispered.

She flexed her bare brown shoulders like a cat in a patch of sun. Her hair shone. Her eyes were very dark brown. She seemed to be floating an inch above the floor . . . And within a year she'd had an abortion in Paris and put her head in a gas oven and been found just in time by the concièrge, according to Mrs Clarke. And now she was going to marry Flight Lieutenant Paul Seago.

'Have you got a card about me, Mrs Clarke? May I see?'

'No, my dear. In any case I keep them in code. For safety, you know.'

'Were you really at my parents' wedding? I don't mean that, but do you really remember it? You go to so many.'

'It was the wedding of the year.'

'I suppose so. I only remember my father a bit. I don't feel as if I knew him. It's so difficult to imagine them falling in love, and marrying, and so on, but here I am.'

Mrs Clarke nodded, more like Nanny Bassett than ever. Certain sequences in the social order of things were as correct and perfect as a proof in Euclid. Without thinking I asked a typical nursery question.

'Were they really in love, do you think? It could just have been Cheadle.'

'They made a particularly handsome couple. Your mother looked radiant.'

'I bet she did. I bet it rained buckets, too.'

'Why should you say that?'

'Oh, I don't know. It was November, anyway. Mummy makes a fuss about the anniversary, and Jane and me were born in August, just in time to spoil the Twelfth.'

Mrs Clarke nodded and went back to her room. I heaved the mechanical elephant into position and tried to think of a way of taking the funeral bits out of my Petronella piece without leaving it as flat as last night's champagne, but the rain at my parents' wedding kept getting in the way. Mrs Clarke had as good as told me they hadn't married for love, but for Cheadle. I don't know why I should accept her word on something like that, but I did. In any case I'd always known, just as I knew about the rain.

When we were about fourteen we came back for one Christmas holidays on the same train. Mummy had orga- nised that, though Jane went to a cheaper school. ('It isn't good for them to live in each other's pockets the whole time.') Mummy got extra petrol for being a magistrate, which meant

33

she could fetch us from the station. It was a beast of a day, black and drenching. Jane and I were sitting together in the back. We came round the Saturn fountain and started up the avenue. I expect all children, coming back from three months away, automatically stare for the first real sight of home. I know I used to. All you see from the fountain is the portico, which goes right up the front of the house. The trees of the avenue hide the wings. On a day like that it's only the pediment and pillars, with blackness behind them.

'It looks like a great mouth, waiting to swallow us,' I said.

'Waiting to swallow *you*, darling,' said Jane. 'It's a stone ogre. Once a generation it's given a girl to eat.'

I didn't think Mummy had been listening, but she called out, 'Nonsense! In any case, next time it's going to be a man!'

She accelerated up the avenue as though she couldn't wait.

I was brooding about this, and I suppose I was thinking about Veronica and my parents' wedding and other disasters, and at the same time desperately trying to make my mind take an interest in Petronella, when I remembered what Tom had told me about finding what he called 'another voice'. Almost without noticing what I was doing I invented an uncle for the little idiot, a cynical old brute to balance her innocent gush. A guardian angel to save her from Veronica's fate. Uncle Tosh. He was running a book on the Season's Engagement Stakes. I can't pretend that I felt him, that very first morning, beginning to leap into life on the paper—he was just a way out of the mess I was in. When I showed the piece to Mrs Clarke she wasn't specially interested, but remarked that if it were true she would win a lot of money off him. On the other hand Tom spotted the possibilities at once.

'You'll find he comes in handy,' he said. 'What about these odds? You'll have readers writing in proving the fellow's certain to lose.'

'I was hoping you'd know about that.'

'You've come to the wrong door. I'm one of your literary Irishmen. The winged horse is the beast I bestride. Sensitive my nature, daring and sweet my thought, but neither mathematical nor hippophatical my bent. Ronnie's the fellow. His brother runs a racing stable. Ronnie!'

'Just a moment,' said Ronnie without looking up. Tom

talked on cheerfully as though telling me an anecdote about some total stranger.

'You know, when Ronnie came down from Oxford all eager to implement the revolution he tried for a job on the *Daily Worker*. Not the least interested in his Marxist fervour, they were, but the moment they found out his connections they snapped him up, gave him the petty cash and sent him out to put it on a horse. Doubled their fighting fund in a fortnight. Come and take a glass of lunch, Ronnie, and expound the intricacies of horse-race betting to little Mabs here.'

We got back to the office two hours later. I'd eaten one flavourless chicken sandwich and drunk a bit less than my share of two bottles of Pommery. We'd ordered the second bottle on discovering that Ronnie was a connection of mine through one of those typical third-cousin-once-removed linkages which come up in the course of conversations about something else—in this case my great-great-uncle's Gimcrack-winner Knobkerrie. He'd had it stuffed when it had to be put down after a training accident, and I think the earliest distinct memory I have of anything is being allowed to stroke its leg, in the billiard room. Tom had been delighted by the discovery and had kept calling cronies over to explain to them that Ronnie and I were related by way of a horse.

There was a note on my desk. 'I have tickets for *Eugene Onegin* at Sadler's Wells tomorrow evening. Please come if you are free. AB.' A telephone number but no address. I hadn't seen the writing before but I knew who it was. I wasn't free, but that didn't matter. I was going. Ah, I could actually insist on going because I could tell Mummy it was part of my job. Uncle Tosh could take Petronella to the opera. Then I wouldn't have to explain who Mr Brierley was.

Still, it might be useful to know. I tapped on Mrs Clarke's door and put my head round. It wasn't a good moment. She was wearing proper spectacles and typing that week's Round on a little white portable. (She used all her fingers, like a proper typist, and was very quick. Letters, even formal ones, she hand-wrote in purple ink on pale pink paper.) She looked up at me over the top of her spectacles—Nanny Bassett again, looking up from her darning, knowing we'd been up to some mischief.

'I'm sorry,' I said. 'This is terrible cheek, but have you got a card for Mr Brierley?'

'I have.'

'Could you tell me what's on it?'

'Certainly not. This is not an information parlour, Lady Margaret. I told you certain things this morning because it was necessary that you should know them, and I thought I could trust to your good sense to tell no one else. As for the gentleman you refer to, I know very little about him as yet, but I strongly advise you to have as little as possible to do with him.'

'I'm dreadfully sorry,' I said. 'I know I shouldn't have asked.'

She nodded icily and went back to her typing.

IV

'That's all over,' said Mr B.

He spoke only just loud enough to hear, as usual, but the grate in his voice cut me short. He didn't want to know. We were having dinner at Skindle's at Maidenhead, at a table by the window overlooking the river. It was no kind of romantic evening though, typical June sulks, with squalls rocking the moored boats and hammering down on to the ruffled black water. What's more Mr B had ordered my meal without consulting me, nothing special, though my half-bottle of hock was delicious. He had a plain omelette and an apple and drank weak whisky and soda. His chauffeur had driven us down in the Bentley while we sat in the back and talked about the magazine. We were still doing so.

I'd been out twice with Mr B since the opera, to a private dinner given by a rich Greek at Claridge's and to a weird evening in a huge white villa near Virginia Water where some of us played vingt-et-un for buttons in one room while next door they were playing chemmy with hundred-pound chips. I guessed that us button-players were there so that we could give evidence if there was a police raid that we hadn't been playing for money, and to delay things a bit so that they had time to hide the equipment in the other room. All three evenings Mr B had been very kind to me, rescuing me from bores, introducing me to people who weren't bores and telling me juicy gossip about them afterwards; he'd listened to what I'd said, too, and seemed amused. Supper after the opera had been oysters and champagne and I'd been thinking, 'Oho, now there'll be his new Bernard Buffet he wants me to see,' when he'd said he'd got some work to do and asked if I'd mind if the chauffeur took me home.

This evening was not like any of those. It was work all through. The magazine. He'd owned it for seven weeks, giving each department a shake in turn. There was a new advertising manager, three men had been sacked from Circulation and one from Accounts, and we'd got a new contract with our printers which they were rather sulky about. He'd left Editorial till last, apart from getting me my job. Now it was going to be our turn, and he was using me as a kind of spy, to tell him about everything before he made his move.

It was extremely awkward. From his point of view, I owed him my job and I was obviously loving it, so why shouldn't he get something back? Besides, we all knew, everyone knew, that something had got to be done. I suppose I'd known it even when I only used to read the magazine in the hairdresser's. There was something dreary about it, something that made you feel mentally constipated. Now that I was on the inside I'd discovered that a lot of the articles and so on were actually pretty clever, pretty tricky to write, but that didn't stop them being dreary. The opposite if anything. They were like an acrobat doing incredibly difficult stunts which everyone's seen too often. The circulation was going down and down. Tom said he'd realised the writing was on the wall when his cronies stopped talking about seeing the magazine in the club and started talking about seeing it in the dentist's. We were all in a way longing for something to happen.

But that didn't make it any easier being a spy. It wasn't just because I liked the people I was spying on. I didn't, not all of them. Bruce Fischer, for instance. Bruce was Art Editor, a big, doughy, blue-chinned man who wore half-transparent nylon shirts which let you see his string vest and hairy chest. A classic edger-up. Only that morning he'd edged me the whole length of the make-up table until I'd used the Gloy brush to write 'No' on his nylon shirt. He'd lost his temper. He was the one who drew the cartoons of the blondes in bed with sugar-daddies. It was a sort of tradition. Right back in the Thirties, in the very first issue, there'd been a terribly daring picture like that and Bruce was still doing them. They seemed to be popular. Readers wrote in with new twists. I thought they were unspeakably dreary, but would I have liked them more if I hadn't thought Bruce was a pretty unpleasant person?

Or Jack Todd? Mr Clarke had appointed him just before the war when the magazine was almost on the rocks, but it was saved by Adolf Hitler. Apparently wars are marvellous for the written word. Ronnie's theory was that whenever civilisation is heading for the rocks everyone tries to reassert its values by doing the most civilised thing they can think of, like going to Myra Hess concerts in the National Gallery, but especially by settling down for a good read. Even so Jack must have had a pretty exhausting war and now he seemed almost like an editorial zombie some of the time, just going through the motions, laughing that awful laugh, buying dreary articles by writers he'd known when they were brilliantly promising, and so on. But then he'd hit a good patch, come up with a dozen fresh ideas, spot new talent . . . me, for instance. He'd liked Petronella, hadn't he? And he was dotty about Uncle Tosh. He'd been so keen on their visit to the opera that he'd made me stretch it out to a whole page in the proper part of the magazine with an illustration by Sally Benbow, and that happened most weeks now. I couldn't help thinking that Jack was a good editor, really, could I?

And Tom? And Ronnie? Whom I did like, who treated me as a real person, junior member of the boys' gang? Who'd taken my side when Bruce had lost his temper—not that Ronnie didn't make the odd bit of accidental-seeming contact now and again . . .

I was worried about both of them, for opposite reasons. Ronnie ran the review pages and wrote the parliamentary sketch. He knew a fantastic amount about what was going on. He could always tell you which ministers Mr Churchill was prepared to listen to and which made him pretend to go gaga the moment they opened their mouths and things like that, but somehow when he wrote it down it came out drab. Tom was the other way round. He was brilliant at noticing the surface of life, what people were wearing and eating and so on, and he had a lovely easy way of writing, but he wasn't remotely interested in what was going on beneath the surface or why things happened. If he wanted to know whether the Viet Minh were on our side or theirs, for instance, he would have to ask Ronnie. I was specially worried about Tom because somehow I sensed that Mr B wouldn't be interested in what he did.

I liked Tom most of all. I had decided, tentatively, that he was 'queer'. Powdering one's nose before a dance of course one gossiped about the men who'd been in the dinner party and who were therefore going to provide most of one's partners for the rest of the evening. All of them would have been to one of the big public schools, and as most of the girls had brothers, quite a bit of information got around. On the whole one welcomed the queers. They tended to like dancing and do it well. They noticed what one wore. They talked more amusingly. They weren't possessive. Above all they didn't behave as though they were going out to bat for the Men's First XI in the great game of sex, all arrogance and nerves, in varying proportions but just as tiresome whatever the mixture. I'd known one of these queers since childhood as he lived only three miles from Cheadle and got asked about a lot, despite having been sacked from Harrow, because he was a good tennis-player. But even he, one vaguely assumed, was going to grow out of it.

Tom (if I was right about him) was not. This made him seem different from anyone else I'd known. And then there was the danger, the daring, involved in that way of life. Only a fortnight before the supper at Maidenhead a well-known playwright had been sent to prison after being found in the arms of a guardsman under some bushes by the Serpentine. Jack Todd had become almost hysterical with excitement at the news, chain-laughing, thrilled by the man's downfall, derisive of the hypocrisy of public life, but obviously inquisitive as a small boy and shocked as a great-aunt. Did *he* know about Tom? Was he in some way getting at him? Tom hadn't seemed to notice but Ronnie had become very jumpy and tried to shut Jack up. Later he'd told me, 'Jack's got it in for old Tom. He needs him. Tom's the flywheel, keeping the machine running when the engine's off. But Jack will do all he knows to stop Tom becoming editor when his own time's up. In fact he'll hang on to that chair till he keels over.'

Now, how much of this could I tell Mr B? Of course I longed to tell him everything, to show how bright I was, how at home in my new adult world. Only I guessed he wouldn't be all that impressed, so I stuck to what actually went into the paper. We were talking about 'By the Way'. This was a series of unconnected paragraphs at the start of each week's paper, beginning with a phrase like 'We notice that . . .' and going on to be ironic or witty or lightly sentimental about whatever Tom claimed to have noticed. He wrote most of them. They looked as easy as pie. You didn't realise till you'd tried that they were incredibly difficult to get right. I was explaining this when Mr B interrupted.

'That's all over,' he said.

I looked up.

'No time for that sort of thing. Not any more,' he said.

'He does them incredibly quickly.'

Mr B gave me his toad look, pulled the mustard pot towards himself, took the spoon and began to smear parallel yellow lines on the table-cloth. I watched, shocked. There was something sacred about clean white linen, about the columns of folded table-cloths in Mrs Hamm's cupboards at Cheadle, some of them stitched with my great-grandmother's initials, as part of her trousseau, and therefore new in 1876, but still perfectly good thanks to the systematic rotation of the columns. Probably they'd all had mustard spilt on them over the years, but Mr B's deliberate smearing was different. Each time he drew a line he reduced the space between it and the one before.

'Our relationship with time is changing,' he said. 'We think of time as a constant, but it's not. It is an accelerating process. In the Middle Ages . . .'

He drew a line on the table, a foot back from where he'd started.

'. . . it might be a century between one serious change in society and the next. It made sense to plant oak trees.'

He began to move the spoon slowly across the rows, an inch above the cloth.

'By the industrial revolution the gap was a generation, by the First World War a decade. Soon we will stop thinking in years and think in months. It affects us all. When our cities were built we invested in a hundred-year future, with sewers and roads and bridges and warehouses that would last. What businessman today will invest in a ten-year future?'

'I've got a friend—the man you rescued me from at that dance, as a matter of fact—who says he's going to be a millionaire by the time he's forty.'

'Perfectly possible, provided he remembers there is no future and therefore no past. The only time is now.'

'What's it got to do with what Tom Duggan writes?'

'He is writing for *here*,' said Mr B, pointing to a space two mustard-lines back.

'A lot of people probably still think they are living there.'

'Do you watch the television?'

'We haven't got one. There's a set at one of my friends'. They can't tear their eyes from it.'

'Exactly. Your people who you think are living in the past are bored with the past, without knowing it. They will move on, all of a sudden, leaving Duggan stranded.'

'In that case, why did you buy the paper?'

He swung round and beckoned to a waiter, then pointed to the mess on the cloth. The waiter took a clean napkin from the empty table next door and spread it over the mess, blotting it out. But I could still feel it was there, shocking, between the snowy layers.

'Why did I buy *Night and Day*?' said Mr B when he'd gone. 'Have you surfed ever?'

'Brrr, no thanks. I've watched people doing it at Brancaster but it takes a north-easter to get the waves up. I don't see the fun in waiting around in a wind that's come from Finland so that you can lie on your tum in the water and let a wave push you ashore.'

'In Barbados we have learnt to do it on our hind legs. It is a healthy activity. You should come to Barbados and try.'

'Oh, I'd love to.'

I don't think I spoke with any special gush. I liked England, and because of the war and problems afterwards I hadn't been abroad much. Two seasons skiing, and bicycles in Normandy, that was all. A squall threshed along the river. The idea of sun and blue waves and warm beaches made my skin crawl with imagined pleasure. I saw Mr B looking at me with his pop eyes half hidden by lowered lids.

'Will you come and live with me?' he said.

Of course my heart gave a bump and I felt my eyes widen. I suppose I blushed, because I do. But in a funny way I wasn't surprised, though I certainly hadn't been expecting him to say anything like that. As I've said, I'd half expected it my first evening out with him, but then I'd come to the conclusion that he liked my company occasionally because I was young and amusing and had a bit of snob appeal, but he'd want somebody much more sophisticated for a lover. And if you'd asked me, when he wasn't there, how I'd react to such a proposal, I'd probably have said that my chief problem would be trying to hide my disgust at the idea. But he was there.

'Be your mistress, you mean?' I said.

'If you choose to put it that way.'

'How long for?'

Now he did the smile.

'Hard to say,' he said. 'Nina left me after two years to marry a farmer in Mull. I kicked another girl out after six weeks and she tried to sell her story to the press.'

'Tried?'

'Stick to the point.'

'You know I'm a minor?'

'Until the tenth of August. I have considered that, but I would like your answer in principle.'

I thought about it. No, I didn't, but I felt I had to pretend to. I could have said no—he hadn't made it seem difficult. I looked at the sodden willows and two swans on the dark water for about ten seconds.

'All right,' I said. 'In principle.'

'You don't want a day or two to think it over?'

I shook my head. Now I was shocked, astonished, frightened. It was him knowing my birthday. It meant he'd been thinking about it in his cold way. The name of the town we were in crossed my mind and that made me go scarlet. He was watching me and raised an eyebrow.

'I wouldn't have guessed you liked puns,' I said.

'I don't . . . oh, I see. If it will set your mind at rest I hadn't intended to make the suggestion this evening. But you looked so delicious at that moment . . .'

'It was thinking about Barbados.'

'We won't be going there for some months, I'm afraid.'

'I don't mind. What shall I call you?'

'My first name is Amos.'

'Does anyone call you that?'

'Only my mother.'

'Is she still . . .'

I could have bitten my tongue off. I don't think a muscle or line in his face changed but I could feel he was hurt and furious. I reached across the table and took his hand. It was as small as mine, but dry and hard.

'I haven't had any practice,' I said. 'I'm bound to be clumsy at first.'

He squeezed my hand, turned it over, looked at it and let it go.

'I'm an ugly little man,' he said. 'Try not to remind me. But I am not yet fifty.'

'You are the most exciting person I've ever met.'

He patted my hand and pushed it away.

'I want to talk about ways and means,' he said. 'I implied just now that I was able to keep my affairs out of the newspapers, but there are, of course, limits. We may have reached them. The combination of British prurience and British snobbery may prove too strong.'

'I wouldn't care.'

'You would, when it happened. Furthermore there is your mother and Cheadle Trust.'

'She can't do anything except persuade the Trustees to cut off my allowance, and that's a pittance. It's all entailed and I inherit when I'm twenty-five.'

'So I gather. But I hear your mother is a formidable woman, and in any case there is no point in creating problems where they can be avoided. I myself am not anxious for publicity. I am not a particularly rich man, though like your friend I intend to be. I operate by persuading richer men that they can trust me to use their money to their profit, and if they were to see my name all over the gossip-columns their confidence might be less. So what I propose is this: you will have to move out of Charles Street . . .'

'I couldn't possibly afford anywhere you could bear.'

'Let me finish. I will of course pay the rent, but you will need to explain where the money is coming from. Todd tells me that these little pieces you've been doing are very popular with readers . . .'

'All I know is people have started sending in grisly imitations.'

44

'All successes have their drawbacks. But they appear to have caught on. I see no reason why you shouldn't produce a little book on those lines. If you judge it right you might do very well. There is a certain type of essentially non-literary small volume which people give each other by the tens of thousands for Christmas. A sensible publisher, recognising the possibilities, might well offer you a fair-sized advance to complete the work in time for him to get it out for the Christmas market. In any case the general public is absurdly ignorant about publishing finances. I don't think any of your family or friends would question the possibility that your advance enabled you to set yourself up in a small flat in the block where I happen to live. The need to have total peace so that you can write the book in a hurry would be your reason for leaving Charles Street.'

'Is this real?'

'You seem markedly more stimulated by the idea than by my previous proposal.'

I laughed and reached for his hand again. He shook his head. We had started to live our secret life, even if the other people in the room were only waiters, or stockbrokers out with their wives or floozies. Hard to tell which was which. There wasn't going to be much doubt in my case. It was extraordinary, now, how much I needed to touch him, to show him I meant yes with something that wasn't just words. To show myself, too, I suppose.

'It's the way I've grown up,' I said. 'Family. You don't let on about feelings that really matter. Except with Jane, of course. She's different.'

'Your sister?'

'I've got two others, but she's my twin. We have unspeakable rows, but we mind about each other dreadfully too. Is it all right if I tell her?'

'Is it necessary?'

'I don't know yet.'

Once more my hand reached towards his but I managed to stop it. Instead I smoothed with my fingers at the napkin. The mustard was gluing it to the table-cloth now, and the yellow lines were soaking faintly through. I looked straight at him.

'Did you ever meet a girl called Veronica Bracken?' I said.

'I don't think so. Why?'

'Nothing.'

'It sounds as if it mattered to you.'

'It might have. Please forget I asked.'

'If you wish.'

He turned to order coffee. I felt shivery and ill, not because of what I'd agreed to but because of the sudden notion that he might have been the man in Veronica's story. My instinct was to go back, for safety, back to the first half of the evening.

'You haven't told me why you bought *Night and Day*,' I said. 'You were saying something about surfing and that got us on to Barbados and then this . . . other thing came up.'

He was lighting a cigar. (The time before, when we'd dined alone, after the opera, he'd asked my permission.) He answered between sucks and inspections of the glowing tip.

'It's the hollow before the wave that matters,' he said. 'If you let that go past you've missed the wave. Then you've got to work like blazes to get your board moving as the wave itself comes. And then you can get up and find your balance and ride the wave. In the sea, of course, you can look over your shoulder and see the wave coming and decide whether it's worth waiting for a better one. But in the metaphor I'm using, where time itself is the wave, all that is hidden and you have only the feel of the hollow to go by. I met a fellow who wanted to sell some shares privately because he thought they were going down and down. I made some inquiries and decided this might be only the hollow before a wave. Now I have to get the board moving. The pun is not intentional.'

'And if there isn't a wave after all?'

'I shall be in serious trouble. As your friend who also wishes to be a rich man could no doubt tell you, it is necessary to take risks. Mostly I risk other people's money, and their trust in me not to lose it, but in order to underwrite that trust, and also to maximise my own share of the eventual profits, I have to risk the capital I have been able to accumulate by riding previous waves.'

'What was the first one? I mean how do you start? I wish some of the Milletts had known. I feel like a sort of mermaid born to sit on a gloomy old rock while your waves come chuntering past. It's worse than that because it's rather a soft

46

rock, and the waves are slowly wearing it away. Sometimes I think I'll be the last mermaid who'll ever sit there.'

I was rather pleased by the way I'd picked up his image and made something of it, but he seemed not to notice.

'It's not so much of a risk to begin,' he said. 'You've little to lose, but you need to see your chance and take it. In my case I was able to help some influential people just after the war and they . . .'

'You were on the Control Commission, weren't you?'

He looked at me.

'I'm sorry,' I said. 'It comes of belonging to a big family. You get used to interrupting each other. I'll try and behave.'

He nodded, still watching me.

'Go on,' I said.

'I think we had better have a definite understanding that we avoid the subject both of my work and yours. Otherwise, where they overlap, you will find yourself in an invidious position. We will begin from this moment.'

'All right.'

'I've told you the only thing that concerns you. I seem to be riding the wave successfully at the moment, but I may suddenly lose my balance and go under.'

'It won't matter. I'll pull you on to my rock.'

Rather charmingly he let me hold his hand all the way back to London while we talked about the Petronella book, but he didn't want to kiss me before he dropped me at Charles Street. Because of the chauffeur, I assumed, though I imagined he must have been used to that sort of thing. *

---

* I am relieved to find that this is almost as far as I chose to go in writing about my sex life. The omission would seem perverse if I had been writing the same story in these days, but in those it would have been extraordinary if I had gone into detail. I do not propose to do so now, but feel an impulse to deal briefly with the question of whether I loved B. The answer is certainly yes. Suppose we were to meet now (I as I am, he as he was) I would probably dislike and distrust him, with good reason. For all his magnetism I would not think him a pleasant or worthwhile person. He was not. But in spite of that, in spite of all changes, I cannot deny that I still, however irrationally, feel for him what can only be called love. Did he love me, though? He never said so. Perhaps that is what this book has turned out, after all these years, to be about.

V

To my amazement, Mummy decided at the last minute that she was coming to the publication party for *Uncle Tosh*, and bringing the family too. I'd hardly seen her all summer, once the Season was over, because she'd gone home to Cheadle. I got my news from Jane who if she was in London came round to my flat on Tuesdays, which were B's regular bridge evenings. Jane knew about B, because I'd told her, but we behaved as if she didn't. I'd untidy the flat to make it feel as if somebody actually lived there, and let her find me doing something domestic like starching my petticoats. I'd cook an omelette, with peaches out of a tin for pudding, and we'd chat in a jerky way, read *Vogue* and *House and Garden*, or play our old private game in which Jane drew Cheadle characters in unlikely situations and I put in the words coming out of their mouths.

I had to go home once, for my twenty-first birthday. It was Jane's too, of course, but you wouldn't have known. By a lucky fluke B had a business trip to Hamburg that weekend. It turned out a thoroughly dire occasion. Mummy hadn't really minded my staying away before the party, though she groused a bit of course, but it meant that she could have a free hand doing things her own way. She wanted a mighty celebration, although I wasn't actually going to inherit for another four years. For instance, I had to get the real sapphires out of the bank to wear, not that anyone would have known, but she wanted to be able to tell her friends. We didn't ask many of my friends, that wasn't the point, because it wasn't really a party, it was a ritual. And it wasn't for me, either, it was for Cheadle. So the guests were mostly the mothers and fathers of other Leicestershire families, gathered to be witnesses at the betrothal of the old stone ogre to his new bride. Then, at the last minute, the ogre turned nasty.

Mummy wanted everything as grand as possible (though also, of course, as cheap as possible) and the grandest thing of all was already there, laid on, cost free, in the shape of the Banqueting Hall. There'd been a minor leak in its roof, which wasn't unusual—there's always a bucket or two standing round somewhere to catch the latest drip. But this time when the builders came out from Bolsover to patch things up before the party they found a complete section of lead that had somehow never been replaced in the 1924 repairs and had been leaking for years on to the huge main bearing timbers, which had been soaking up the leaks so that they didn't show up below, and now the timbers were rotten through, and a lot of the other woodwork as well. The architect Mummy got out said that there were tons of baroque plasterwork up there held in place by cobwebs, and the Banqueting Hall wasn't safe to walk through, let alone to dance in. In fact we danced in the Long Gallery, which was much better anyway because the wooden floor is easier on your feet than marble, but for Mummy it wasn't the same thing. It wasn't part of the ritual, and in a mysterious way she decided that it was all somehow my fault.

It was my fault because I hadn't been there and the ogre was sulky. Of course she didn't say this—I sometimes think she hasn't any imagination at all—but it was what she felt. Now it was my duty to leave London and come and help her in the crisis. We had three absolutely record rows, but she found she couldn't beat me down any more. I was free. It was all happening outside me. (When I did get down to Cheadle I was much more interested in pumping Wheatstone for stories about my great-great-uncle, a truly fearsome old savage, which I could adapt for *Uncle Tosh*.) It was like one of those dreams when you are actually aware you are dreaming; monstrous things threaten you but they only frighten you on the surface because you know you can kill them by waking up. That's what distinguishes a proper nightmare, like the Hansel-and-Gretel one I used to have. While it lasts, it's real.

What was real for me was my happiness, my job, Pet-ronella, my life with B. He was a congenital early riser, which I'd never been but took up because it was the only way I could cram everything in. We would get up at six, however late we'd got to bed, and off he would pad to his rowing machine and his sun-lamp. I would dress, switch my telephone through and go up to my flat and write for two hours and then have breakfast. He would telephone me at half-past eight to tell me where he would be during the day and what we were doing that evening. (If *I* had an engagement I'd have to have told him several days before.) He'd be very brisk, as though the only point in telling me at all was so that I'd know what to wear and whether to have my hair done. Then I'd catch a bus to Westminster and a tram along the Embankment and walk up through the Temple to Shoe Lane and the office. In spite of what B had said to me at Maidenhead nothing much had changed in the editorial department. Tom was still writing 'By the Way' and Bruce was drawing his sugar-daddies in bed with blondes (which now had a ghastly fascination for me, though I still didn't think they were funny) and Mrs Clarke was writing the Round in the same unbelievable way. But, perhaps because I was so happy, I felt as if things were cheering up. The circulation was still falling, but not so fast, and I thought that fewer issues now had that musty, dead-mouse smell which used to hang around most of them when I'd first come to the paper.

In the evening I would go back to my own flat and change out of my office clothes. Then I would go down to B's, shower, do my face and hair, put on a frock and read till he came home. I kept most of my clothes down there because he liked to watch me dressing and undressing. And he liked me to be well dressed when we went out, so he'd opened accounts for me at Victor Stiebel and Harrods and a few other places. I wasn't extravagant with them. I walked a sort of tightrope in my own mind. For instance we'd slipped over to Paris so that Petronella could do the Autumn Collections and I'd fallen for a little Dior suit, dark grey silk with black lapels and cuffs. I longed for it, and I felt B guessed there was something I wanted, but I couldn't ask. It wasn't a question of his paying for it, even—I could actually have afforded it out of my own money, but I would have needed his help to work some kind of currency fiddle to buy it, and he was obsessive about that. He grumbled all the time about the £25 limit but he stayed inside it with a sort of obsessive stinginess which was quite out of character. At home he was generous without being lavish. He paid the rent of my flat and settled my accounts because doing so allowed us to live in the way he wanted, but the bargain between us didn't lie in that, any more than it lay in my being young and reasonably intelligent and pretty in my piggy way. For me it lay in feeling happy and alive in his company. For him I suppose it lay in knowing that I didn't think of him as an ugly little man.

Not that it was all perfect, all the time. He could be desperately moody, and once or twice a total beast. I suppose I'd better put one of these times down, because I want him all, and that's part of him too.

We were due to go to the theatre. We had met by accident earlier in the day, because I'd gone to Sotheby's to get material for a Petronella piece about a sale of Old Masters, and B had been there. I'd caught his eye across the room and smiled at him. He hadn't smiled back, but he wouldn't. So I was waiting for him in his flat that evening, already dressed for the theatre and eager to chat about the sale. I thought he'd be amused about my going to something like that on my own because I never used to until he started to try and educate me. When Jane and I were born the ovum seems to have split with all the aesthetic genes in her half. I expect that's scientific nonsense, but it's how it worked out. I got the words and she got the pictures. Of course I knew some names and could do a bit of simple chat, but I could never actually *see* that a Rembrandt self-portrait had anything more to it than a good coloured photograph. I'd gone to that particular sale because there'd been a couple of Canalettos in it. We've got six at Cheadle so I wanted to know what they fetched. 'Selling the Canalettos' is family shorthand for taking desperate measures in a financial crisis.

When B came in I gave him his drink and asked whether he'd bid for anything. He went and stared out of the window, emptied his glass and poured himself another without saying a word. By then I knew that something was wrong, but I wasn't prepared for it when he swung round and asked in his harshest voice why I hadn't been at the office. I explained about the Petronella piece and was trying to say I thought we'd agreed not to talk about my job, but he went off on another tack, saying that it was pointless for me to write about pictures because I was too stupid to understand anything about them. The only pictures in the flat were a couple of sea-scapes, fishing-boats in rough seas, which I actually liked because they reminded me of a painting in one of the West Wing rooms at Cheadle where I used to hide under the bed to read. I made the mistake of saying so. B said they were rubbish and he was going to get rid of them next day. Then, deliberately I thought, he set about reducing me to tears. I thought he'd decided to 'boot me out' but after all that he insisted on going to the play, which turned out dire. He never referred to the incident again. It might almost have been some kind of brainstorm, except that he did get rid of the sea-scapes and next time he came back from Germany replaced them with a horrid little picture of the head of Christ, grey with death, and Mary's head huddled against it, clumsy and grey with grief. Naturally I didn't risk saying anything about it, or any of the other pictures and knick-knacks he began to import.

I took it as a warning. I knew it meant something, and I told myself it was his way of making sure I didn't take my luck for granted. I didn't, and I suppose that made me enjoy the happiness all the more, so it may have been worth it. (Apart from that it meant that B stopped trying to educate me and when we went to Private Views let me wander about eavesdropping on the perfectly extraordinary things people say to each other in art galleries.) That was the worst time. Usually I could cope with him by treating that part of our affair as a sort of game. If he didn't like something—a dress for instance —he'd be brusque or even rude about it, and that meant I'd lost a point. If he was pleased he didn't tell me, but I learnt to know, and scored myself one.

Though I'd signed the publisher's contract and written and rewritten every comma and read the proofs and so on, somehow I never really believed *Uncle Tosh* was a real book until the publication party. We held it at the *Night and Day* offices in Shoe Lane. It was what Petronella would have called a hoot, because everyone seemed to think it was a perfect opportunity to work off hospitality debts, and the list grew longer and longer. We cleared the big middle room but it soon became obvious that that wasn't going to be enough so I had the cheek to ask Mrs Clarke if we could use hers too, and she said yes. I'd been half hoping that B would subsidise the drinks—the publisher's budget would have run to about half a glass each—but I couldn't ask and he didn't offer. In fact I didn't even know whether he was coming—during our usual morning telephone confab he'd just said he was meeting someone and might perhaps bring him along. In the end Jack Todd authorised Accounts to help, and I topped up with some of my advance, but we were still short, so Ronnie mixed the drinks.

The drink, I mean. It was take-it-or-leave-it. Apparently left-wing politics make men expert in how to get stoned on a shoe-string. It was mostly Algerian white wine, with Moroccan brandy to give it a kick and a couple of other things to hide the taste and cochineal to turn it bright pink. We told the guests that it had been created specially for the occasion and was called Petronella. Jack Todd had used the party to invite a lot of his lame dogs—quite well-known names, some of them, in an is-*he*-still-alive sort of way—which gave the occasion what Tom called a certain cobwebby literary cachet. It made me giggle to see those mottled noses sniffing warily into their glasses, though I heard one of the old boys mutter that at least it was a bit stronger than what publishers usually produced.

Then the publicity man at the publishers had said it would be a good idea if I got some real debs along—the Susans, he nicknamed them. I chose ones who looked the part and could talk Petronella. One of the things that had happened during the summer was that she'd really caught on. For instance Selina had come back from a weekend in darkest Worcestershire and told me that two girls had physically fought over *Night and Day* when it arrived because they wanted to see whether Petronella had come up with anything new for them to work into their repertoire. Some of the Susans could talk Petronella for twenty minutes non-stop, which I certainly couldn't; she came to me sentence by slow sentence on my typewriter in my little empty-feeling flat at the top of Dolphin Square in the early morning. By now there was an accepted Petronella voice, a breathless but metallic quack, just right. A few young men tried to talk Uncle Tosh, but I never heard a good one.

And then there were the professionals, reviewers and gossip-columnists and even a few ordinary reporters who'd been sent along by their editors to do a story about this titled idiot who'd written a book. The jacket said '*Uncle Tosh* by Petronella' but I'd sneaked in an Acknowledgement in which she thanked darling Margaret Millett for helping her with the speling. This was the first time we'd publicly admitted that I was the author of Petronella, though there'd never been any real mystery about it after the first few weeks. By the end of the Season I was getting invitations from women I'd never heard of saying it would be absolutely divine if Petronella would come and be foul about their party. I remember moaning to Mrs Clarke about how difficult it was to keep her innocent, and Mrs Clarke smiling in her seen-it-all way. But the press hand-outs for *Uncle Tosh* didn't just use my name; they made a song and dance about the title, and the Cheadle inheritance and all that. I didn't mind, because it was terrific publicity, though Mummy was going to loathe it when she saw the papers next morning. Anyway, these extraordinary men turned up at the party expecting me to be *like* Petronella. I suppose people who rely on facts really rather distrust the idea of anybody making things up out of their imagination. They feel threatened. So I threatened them a bit more by explaining that Petronella was best understood from a post-existentialist standpoint, and telling them about the underlying parallels with Camus. (I could keep that up because B had told me to read Camus.) Then I introduced them to one of the Susans, so they got their story after all.

I was talking to a *Manchester Guardian* journalist who had rather called my bluff by knowing about Camus and wanting to explore the parallels when Tom came up and said, 'Mabs?' You get used to the question mark when you have a twin sister. That was the first I knew that the family had arrived.

'Jane, actually,' I said.

He peered at me and shook his head.

'I am forced to reject the imposture on external evidence,' he said. 'There's a girl in Dorothy's room in a gold dress like yours calling herself Margaret Millett and expounding the nuances of the dialect of your tribe. Journalists are taking notes of what she tells them. I have heard her declare that the word 'potato' has no plural. One speaks of a brace of potato. The scribblers are taking it for gospel. That's not in your book, that I remember.'

(Tom had been an angel and copy-read *Uncle Tosh* for me. He'd made masses of useful little suggestions, but the thing that had really fascinated him, like a scab he couldn't stop picking, was Uncle Tosh's list of words. I'd only put this in to fill up the end of a chapter, dividing the words into 'Us' and 'Ponsy'*—mostly quite obvious ones like saying 'luncheon' and not saying 'toilet'. Things Mummy had always insisted on, though she'd made up her own rules—some of our friends, for instance, thought it was a bit ponsy to say 'Mummy' but she said that was nonsense.)

I felt a gush of fury that absolutely astonished me. By Tom's eyes I could see I'd shown it. I snapped something at the Camus-man and began to shove my way out of the room. The crush slowed me down enough for me to feel I'd got some sort of control back by the time I'd pushed along the corridor to Mrs Clarke's room. Jane was a few feet from the door, facing it. There were two men talking to her. One of them did have a notebook. She'd been watching for me, and smiled like a pig-faced cherub.

'Hello, Jane darling,' she said. 'I hope you're enjoying my party.'

---

* About three years later, when that U and Non-U business got going in *Encounter*, people remembered my book and asked me where the word 'ponsy' came from. I used to tell them that it was really 'poncy' but Petronella had spelt it wrong, and if they then said it didn't mean that I explained that my great-great-uncle applied the word to anything he disapproved of, being a man of limited vocabulary, and that we'd picked it up and used it without knowing what a ponce was. The bit about my great-great-uncle was true, but in fact we'd adapted the word to fit poor Miss Pons, who had come to us as a governess and fully lived up to her superb references, except for insisting that we used a vocabulary my mother had absolutely forbidden. Many people assume that 'real' aristocrats are not snobs. This is rubbish in my experience. The truth is that they guard their exclusiveness ruthlessly, but in obscure ways. Though Miss Pons was much the nicest governess we were ever likely to get, all four of us agreed that my mother had done right to dismiss her. I couldn't explain about Miss Pons in 1956 (was it?) because she was probably still alive.

I stared at her. I remembered she'd rung me to ask long or short, and I'd told her what I'd be wearing. She'd got hold of a gold frock from somewhere. I'd never seen it before and it looked a bit tight under the arms. It wasn't the same as mine but near enough for a man not to notice. I have to explain that there was nothing unusual about this. We often played that kind of trick, on each other, on our friends. Jane had once come home to Charles Street and told me I was now engaged to a young man she knew I was utterly bored with. She'd shown me a ring to prove it. I'd got almost hysterical with panic, though I knew it couldn't be true. (In the end it had turned out that she'd spent the evening trapping him into telling her how much he preferred me to Jane and how anyone who really cared for me could tell us apart at once, and then as he was paying the bill she'd told him who he'd been talking to.) Now I was perfectly well aware that Jane just thought she'd have fun doing something like that again—she couldn't have understood how it mattered to me, in fact I hadn't understood myself till that moment. Or perhaps I hadn't realised how quickly my private self, the self that had nothing to do with family and Jane, had grown, and grown apart, since I'd left Charles Street.

Jane saw what had happened. Her eyes stretched. Her nostrils widened into piggy pits. Sharp red blotches appeared on her cheeks. I knew that I must be wearing exactly the same hideous mask, but I couldn't do anything about it. The men stared.

'What the hell do you think you're up to?' I snapped.

Jane produced a grimace that was meant to be a smile.

'I'm afraid Jane can be pretty stupid,' she said to the man with the notebook.

The man looked embarrassed, but eager and inquisitive too. His ratty little eyes flicked from face to face. I started to screech. I don't know what I said.

When something like that happens in the middle of a noisy crush there's a funny effect of silence spreading away from the centre where the rumpus is, as more and more people realise that something's up. This had just begun to happen. I was fighting to get back into sanity, but all I could see was Jane's face, working like a spell, turning me against my will

56

into a screeching pig. I was just about to ruin my own party. Jane's face was framed against the back of a man with a large, pink, bald dome and yellow-grey hair trailing down over sticky-out red ears—one of Jack Todd's mangy lions. He became aware of the pool of silence spreading over him and turned to see what the fuss was, but somebody shoved him aside and barged through. It was Mummy.

The screech stuck. She came forward wearing the smile she uses when there are guests and everyone has just heard a pile of plates go down outside the pantry.

'*There* you are, darling,' she said. 'What an interesting *lot* of people. Please introduce me to your friends.'

'You'll have to ask Jane,' I said.

Jane looked in the other direction. The pig-mask was melting away.

'Your daughters are fantastically alike, Lady Er,' said the man with the notebook. 'Can anyone tell them apart?'

'So people say,' she said. 'I think they're *quite* different. This is darling clever Mabs, and this is darling clever Janey.'

She put her arms round us and drew us close, uniting us in love on the maternal b.

'I wonder if you could tell me, Lady Er, if your family always talk about, what was it, *traddling*?'

'Traddling?'

'And a brace of potato?'

Mummy laughed.

'Oh, dear no. That was only old Major Ackers. He was a bit . . .'

The man twitched his notebook up.

'A bit what?' he said.

Mummy stared at him.

'Aposiopesis,' I said.

'Oh, Ar, Eff,' said Jane at the same moment.

'You mustn't tease the poor man,' said Mummy.

I thought journalists were supposed to have thick skins. With real satisfaction I watched the sweatbeads glisten on his cheek. The unity of Family is extraordinary. My fury with Jane was still grinding away inside me and I was tense with Mummy's touch, but for the moment the three of us were like some tribe who have caught an intruder on their sacred ground and are now dancing round him while he roasts alive. This was *my* ground, *my* party, my triumphant celebration of freedom from the thraldom of Cheadle; but suddenly here we were, the three of us, as if we'd been putting on our hats for church outside the Morning Room and agreeing without saying so that we were going to have to keep at arm's length that pushy new family who'd just moved into the Old Rectory.

The man put his notebook away. He was going to vote Labour for life, I could see, and what's more he was going to write the cattiest story about me that he could get past his Features Editor. (I was wrong. It turned out an absolutely grovelling piece, as if he'd really loved what we'd done to him.)

Mummy let go of Jane but not me and by swinging a few inches round managed to split us off completely from the others.

'I hope you'll introduce me to your friend, darling,' she said.

'Tom? He's in the other room.'

'The one who settles your account at Harrods.'

She smiled at me, the-witch-who-will-find-you-in-the-end. Ever since I could remember she'd been able to do this. The trick had two parts. The first was finding your secret, and the second was choosing the moment to tell you. There was a tone and look for it, a sad little voice, a sad little smile, eyes bright as glass beads. No anger, only contemptuous pity that you should think you could hide from her, ever, anywhere. Of course she never told you how she found out.* The punishment was usually fair and came with a great swoop of relief.

---

* I worked it out years later. It had been my fault for being too pig-headed about the nature of my relationship with B to give a false name for my accounts. My mother had one at Harrods but used it so seldom that I'd forgotten. Hers was in the name of Countess Millett, but she always referred to herself as Lady Millett and had done so when she'd ordered an emergency wedding present for someone; so the item had got on to my account, which B had settled without question. When my mother had telephoned to ask why she hadn't had the bill the confusion had persisted long enough for somebody to try and clear things up by telling her who had signed the cheque.

I have just been down to wake her up and give her her pill. It was one of the mornings when she doesn't know me, except that she took it. If anyone

I was nine again, reading Mumfie under the bed in King William's Room when I was supposed to be helping Samson weed the Bowling Green path. Sick-mess in my throat and all my skin a layer of chilly rubber. I discovered that beneath my recent happiness and exultation—part of it, adding to its excitement—had been the certainty that this was going to happen. Of course I'd sometimes wondered what I'd do or say if she found out, but that's not what I mean. The rhythms of my life decreed that she had got to find out. In dreams of escape you glance back along your secret path and see that at the entrance you have left your pullover, caught on a blackthorn, a huge and obvious clue for the lion-faced people to find. You left it there on purpose, though you didn't know, because that is the logic of the dream.

I refused to meet her look. She still had her arm half round me, resting on my shoulder. Straight in front of me was Mrs Clarke, talking to a tall thin stooping man I didn't recognise. Ronnie came up to them with a fresh-mixed jug of Petronella.

'I do think I'd better talk to him, don't you?' said Mummy.

I put my hand up and lifted hers off my shoulder. She didn't resist, but let it fall.

'He isn't here yet, as far as I know,' I said. 'I don't know if he's coming.'

'But when he does?'

'If he does.'

'Don't forget, Mabs.'

No punishment. None at all.

'All right,' I said. 'Come and meet this new cousin I've found.'

I introduced her to Ronnie and Mrs Clarke, and the three of them hived off leaving me with the tall stooping man. He turned out to be the head of the firm which was nominally

---

else had tried to give it her, other than Fiona, she would have spat it out. Even so only about half the water I give her to wash it down with goes in. It struck me while I was mopping up that in all our lives together there had been two special rituals which had bound us to each other—when I was young, the witch-ritual; now the pill-ritual. Coming back to finish my stint I re-read the paragraph to which this footnote is attached and felt it to be almost extraordinary, a measure of my then freedom, that I had been able to write it in the past tense.

publishing *Uncle Tosh*, though we'd done all the real editing and so on in the office. I'd only met a couple of his underlings —*Uncle Tosh* must have seemed very small beer to a man used to publishing two-volume biographies of Rilke. He was an edger-up, but in a different dimension from Bruce Fischer. He used his height to crane over you and then came smiling down, like a rook eyeing turf for leather-jackets. Luckily my frock had a high collar. He told me that now the subscriptions were in he'd decided on a reprint. When something good happens in publishing, it is always the doing of whoever tells you about it; something bad is always the fault of the system, incurable. I tried to look starry-eyed with gratification. Mercifully one of the mangy lions came maundering up, with suggestions for an autobiography. Any other time I would have hung around to see how the publisher fought him off, but I edged away.

Jane wasn't even polite to the man she'd been pretending to talk to. She swung round and grabbed my wrist.

'What was that fratch for?' she said. 'I was having fun.'

'Sorry. You couldn't have known. I tried not to.'

'They didn't know *anything*. I could have got away with . . .'

'Careful, darling. It's coming back.'

'Oh, all right. You might have warned me when I rang up about the frock.'

'Didn't think of it. There's such a lot of my own life . . .'

'Who's Mummy talking to?'

'The man with the jug is Ronnie Smith. He's a sort of fourth cousin. A Communist. Works here. I like him.'

'Mummy doesn't. She's in a filthy mood about something, Mabs.'

'She's found out about me and B.'

'She hasn't! How?'

'No idea.'

'What are you going to do?'

'Nothing. I suppose she might try and have me declared insane, or something, or break the Trust in your favour, but I don't think she'd get away with it.'

'Anyway it's you she wants, Mabs. You've always been the one. Is he here?'

60

'Haven't seen him. He may not come. He wasn't sure. She says she wants to talk to him.'

'What on earth about? Oh, if it were anyone else, Mabs, wouldn't it be bliss to eavesdrop?'

'She'll tell him to give me back and he'll say no. I don't think she's met anyone like him before. Listen, darling, suppose she reacts by making life hell for you . . .'

'Why should she?'

'She'll have to take it out on someone. Anyway, you could come and live at my flat if you wanted. I'd have to ask B, of course.'

'I don't think . . .'

Close by my shoulder I was aware of one of those minor jostlings you get when somebody tries to head for another part of a crowded room. It was my publisher, escaping the autobiographical lion. Jane and I had been standing at an angle so that we could mutter into each other's ears, isolated by clamour. This stirring forced us to turn and I found myself face to face with Mrs Clarke, apparently waiting to come through between us. I'd last seen her in quite the other direction, talking to Mummy and Ronnie. She had a photograph in her hand.

'Oh, Lady Margaret,' she said. 'Do you think your dear mother would be kind enough to sign a picture for my collection? I've been looking through the file for a good one.'

She spoke perfectly naturally, as if she hadn't overheard a thing. She'd had a lot of practice, of course, but I didn't think she could have. Mummy was sure to say something unspeakable to her about the photograph. I tried to head her off.

'She's in rather a dicey mood just now,' I said. 'Have you met my sister Jane?'

'I knew it must be,' said Mrs Clarke. 'You're an art student, I believe, Lady Jane. Such a worthwhile accomplishment in a woman, being able to paint and draw beautiful things.'

Jane's 'art' at that stage consisted of welding iron bars and plates to each other until she'd got something like a section of gaunt skeleton with bits of machinery muddled in, and then dipping the result into acid baths to make it go into interesting pits and nodules. She could be very intense about it, and sniffy about pictures and sculptures ordinary people liked, but I'd told her I approved of Mrs Clarke so she was a saint and swallowed her aesthetic pride and talked about our great-grandmother's watercolours of Italy which hung—hundreds of them—around Cheadle in back passages and bedrooms and were supposed to be rather good for an amateur. In spite of what I'd said to Jane I was really very shaken and worried and longing for B to come. I eased myself away and went off to look for him.

The other room was just as crowded and even noisier. We had hooked the swing doors open, but it was as though they were still exerting their influence, separating the civilised from the rowdy. Most of the Susans were here, quacking away, and the men seemed to look younger too. I weasled my way round, but it wasn't easy. For a start B was too short for me to see him over people's heads, and then I was constantly being stopped and asked to settle arguments. It was amazing how that word-list had got everyone going. We'd put a stack of the book out on the landing, just to prove that it was real, but they'd all been snitched. People were holding them open and consulting them so that it looked like a roomful of foreigners trying to carry on conversations with the help of phrase-books. Then people tended to assume that the Susans knew all the answers, as if they'd been born with silver dictionaries in their mouths, when in fact some of them came from decidedly ponsy backgrounds—though girls have a fantastic knack for picking up tones of voice and getting them right. The extraordinary thing was that though I was really aching to find B, and though I also thought my word-list was just a bit of nonsense I'd shoved in to make up space, as soon as anyone asked me about a particular word I couldn't help talking as though it really mattered. I got into a long argument with Priscilla Stirling, who certainly wasn't one of the ponsy ones, about 'mirror'. Perhaps because the Petronella drink was stronger than people realised no one seemed at all bashful about discussing the subject, though they did so with a kind of inquisitive glee, like schoolgirls talking about sex. It must have taken me twenty minutes to find out that B wasn't there after all.

I met Tom out on the landing. He raised one eyebrow at me, making his face look suddenly very Irish. Ronnie used to say that Tom was really a wild Celt who spent his time trying to pass himself off as an English gentleman-scholar. When he reverted like this it was a sign that he was moderately drunk, though a stranger mightn't have known.

'Mabs,' I said. 'Jane's has got short sleeves and no collar.'

'Easy as that?'

'Unless we sneak off to the loo and swap.'

'I shall write a thesis proving that Shakespeare was terrorised by the twins next door when he was a baby. It would explain quite as much as the usual theories about his mother. And then there was Casanova . . .'

'Supposing it was true.'

'Mabs, you ought not to know about that.'

'It tends to come up. I didn't think you, though . . .'

'Cheap liquor cheapens the accompanying conversation. Haven't you noticed? We are all going to have appalling hangovers.'

He finished his glass and smacked it down on the table where the books had been. He was drunker than I'd realised, and upset about something too.

'What's the matter, Tom?'

'Noticed Jack's not here?'

I hadn't, though I should have. At a gathering like this the laugh would have been almost continuous, and audible too through the racket.

'He's leaving,' said Tom.

'Leaving?'

'Told us not to tell you. Said he didn't want to spoil your party.'

'You mean resigning?'

'Sacked.'

'No!'

'Better for him, apparently. Allows him to claim compensation on his contract.'

'But when . . .'

'Been brewing. Letter on his desk this morning making it definite.'

'From Mr B?'

'Who else?'

Then he must have written it yesterday. We'd eaten alone

63

last night, at the Escargot in Greek Street. It sounds dull, but it had been a lively, easy evening with a lot of talk. We'd gone back to the flat, slept together, kissed when we woke. Surely he could have . . . Perhaps he didn't want to spoil my party either . . . Then couldn't he have waited one more day?

'Who's going to . . . I mean are you . . . ?' I said.

'Not been told. I'd like the job. When this sort of thing has happened in the other departments Brierley seems to have had a man ready.'

'Oh. But you'll stay, won't you?'

'Will you?'

'Of course. If he'll have me, I suppose. I absolutely adore being here.'

'It may not be the same.'

'Please stay, Tom. It certainly won't if you go.'

He laughed, but then his eyes left me. Some of the guests had started to go but others were still arriving, so the terrible old lift was groaning up and down almost continuously. I'd been standing with my back towards it but turned to see what Tom was looking at. B was coming out of the lift, talking to a youngish man whom I recognised but couldn't put a name to for an instant. Then it came to me. On the stage, about a fortnight before, acting in a revue called *Backbites*, which I hadn't thought specially funny but was being talked about because it was different—not just gently bitchy in a revueish way, but rude about real people as though it meant it. The Lord Chamberlain had refused to pass some of the sketches. This man, Brian something, was supposed to have written the unkindest bits as well as being one of the principal actors. B brought him towards us.

'Brian Naylor, Tom Duggan, Margaret Millett,' he said. 'They're on the literary side.'

Mr Naylor was a round-faced, stupid-looking man with short gingery hair and small gold-rimmed spectacles. On stage he used a monotonous flat voice with drawling vowels —Midland, somebody had told me. His main joke was to apply this oafish-seeming approach to touchy subjects. For instance he'd done a monologue about how he didn't mind his Jewish dentist poking around among his molars but he was disgusted by the idea of letting him hack divots out of his favourite golf-course. Part of his technique was not to smile at all. It all seemed such an act that I was surprised to hear him speak now in exactly the same voice.

'This is a typical press day, I suppose,' he said.

Tom was looking greyish but answered in a normal voice.

'It's a party to celebrate the publication of Mabs's book.'

'So you've written a book, Margaret?'

'Only a little one,' I said. Wrong answer. Wrong tone. I felt totally bewildered.

'A vade-mecum to the upper reaches of the class system,' said Tom. 'No social climber should be without it.'

'Is there anything to drink?' said Mr Naylor. 'Scotch, for preference.'

'Find Mr Naylor some scotch, Duggan, and introduce him to the rest of the staff,' said B.

He turned to me.

'Congratulations,' he said.

'Thank you. It's going very well.'

He was actually about to move off when I stopped him. He was furious. Nobody else would have known, but I did. He thought I was going to say something about Brian Naylor.

'Mummy's here,' I muttered. 'She wants to meet you.' His eyes opened very slightly.

'I don't know how,' I said. 'Something to do with my account at Harrods.'

He nodded. He still wasn't pleased, but it was better than if I'd tried to use our affair to interfere with office matters.

'Look after me,' I whispered. 'Please.'

'Out here, then.'

She was near the door in Mrs Clarke's room and had obviously been watching for me. As soon as I appeared she came forward. She had a horrid look of triumph.

'Some woman has just asked me to sign a *photograph*, darling,' she said.

'Oh dear. I hope you were nice to her.'

'I made it clear that I would do no such thing.'

'A lot of your friends have. She's got a whole collection.'

'I am not a stamp. Are there any more of your interesting friends you'd like me to meet, darling?'

'One more,' I said.

I led her back between the swing doors.
'Is that him?' she whispered. 'Oh, darling, how could you?'
'Very easily, if you want to know.'
I introduced them formally and let them get on with it.

VI

Tom had been right about the hangovers. It was worse because the next day, Friday, was press day and there were proofs to read. We hung around and waited for them to arrive from the printers. Brian Naylor seemed to have made a bad impression on everyone, even Bruce Fischer, whom I'd stupidly assumed to be rather the same kind of person because they came from the same sort of provincial lower-middle-class background. Then Ronnie found a review of *Uncle Tosh* in the *Spectator* and I took it away to my desk outside Mrs Clarke's room to read and re-read. It was only six lines at the end of a much longer review of Stephen Potter's *One-Upmanship* but I didn't mind. The man said it had made him laugh. I thought it was such a silly little book (no I didn't, but I assumed everyone else would) that it was terrific to have it reviewed at all.

When Mrs Clarke came through I jumped up and started to try and apologise for Mummy being foul to her about the photograph. She looked puzzled.

'I am quite used to people being a little eccentric, my dear,' she said. 'It's their privilege, I always say. I thought it was a very lively party. Isn't it surprising what a mixture will go, sometimes? Did you meet this Mr Naylor?'

'A bit of a skeleton at the feast, I thought.'

'Oh, I do so agree.'

'None of us are what you might call enthusiastic.'

'Such a pity. I wonder if it mightn't be possible for someone to explain to Mr Brierley what a mistake he's making.'

'Oh. It would be difficult. Once he's made up his mind. I imagine.'

She didn't seem to notice my stammerings.

'Such a pity,' she said. '*Quite* the wrong person.'

'Perhaps he'll learn.'

'Let us hope so. But oh, my dear, I'm so pleased for you that your book has turned out so popular.'

'Isn't it lovely? Absolutely super, in fact. Would you like a signed copy?'

'That would be very touching, if you can spare one.'

'You can keep it in the loo to show people what you think of it.'

'I shall keep it among my proudest possessions.'

Being an author was turning out an expensive affair. You get six free copies, and at least twenty people seem to expect you to give them one. So you keep having to buy your own book to give away. We smiled at each other through our hangovers and I felt I'd partly made up for Mummy's beastliness about the photograph. Actually I doubt if Mrs Clarke had a hangover—she was far too experienced a party-goer—but she didn't look well. She was wearing her powder like snowfall on the Pennines, deep drifts softening the ridges and wrinkles, but they were still much more obviously there than usual. If I hadn't been so preoccupied with my own inner weather I might have realised that she'd had a bad night, or something, and so was less in control than usual. She half turned as if to go on to her room, but then faced me again.

'My dear,' she said. 'I have become very fond of you. I think you are a sweet, clever girl. But I think I must say this. It is very important to know where money comes from.'

'Are we talking about a friend of mine?'

'I believe so. You see, everything that we care about depends on the right people having the money. The world you and I value will cease to exist without that.'

'Do you think so? I mean it's often all started with wrong people, hasn't it? The original Millett was a master dyer, but he really made his pile out of loot when the monasteries were dissolved. And even now, well, look at the Lanners. So respectable you could stuff sofas with them. But old Greg Lanner was just a South African bandit who was lucky not to get himself hanged several times before he found that goldmine. I bet you half the people you write about in the Round really owe their money to ancestors who weren't much better than him.'

'I do not think it is fair to hold that against the present Lord and Lady Lanner.'

'But it's still where the money came from, isn't it? I

suppose you could say the system's a bit like a glorified sewage farm. You put in dirty money one end and as it washes through the generations—you know, like filter-beds, with those arm things going round and round—it gradually gets cleaner and cleaner until it's fit to set before the king.'

I thought this was a lovely image—it had come to me on the spur of the moment. Pity I'd finished *Uncle Tosh*. It would have been just right for him. Mrs Clarke sighed.

'My late husband was very clever about money,' she said. 'He had a lot of excellent friends in the City. Naturally, I have been asking them what they know about the gentleman of whom we are speaking.'

'I thought it was sugar. Something to do with by-products. And before that there was a plantation in Barbados. I thought.'

'I know Barbados quite well. I go to the West Indies most winters. They like to read my accounts of their doings. But I can tell you that although there was some money to be made from plantations during the war, since then it has been very difficult. And in any case it was only the well-managed estates . . . There is some very strange blood, besides . . .'

She was obviously finding it difficult. So was I. Luckily at that moment the boy arrived from the printers with several pages of achingly tiny type about next week's cinemas and theatres for me to check and correct.

B had said nothing to me about Mummy after the party and I hadn't asked. We'd talked about other things, but I'd known from small signs that he felt I'd gone beyond the terms of our contract. Mummy had left without saying goodbye. I'd have liked to try and make contact with Jane, but she was going down to Cheadle for the weekend, while B and I were off to a bridge congress in Hastings.

This turned out totally dire. It sheeted with rain. B was playing with an unfamiliar partner and they kept having misunderstandings which he couldn't grumble to me about because I wouldn't have understood a word. There were no reviews of *Uncle Tosh* in any of the Sunday papers. We got back to London, both in a vile mood, at three o'clock on Monday morning. B got up at six to do his exercises, so out of sheer obstinacy I went up to my flat to write. I'd started straight off on another book as soon as I'd finished *Uncle Tosh*, not because I had a passion to write it but simply out of the habit of doing that sort of thing then. It had begun as a kind of cod romance, set in Edwardian times, strongly influenced by *Cold Comfort Farm* but peopled with marchionesses and sinister millionaires; then, mysteriously, I'd found myself actually believing more and more in my own grotesques and I was beginning to think that I would have to take the leg-pulling element out and turn it into a proper novel.

There was a folded scrap of paper on my doormat. Jane's writing. A page from a pocket diary.

'Where are you? Must talk. Can't ring from Ch. St. Will come to *N & D* 10.30 Monday.'

Blearily I settled down at my typewriter, but I'd done less than a couple of pages when the telephone rang. It was B.

'You're early,' I said.

'Can you come down? Now.'

'All right.'

He was in his dressing-gown reading a company report. A large cup of very pale coffee steamed beside his armchair—he was waiting for it to get completely tepid and then he would drink it. On the low table beside him were several neat piles of letters and other papers. The ripped envelopes lay on the floor. He picked up one of the letters and glanced through it. Mummy's handwriting was large and jagged. You could recognise it from yards away.

'I'm terribly sorry,' I said. 'It really isn't fair on you.'

He did his toad smile.

'Believe it or not she's trying to blackmail me.'

'But it hasn't got anything to do with you. It's entirely my look-out.'

'For money.'

'Oh. How much am I worth to her?'

'No exact figures. She appears to think that as I have taken something out of the Cheadle estate I ought to put something back, in the shape of a new roof to the Banqueting Hall.'

'She's disgusting.'

'There is a hint of other elements in the transaction.'

'I've a good mind to go straight down to Cheadle and beat her up.'

'She appears to be still in Charles Street.'

'Terrific. I can . . .'

'No.'

'You aren't going to take her seriously!'

'I am not going to take her proposal seriously. But she might be in a position to make a nuisance of herself at this particular moment.'.

'Oh.'

People keep saying it's a small world, when really it's a lot of small worlds, with less overlap than you'd think. Moving in with B I had changed from one small world to another, though to outsiders they might have seemed almost identical. The fathers of many of my friends might sit on the boards of companies on which B's allies and enemies also sat, but they were not the same sort of people. My friends' fathers, whether they said so or not, were waiting for England to return to the kind of place it had been before the war. Mr Churchill belonged to that period and Mr Eden, and now that they were in power my friends' fathers were impatient for it to happen. The war itself and the struggles afterwards had been only an interruption. But for men like B the Thirties were dead history—deader even than they were for me because of my connection with those times through Cheadle and the people there, such as old Wheatstone. For these men the war and the period since had been the start of things. That was when they had begun, one way and another, to spot their opportunities and make the most of them. They were impatient too, but to go on, not back. They weren't impressed by Churchill and Eden. Their hope lay in the younger politicians who were going to clear away all the left-over restrictions of wartime—B had a particular bee in his bonnet about currency control—and let those who could get rich.

Of course there were occasional overlaps. These could be embarrassing, and hilarious. There'd been one dinner-and-night-club evening at which Sir Drummond Trenchard-Yates turned up with a marvellously bosomy and brassy blonde, the sort Bruce Fischer kept drawing. Aunt Minnie Trenchard-Yates was really no relation of ours but that's what we'd always called her because she was Mummy's closest friend, a tiny, smiling, sweetly tough woman I'd known since I could remember. Sir Drummond had got rather grand, Director of the Bank of England and so on, and he huffed and puffed a bit when he saw me, rather as though bringing his blonde had been like coming to the party wearing a black tie when he should have been in tails. He kept explaining that the blonde was his secretary, and that she was wonderful at putting his spelling right. Later that evening, having apparently decided that I was the other kept woman in the party—the remaining three seemed to be more or less wives—she poured out her heart to me. It was too sad. She seemed really fond of Sir Drummond and was longing for Aunt Minnie to divorce him so that she could marry him and become what she called 'a real person'. I hadn't the heart to tell her that Aunt Minnie would never let it get that far.

That sort of thing didn't happen often, and though the men mightn't be as awkwardly placed as Sir Drummond, they still behaved as if they all belonged to a sort of huge, vague club, whose basic rule was that the members didn't tell their wives about each other. But clubs have snags, as well as advantages. Suppose Mummy were to talk to Aunt Minnie about me, and then Aunt Minnie snapped her fingers at Sir Drummond —well, I couldn't imagine Sir Drummond sitting on one of his boards and putting forward a coherent financial argument against some enterprise of B's, but I could imagine him going a bit red and pulling his moustache and saying, 'Don't care for the feller myself. Heard something the other day . . .' And that might be enough. It was what Sir Drummond was for, after all, being a sound chap and hearing things.

I'm only using Sir Drummond as an instance. There were a dozen people Mummy could get in touch with, any of whom might have been able to put a spanner in B's works. The point is that B couldn't afford it. Though I gathered things had been going rather well these last months he was still always desperately short of money. He had a huge overdraft. He lived like a rich man, spent like a rich man, but if he'd been forced to sell up at certain moments he'd probably have been bank-rupt. It was other people's money, and it all depended on other people's confidence.

He was reading the letter again.

'I never really believed you, you know,' he said. 'I put her down as a stupid woman.'

'Oh, she is, in some ways. But she's brilliant at people. If you've got a weak spot she'll find it. What are you going to do?'

He caressed a little bronze sculpture he'd brought back from his last trip to Germany—more like an egg than a head, though it had a nose and eyebrow-ridges.

'Nothing for the moment,' he said. 'Don't let's talk about it any more. I've got work to do.'

'Just one thing. I'm terribly sorry. It's family still. Jane. I found a rather desperate-sounding note from her when I got downstairs. I think Mummy may be giving her hell. I wondered if you'd mind if she came and lived in my flat for a bit.'

He tested his coffee with his finger and licked it clean, glanced for a moment at Mummy's letter and then stared at me, slowly, all over. I was baffled. He might have been irritated or furious, even, but it wasn't like that. It was more as though he was seeing me for the first time and making up his mind whether to buy me.

'It is gratifying to feel that there is one person in the world who trusts me,' he said.

I didn't understand at once, though Jane and I were used by now to the idea that some men get excited about twins. Casanova wasn't the only one. I felt myself do one of my pillar-box blushes, but I made the words come.

'If you really wanted to,' I said. 'I don't know what she'd say.'

I had to wait while he took a long swig at his disgusting coffee. He did it on purpose, for pleasure, getting his own back in a small way for what Mummy had done to him. It struck me that he might even want to show her what he thought of her attempt to blackmail him by taking Jane away from her too.

'I think it's time we had a treat,' he said at last. 'Thank God Barbados is still in the sterling area.'

Mondays were always a bit desultory. The true week began on Tuesday, when the outside contributors came in for the editorial conference and Jack Todd made up his mind about the main features of next week's issue. Haggard from the weekend at Hastings I read would-be-funny manuscripts —always an extra large batch in the Monday post—and passed on about one in ten to Tom. Ronnie found, in the *Daily Worker* of all places, a review of *Uncle Tosh*, treating it as a text for a satiric blast at the moral bankruptcy of capitalism. I guessed Ronnie had used his connections to get it mentioned at all, but I was still pleased, though it wasn't a review that was going to sell many copies. The others were more interested in a gossip-column paragraph in the *News Chronicle* about Jack Todd leaving and Brian Naylor taking over. It hadn't been officially announced yet.

Jane turned up wearing her art-student uniform—ponytail, chunky sweater, wide corduroy skirt. She looked about as haggard as I felt. Coffee came round at that moment. Although she'd been so urgent about talking to me she didn't pick up my hint about moving off to somewhere private, but lolled against the make-up table in the middle room, leafing contemptuously through the proofs of not-yet-used cartoons which she'd found in an open drawer. Nellie came in and said that Jack Todd had decided to take the day off because of not wanting to be pestered by journalists ringing up to ask about the *News Chronicle* piece; but poor Tom—he'd obviously had a bad weekend and now had a greyish, sweaty look, as though he was going down with flu—was pretty well anchored to his telephone, fending off inquisitive Fleet Street cronies. I let Jane finish her coffee and then dragged her away to look for somewhere where we could talk.

The waiting-room was occupied by a pipe-puffing cartoonist who'd come to show his portfolio to Bruce Fischer. Mrs Clarke was in her room. My desk, out in the corridor, seemed far too public. Then I remembered what Nellie had said about Jack Todd not coming in so I put my head round the secretaries' door and asked if we could use his room for twenty minutes. Nellie said she supposed so.

As soon as we were alone I put my arm round Jane's shoulders. She didn't respond.

'Darling, I'm desperately sorry,' I said. 'I'm sure it's all my fault.'

'What is?'

'Whatever's happening.'

'Yes, I suppose so. I suppose you couldn't have known.'

'I guessed.'

She loosed herself from my arm and moved away.

'You guessed *this*?'

'What?'

'I thought she'd written to him.'

'He didn't show me the letter.'

'Oh.'

'I gather she wants him to pay for the Banqueting Hall roof.'

A long pause. I sensed a deep reluctance in her. Apparently she'd been expecting I would have read Mummy's letter. For some reason it was difficult for her to begin without that.

'Do you do everything he says?' she asked.

Quite unreasonably the thought crossed my mind that she was about to make the same ghastly suggestion I'd thought B'd been hinting at that morning. I couldn't see any possible connection between this and our problems with Mummy.

'Almost,' I said.

'If he told you to go away?'

'That's part of the bargain.'

'Oh.'

'But if I thought he was doing it because of Mummy, I'd fight.'

'I thought you would.'

'What did she say to him at the party? Do you know?'

'She asked if he was going to marry you. He said of course not. He said you understood that. She told him he'd got to send you home. I don't know what he said. She was raging.'

'He's ruder than anyone I've ever met when he wants to be. What do *you* think, Janey? About B and me, I mean? Do you mind?'

This was something we'd decided without discussion not to talk about. It was too tricky. In spite of our endless rows, Jane was the only person I'd ever properly loved until I met B, but I knew I couldn't count on her feeling the same. It was so much easier for me. Almost everything that had happened to us, all our lives, had been unfair on Jane, and the only excuse had been that I was the sacrifice. In the end she might be free, but I never would. Even that makes it sound a better bargain for her than it really was—nobody could call inheriting Cheadle a specially painful sort of sacrifice. And now, well, part of the unwritten contract was that the central ritual of the sacrifice would take place on the day I married, and thus brought a man home to look after Cheadle and sire another generation on me, so that the sacrifice could be repeated in thirty years' time; and a vital part of the magic was that I must go spotless to that altar. It may seem a bit loopy to talk like this, in this day and age, but though Mummy would have been completely incapable of expressing herself in those terms, it was how she *thought*, and so, in spite of ourselves, the way Jane and I thought too. * By having an affair with B I had broken the contract and spoilt, or at least risked spoiling, the magic, but I was still going to inherit Cheadle. And on top of all that I was having a glorious time. Jane wouldn't have been human if she hadn't minded.

'She wants him to let you go and have me instead,' she said.

'What?'

'She hasn't actually said so, but that's what she wants.'

I didn't understand at once. It was such an obviously impossible suggestion, she must mean something else. Then I remembered B saying 'There is a hint of other elements in the transaction.' I remembered him looking me over, like a slave merchant, after I'd made the suggestion about Jane moving in upstairs. He'd been wondering whether I knew, somehow, about Mummy's idea, was part of the scheme, and was making a first move towards bringing it off. And then he'd decided that I wasn't, and he'd said what he had about being trusted. The extraordinary thing was that when I did understand I didn't blaze into one of my rages with Jane. I was appalled. Sick. Chilly with shock. Jane was watching me.

'I don't want him,' she said. 'I don't want that. She can't make me.'

---

* And I, at least, still do. Not about the literally virgin bride, of course, but at a deep and primitive level something that has the same ritual meaning, something to do with innocence, and also with being chosen—not by my mother (or now by me) but absolutely. Chosen, like that. I accept that this is probably only a way of rationalising what I have now become, but that makes no difference to the nature of the feeling.

Her voice was creaky with tension.

'You can have Cheadle,' I said.

'What on earth are you talking about?'

'You can be Mabs from now on,' I gabbled, 'and I'll be Jane. Like we've done before, only we'll keep it up for the rest of our lives.'

'Are you serious?'

'Yes, absolutely. Don't you see . . .'

And I was. It was a totally absurd suggestion. Mummy would have known at once, for a start, and there were all sorts of other things which made it impossible, but all the same I did mean it. If I had the choice, I would give up my rights to Cheadle for ever rather than give up B, even though he might choose to turf me out next week.

'Don't be bloody stupid!' she snapped. 'I don't want anything you've got. I don't want him. I don't want Cheadle. I want myself. Me!'

The pig-mask had started to form, but then her glance shifted. She looked over my shoulder for an instant, twitched herself round, swirling her skirt out, and leaned panting with her hands on the edge of the desk, her pony-tail hanging down to hide her face. I turned and saw Brian Naylor standing in the doorway.

'I trust I don't intrude,' he said in his flat, oafish voice.

'I'm sorry,' I said. 'I didn't realise . . . Nellie said . . .'

'Having a wee bit of a tiff, are we?'

'Mr Todd's not coming in today.'

'A great loss. A great, great loss to us all.'

'This is my sister Jane. We had an urgent family problem we had to talk about. I'll find somewhere else.'

'Hello, Jane. Don't go. The feminine touch is called for. Tell me what you think of the furniture and fittings in this salubrious accommodation.'

'Dreary,' said Jane, barely looking up.

'Dreary. That is your considered opinion.'

'Yes. Can I go now?'

'Not quite appropriate for the editor of Britain's foremost humorous weekly?'

(He was quoting from the slogan of an advertisement we were running as part of a circulation battle with *Punch*, but his leaden intonation—as with almost everything he said—implied the opposite of what the words seemed to mean.)

'You'd better get Heal's in,' Jane muttered. 'Tell them Swedish.'

'Heal's. Swedish.'

'Elephant-grey carpet and dead white walls and stainless steel floor-lamps and natural linen curtains and Bernard Buffet prints and Örrifors glass. Can I go now? I'm trying to talk to Mabs.'

'In office hours.'

'*Her* office hours.'

He strutted over and put his arm round her. It seemed as long as an orang-utan's. His right hand, hairy-backed, clamped on to her breast. Bruce Fischer was a model of finesse by comparison. Jane went Millett scarlet and tried to hoick herself free but he gripped her wrist and winked at me.

Jack Todd wrote his own articles longhand and kept a large bottle of Quink on his desk for the purpose. Probably because I remembered my success with Bruce and the Gloy pot I snatched it up and undid the top. Mr Naylor saw and let go of Jane to grab at it. I snatched it away but he caught my other wrist. Jane swung at him round-arm from behind, hitting him high up on the side of the head. I don't know whether without that I would have thrown the ink or merely threatened him with it, but his sideways stagger—Jane had muscles like a blacksmith from her sculpting—pulled me half off balance, so that my arm holding the ink-bottle threshed instinctively forwards. The ink shot out in a fountaining arc, starting on the curtains, spraying across the wall and a bookcase and finishing on Mr Naylor's trousers. He looked down, then at the mess on the wall. He straightened his specs, rubbed his head where Jane had hit him and laughed—an open, cheerful sound.

'If we'd rehearsed that we'd never have brought it off,' he said. 'Is that stuff washable?'

I looked at the label.

'Yes.'

'God, what a mess.'

He laughed again.

'It was your fault,' I said. 'Being editor doesn't give you *droit de seigneur*.'

Instantly he lapsed back into his stage face and voice.

'I will try and remember that, Margaret.'

'Good,' I said. 'I'll get someone to clear up.'

I found Jane in the corridor, said, 'Hang on a tick,' and poked my head round the secretaries' door.

'I've spilt Mr Todd's ink, Nellie.'

'You haven't! Over his desk?'

It must have been a regular occurrence, though I didn't remember it happening. Nellie whipped a drawer open, snatched out a folder of blotch and rushed past me. Just inside Jack Todd's room, though, she stopped dead. Over her shoulder I could see Mr Naylor. Not unnaturally he had taken his trousers off. Nellie, a large, pale girl of about thirty whose salient characteristics were efficiency and devotion to Jack Todd, hesitated a second, flung the blotch at Mr Naylor and rushed back out.

I don't imagine she meant to use the blotch as a missile. She was only trying to get it into the room and herself out again as quickly as possible. He wasn't a specially indecent sight as his shirt-tails covered his pale, hairy legs almost to the knees. The blotch had struck him in the chest and strewn itself at his feet. Ink was pouring in rivulets down the spines of the books beside him. He was laughing again, and I was too.

'How long do you keep this up?' he said.

'I don't know. I'm sorry.'

'Nothing to be sorry about. Where I come from we tar and feather strangers. I think I'm going to like it here.'

I yelled to Jane to come and help, and while she blotted the worst bits I telephoned the commissionaire, Sergeant Sawyer, and told him there was a mess to clear up urgently. Then I asked Mr Naylor for his measurements and took Jane with me along to a men's outfitters in Ludgate Circus where we bought him a cheap pair of grey flannels. On the way we talked quite placidly about what we were going to do. The silly little bout of action seemed to have cleared my mind. I understood something about Jane which I'd never really seen before. She'd often sworn she wasn't jealous of my luck in being born first and I hadn't believed her, but it was true.

Provided that in the end I did what Mummy wanted Jane didn't mind how much special treatment I got, or how much fun I had. She didn't mind my having an affair with B, because it wasn't going to last for ever. I would come back in the end. But what I'd said about swapping places, stupid though it was, had truly frightened her, because it showed that given the chance I might somehow slip away for ever. Her reward, what had made the whole arrangement tolerable for her, had always been that in the end she was the one who would be free. In their different ways Mummy's wicked scheme and my own dotty idea, though neither of them could possibly work, had been images—nightmares—hinting that her freedom might not be there, ever, after all.

We didn't talk about this, directly. I told her we were going away for a week to Barbados and I'd give her a key of my flat in case she wanted to go and live there for a bit, and I tried to make her see that the best way to think of Mummy was as a sort of blood-curdling old witch who loses all her power as soon as you realise that none of her spells actually work. There was nothing, however she raged or wheedled, she could actually do. I didn't tell Jane what B had said about Mummy being in a position to make a nuisance of herself just then —that was none of her business.

VII

'You'd better come and meet my mother,' said B.

It was one of his typical tricks, to spring something on you and watch you jump. I was used to it, but he caught me this time. We had been in Barbados five days and met a number of B's acquaintances—a much more ramshackle and dubious collection than his friends in England, and not at all the sort of polo-playing Barbadian Mrs Clarke wrote about in her winter excursions to the islands, either. There'd been a numbingly boring American businessman who could only talk about expanding the island's tourist facilities, an almost wordless lawyer, a voluble half-Indian building contractor, and so on. I hadn't had any sense that B had enjoyed these meetings—in fact he disliked and despised the people as far as I could make out, but he was strangely patient with them and refused to tell me afterwards the sort of gossip about them which he would have amused me with after similar encounters in England. None of them had even hinted that his mother was on the island.

'Take off that nail varnish and find something quiet to wear,' he said.

'Do you really want me to come? I'll be perfectly happy . . .'

'Yes. It'll be a help.'

'All right.'

She lived in a new block of flats overlooking the harbour at Bridgetown. The place was obviously expensive—bowls of flowers in the entrance lobby, thick carpet, the chill of air-conditioning, smooth-running lift. But when B opened the door of a top-floor flat with his own key I realised that I was crossing a frontier—between times, or civilisations, or something vaguer. The hallway reeked of spiced cooking. Its walls were white-painted, like those outside, but the furniture consisted of a monstrous black armoire, heavily carved, and beside it a cane chair with one of its legs mended with a

81

splint. In the distance a strange big voice was ranting through shouts and bursts of music. We passed an open door where a small black man, grey and wrinkled, was stirring an old iron cooking-pot on a modern electric cooker. B raised a hand in greeting to him, and the man's face, wreathed in the spicy steam, split into the traditional water-melon smile. I smiled back, of course, but the scene through the door heightened the sense of having moved into a country much more foreign than the Barbados outside. The worn old face, the smile, the stoop over the pot, the pot itself—older possibly than the man—belonged to an illustration to some book in the Cheadle nursery, one of Daddy's perhaps, or going back even a generation beyond, a G.A. Henty about adventures in the American Civil War. Or pirate-hunting, a century before, among these very islands. Some images don't change. The man in the kitchen was the old slave who happened to hold the clue to where the treasure lay.

B opened the door for me at the far end of the hallway. The voice came blasting through, recognisable now as that of an American revivalist preacher. The cries and music came from the congregation. B crossed the room and switched the wireless off. I stood by the door, peering through dimness made duskier still by the dazzle of morning sun between the slats of blinds. There seemed to be nobody in the room, but it was hard to be certain because of the clutter of furniture—screens, little tables, chairs, lampstands, a piano, sideboard, and vague shapes whose purpose I could only guess at because of the way everything drapable seemed to be draped in beautiful old silk shawls the colour of ivory, fringed and embroidered. Though most of the large furniture was as black and heavy as the armoire outside, the shawls seemed to light the dim room with their own vague luminescence, like snowfall in a winter wood at dusk. The room was stifling.

B strolled across to a *chaise-longue* and stood looking down at the muddle of cushions and shawls on it.

'Wake up, Mother,' he said.

'I am wide awake,' said a vigorous old voice, 'and listening to the Word from the lips of the Reverend Patterson. Why did you silence him?'

'Why don't you use the air-conditioning? It's far too hot in here.'

'Noisy nuisance. Why did you silence him, Amos? Why will you always be deaf to the Word?'

'I've brought a friend to see you.'

The *chaise-longue* arranged itself. A yellow hand emerged from the cushions and clawed a corner of shawl aside to reveal a large wrinkled face, even more toad-like than B's, and some wispy yellow-grey hair. Surely if B had known he might find his mother in this kind of state he could have left me waiting in the passage and given her a moment to pull herself together, but being B he enjoyed such confrontations. I was cross enough with him already for making me take my nail varnish off just after I'd spent twenty minutes putting it on.

Mrs Brierley didn't seem at all put out. Two or three of the cushions became her body as she heaved herself into a sitting position, slapping B's hand aside when he tried to help her. She patted her hair, tugged her shawl, and then, sitting primly on the edge of the *chaise-longue*, rotated her head like an owl towards me and rotated it back as I walked round to stand where she could see me better.

'Miss Millett, my mother,' said B.

She inspected me. The whites of her eyes were yellow and bloodshot but the dark brown irises seemed unbleared. She was very short, but fat, and smelt pungently of Pears soap. The likeness to B was strong, not just in her general ugliness but also in the feeling of self-willed energy that beamed from her.

'How do you do?' I said.

'You are welcome,' she answered, not with the snap she'd used in speaking to B but with a slight drawl. She patted the *chaise-longue*.

'What is your denomination, Miss Millett?' she said as I sat down.

'Church of England, I suppose.'

'Neither hot nor cold, but better than nothing. Do you attend?'

'When I'm at home. I haven't found a church I like in London, I'm afraid.'

'What do bricks and mortar count for? It is the preacher, the man with the Word on his lips.'

'I like the singing best.'

'You have never heard singing.'

'Oh, I don't know . . .'

'A thousand negro voices under the stars, gathered after labour to praise the great Creator.'

'That must be terrific.'

'It surely was. The Lord was there among us.'

'Let's have a drink,' said B.

Mrs Brierley reached down to the floor, picked up a satin-covered shoe and used the heel of it as a mallet to strike the brass gong on the table beside her. The old black man must have been poised at the door, ready, because he came in immediately carrying a silver tray with three glasses on it. He was wearing a clean white jacket now, but the same old linen trousers, shredded at the ends like those of castaways in desert-island cartoons. His feet were bare. He held the tray for Mrs Brierley who sniffed at the glasses in turn.

'Maketh glad the heart of man,' said the old man. 'For thy stomach's sake.'

Mrs Brierley smiled B's toad-smile and licked her lips, the way I always thought B was about to. She handed me a beautiful tall thin glass, slightly chipped and only about half full. She then chose a large cheap tumbler for herself, brim full, leaving B another old glass, larger and coarser and fuller than mine. I took an incautious sip, thinking it was going to be sangaree, a weak, cold, winy concoction I'd been drinking in bars. It turned out to be some kind of sweet-sour punch, with twice as much rum in it as I was ready for. B had been watching me, amused.

'My mother drinks rum under doctor's orders,' he said. 'I drink it because I like it. Thank you, Jeremy.'

'Were you born on a plantation, Mrs Brierley?' I asked.

'Born and reared among fields that bore my name. Born in the old days, reared in the old ways, a Halper of Halper's Corner.'

'It sounds marvellous.'

'It was hell on earth, Miss Millett. The Devil walked those fields in the shape of my father, a wicked, lustful, foul-mouthed, drunken atheist. My mother would stumble into my room at midnight to weep by my cot. When she died, many thought it was murder. The other planters would not speak with my father, or have me to their houses. I grew up alone, reared by the devil to be one of his kind.'

'How ghastly,' I said, though actually she made it sound perfectly thrilling, and meant to. 'Do go on.'

'When I was seventeen a man of God came to us, sent from England to do mission work among the negroes. I saw him stand face to face with my father and wrestle there for his soul. My father laughed and swore and turned away, but my heart went out to that young man. I began to toil by his side in the work of the Lord among our poor Negroes, and before the time came when he was called back to England I betrothed myself to him in secret. I promised him I would follow him, but for eight years my father would not let me go. I had no money, no friends but our Negroes. Though I wore silk and lace and walked along the cuts between the cane fields with a servant to carry my parasol over me, I was no more free than an ape in a cage. For eight long years I continued the Lord's work which that young man had begun, bringing the Word to our people where they laboured in the fields. One day the Lord moved me to speak to an old Negro of my sorrow, and thenceforth he and all our people put a portion of their small wages aside, little by little, to help me. In their poverty and in their wretchedness they sought to prove how nobly the seed we had sown among them brought forth its harvest of good works. At last we had gathered enough to pay for my passage to England. One day as I walked among the fields, with my father watching from the verandah, I went into one of the huts, as was my custom, to read the Word of the Lord, but instead I changed clothes with a child of that house and we put flour upon his face and he walked out under the parasol, going from hut to hut, while I was stolen away by the back and hidden in a cart they had ready with my cases, and taken to the harbour and put aboard the steamer for England. As we crossed the harbour bar I saw my father come raging down to the quay.'

'What a romantic story! But what about the people who'd helped you?'

She held up her pudgy, crook-fingered hand, palm forward. I realised this was a party piece, which had to be told in its proper order with its proper words, like a church ritual. She talked with a slightly nasal drawl, which didn't sound American or like anything else I'd heard, and sipped purse-lipped from her glass between sentences. I could imagine black faces, fire-lit, ringing her, as she sat in a space between shanty houses, and the stars overhead, and the punctuating cries of 'Hallelujah' and 'Praise the Lord'.

'I sailed to England,' she said, 'and found my betrothed in Halifax, where I joined myself with him in the work of the Lord. Our son Amos was given to us. Ten years passed, and there was war and the breaking of nations, but we toiled on in the stony field the Lord had made our portion. For five and thirty years we toiled with small reward. Each year at the time of the Lord's birth I wrote to my father and sent him tracts, begging and warning him to repent of his wicked ways, but he sent no answer. Then there was war again, and our son Amos was called to fight. Within a year there came a letter from a lawyer in Bridgetown saying that my father had died and Halper's Corner was now mine, subject to heavy mortgages. I spoke with my husband and we made plans to return to the place where we had met and take up the work we had begun there, but because of the war we could not travel, and then within the year the Lord called him to His side and I was left desolate. My son Amos was in Italy. I had none to turn to. But at last the war ended and I gathered my possessions and sailed home to take up my inheritance. All was in ruin. Though the war had given fat years to sugar planters, there had been none to manage Halper's Corner, and with peace the lean years came. Only one seed still prospered. The Word of the Lord that with my husband's help I had sown among our people was now a strong green tree. Many remembered me and rejoiced at my return. They told me that my father had died as he had lived, ninety-five years old, raging in sin. They told me too that on my escape his fury had been terrible, so that he might have slain my helpers with his own hands, but foreseeing this they had persuaded the doctor from Holetown to come up, giving other reasons, and this man, though a feeble vessel, constrained my father by his presence. And the other landlords around were happy to thwart my father, so it was not difficult to hide my chief helpers, the boy who had carried my parasol, and the boy who had worn my dress. He stands before you now, my brother and servant Jeremy.'

'The Lord shall deliver me from every evil work,' said Jeremy.

I hadn't realised he was still in the room, but he was, standing by the door and listening eagerly to the story. He smiled again when I caught his eye. There was something familiar about the smile which made me blink inwardly, and see him with different eyes. The likeness was nowhere near as strong as that between B and his mother, but it was there. When Mrs Brierley had called Jeremy her brother, she had meant it. Stepbrother, anyway.

'How marvellous!' I said. 'Did you manage to get the plantation going again? Was it very beautiful?'

She looked at me half-sideways over her glass. Knowing B as well as I did I thought she was pleased. I guessed he had brought me along because it would give her somebody new to tell her story to. Judging by the few words they'd said to each other so far, they didn't find tête-à-têtes very easy.

'If Amos had stayed we might have done it, with the Lord's help,' she said.

'We'd have needed that,' said B. 'Sugar's been in the doldrums for five years. The places which had built up a bit of fat during the war have managed to keep going, but Halper's was run right down and mortgaged twice over.'

'Now they are giving us the Commonwealth Sugar Agreement,' said Jeremy. I expected him to add 'Hallelujah,' but he didn't.

B shot him one of his looks. I thought he was about to snap at him to clear out, but perhaps he wasn't quite prepared to take that line with his step-uncle. Instead he just growled, 'Too late. Tell Miss Millett what it looked like, Mother.'

'Ah,' she said. 'It is an old house, built by my forebear Cleck Halper in the year of our Lord seventeen hundred and twelve. Built and well built, but my father neglected it. I did not think it beautiful when I was a child, but when I returned and saw it in its ruin my heart went out in grief. The fields around are fields of cane, with cuts between, beautiful in the green and gold of their season. And beyond the road is a little bay with a beach, where my mother used to take me when I was a child and teach me my letters in the sand. That was surely beautiful, according to the beauty of this world.'

She was talking now in a much less here-endeth-the-second-lesson style, but with her drawl more pronounced. I thought perhaps this was part of the story that she didn't often tell.

'It sounds lovely,' I said. 'Can we go and see it?'

'Waste of time,' said B. 'Miss Millett is going to inherit an old house, Mother. That's why she's interested.'

'Lay not up for yourself treasures upon earth,' she said.

'It seems to be more a case of laying up for yourself troubles upon earth,' I said. 'Besides, I didn't do the laying up. It all happened before I was born. Perhaps one day I'll run away for love, like you did.'

In fact B made very little fuss about driving me out to Halper's Corner. I felt that he actually wanted to go, but at the same time not to seem to want to. It was difficult to be sure. He'd been more than usually unpredictable these last few days.

The house we were staying in—I never found out who it belonged to, but B said it wasn't his, and it had a used feeling, half-full bottles in the drinks cabinet, recent copies of *Life* and *Harpers*, servants and a gardener—also provided a vast squashy American car, a convertible. We drove up the West Coast Road in the middle of the afternoon. B was in one of his withdrawn moods, so I fantasised about being a film star being taken by my director to look at the location for a lush plantation romance—brutal planter, sullen-seeming daughter, noble young missionary—there'd have to be an alternative lover, of course, spit image of Mark Babington—*he* would be the one who rode frantic to the quay as the ship sailed for England—finish in misty glow as lovers embrace at Liverpool with Salvation Army Silver Band for background, and skip the grinding years in Halifax—not Hollywood material . . .

Before I'd come to Barbados I'd created it vividly in my mind's eye, white beaches and palms round the fringe, and a hinterland of steep jungly mountains, brilliant with parakeets and hibiscus. Quite wrong. It turned out to be a land-scape rather like one of the duller English counties, rolling, undistinguished hills given over to farming. It obviously wasn't England, because of the blueness of the sky and the blackness of the people and their crowdedness and poverty, and the height of the sugar cane in the fields; the beaches and hibiscus were there too. So one was abroad, but not very. Mrs Brierley's flat still felt far more foreign than anything else I'd come across. Up the West Coast Road, where the land was poorer than elsewhere, there were certainly unfarmed patches, but even these had a scrubby, battered look. The sheer number of people on the island meant that there was almost nowhere really wild and lonely. It was all a bit like a town, with fields instead of houses. I had prepared myself to be disappointed well before B turned up a track between cane-fields. The lie of the low hills enclosed a flat triangular area. The sea dropped out of sight behind us and for once I felt here was a place of isolation. A black man on an old bicycle came bumping down the track towards us, pulled aside to let us pass and gaped as we went through. A hundred yards further on, as the track rose to one of the boundary hills, it was barred by rusted iron gates hanging askew between a pair of grand stone gateposts. B stopped and we climbed out.

The gates were padlocked, but a footpath had been beaten through a breach in the stone wall, so we followed it round and up what must once have been the sweep of a carriage drive but was now only a path one man wide and barely kept open, through the tangle of sweet-smelling undergrowth, lush with feeding on its own decay and raucous with insect life. The tops of three vast palms were visible above the bushes, but no sign of a roof or chimney.

I led the way until the path opened into a clearing. As I approached it I could see a tethered goat, but then a black boy leapt across the gap with his left elbow and shoulder angled forward and his right arm flung stiffly back, the hand clutch-ing a battered old ball. A couple of seconds later I heard the snap of the ball on to a bat. I walked on into the clearing and there was the house. It was stone built, three storeys high. A double curve of stone steps rose to the broken front door, and the porch had been extended on either side to make a deep balcony the whole width of the house, the verandah where Mrs Brierley's father used to sit and watch as she carried the Word of God to his labourers down below. There had been three grand Dutch-style gables at roof level, but the whole south-west corner of the house was in ruins. Once there had been four of the big palms, symmetrically planted at the corners of the building. Three great smooth trunks still rose in place, but the fourth had fallen and lay with half its roots in the air and its trunk slanting up through the wall of the house as if it had poked its head in through the window to see what was happening in the nursery. The falling masonry had smashed through the verandah roof that end, but on the other side it was still intact and the verandah seemed to be used now as an open-air kitchen, with the black iron chimney of the stove lashed to a filigree pillar. In the clearing two more goats grazed, and chickens clucked in dust baths. Beyond the corner of the house an old man was hoeing a vegetable patch. Nearer were the cricket players, two boys and a girl.

The girl saw me as she straightened from picking the ball up. Her hesitation made the bowler turn. He was black as a boot, but the girl was paler, as was the younger boy with the bat. Both of these were quite clearly Halpers. I realised that when Mrs Brierley had described her father as lustful she'd had some evidence to go on. The bowler stared at me for a moment, then turned and shouted to the man with the hoe, who shaded his eyes and gazed before coming slowly towards us.

'The tree came down in the '44 hurricane,' said B.

'It's too sad. They must have been planted when the house was built.'

'I should think so. Hello, you're Philemon, aren't you?'

'Yes, please, Mr Halper. Glad to see your face, Mr Halper.'

'My name's Brierley,' said B in a bored voice, watching the cricket, without seeming to be interested in that either.

'Do you remember old Mr Halper?' I asked.

'Sure I see Miss Mary's father.'

'What was he like?'

The old man glanced towards B and pointed. Like that.

'Die way he live,' he said. 'Drunk and cursing. Bring ruin on us all.'

'Rubbish,' said B, who couldn't have seen the gesture. 'He kept things going his own way till he was getting on ninety. It was my mother running off and leaving him with no one to help did the damage. She should have stuck it out here. Seen enough? Let's go.'

'You tell me what going to happen, sir?' said Philemon. 'Nobody know what going to happen.'

B gave him a bleak look.

'Your guess is as good as mine,' he said, and turned away. Philemon shook his head and hobbled back towards his vegetables.

Because of the narrowness of the track I couldn't talk to B properly till we were in the car.

'You didn't have to be quite so foul to that old man,' I said. 'Surely you've got some idea. It's his whole life, after all.'

'I thought I did but now I don't,' said B.

'You're hating this, aren't you?'

'I decided you'd better see it.'

He didn't start the car but sat brooding at the even acres of half-grown cane.

'Apart from the house it doesn't look all that run down,' I said.

'Not bad, I gather.'

'Oh, I thought you'd sold it.'

'Not yet. No point. Get nothing for it with the sugar market shot to hell. I've been waiting for a turn-up, paying off the mortgages and meanwhile working it up into a state where it will fetch something.'

It didn't sound at all B's style to pay off mortgages before he had to, but I didn't say so.

'What's this sugar agreement Jeremy was talking about?' I asked. 'I noticed you shut him up.'

'Commonwealth Sugar Agreement. Becomes operative next year. Should stabilise the market, and then I can sell and sort things out.'

'Is it yours or your mother's?'

'Mine, effectively. I bought her an annuity in exchange. She got much better terms than she'd have done if she'd simply sold it then, so I don't want her now getting it into her head that she should have hung on. None of us knew this agreement was coming up. It was only passed last year. Shall we go?'

He sounded relieved, as though this was what he had brought me out here to tell me. For some reason it had been worrying him, and might even explain his recent edginess.

'All right,' I said. 'Can we look at the bay, though, first?'

'What bay?'

'The one where her mother used to teach her her letters in the sand.'

'You don't want to see that. It's just a bay.'

'Please. As we're here. It was important to her, wasn't it?'

'You liked the old frump?'

'I think she's terrific. After a life like that.'

'I don't owe her anything.'

'I expect other people's mothers tend to seem OK. A lot of my friends can't see what's wrong with mine. But don't you have a hankering, darling, to see the house in order again?'

'Not worth the effort.'

'That's not what I meant. Suppose your fairy godmother were to wave her wand and there it was, roof mended, garden spick, all four palm trees standing, and you sitting on the verandah smoking a cigar while a shiny black butler brought you your punch on a silver tray?'

'No,' he said, and started the engine.

We drove bumpily down to the main road, headed north, and a quarter of a mile later turned left along a fresh-laid concrete track towards the sea. It wound between dunes, bare sand in some places, and in others spiky plants like yuccas, scrubby bushes and a few palm trees. At the shore-line—a dazzle of white beach between two wooded headlands—it curved back and climbed a low outcrop a hundred yards inland. Up there there were signs of work, obviously connected with the newness of the road. I could see a jeep, and the tip of a crane. Apart from that the bay was, as Mrs Brierley had claimed, beautiful according to the beauty of this world.

'It's a long way from the house,' I said, thinking what a release it must have seemed to mother and child, so far from the brutal troll who ruled the cane-fields.

'My great-grandfather bought it to dredge so that he could ship his cane straight out,' said B. 'That was always the chief problem—too far from the factories. But he was caught by the 1876 slump.'

'What's happening up there?'

'New hotel, mainly.'

'How dreadful.'

'Don't be a snob.'

'I am a snob. I can't help it. It's like the idea of trippers trooping round Cheadle. We do have open days, but the family all hide and pretend they aren't happening. Don't you feel that at all?'

'Why should I? I was born and brought up in Halifax. People who live most of their lives in places like Halifax consider it an excellent idea that hotels should be built by otherwise useless beaches for them to stay at.'

'That's not what I meant.'

'I know. You're trying to make me say that because my family have kept it as a wild bay for eighty years I should continue to do so. You forget that we originally bought it for commercial exploitation. In any case your whole idea is based on a misconception. I am the man who was born in Halifax. Any feelings I have are appropriate to that man. In fact my feelings towards Halifax are that it was a place to get away from and never go back to. But the man I am could not have been born here. Suppose my mother had not run off and joined my father, she would most likely never have married. But if she had, and had then had a child, that child would not have become me. Even if the father had been my father, that is still true. We are who we are by the accident of a moment. You ought to know that. You are one of a pair of twins because of a momentary readjustment of molecules in a uterus twenty-two years ago.'

He lolled back on the soft bench-seat of the car, his brown face more toad-like than ever because of his impenetrable sun-glasses. His voice too had the reptilian creak which came when he was talking about something important to him. I had learnt more about him today than in all the rest of our friendship. I even knew his age, born ten years before the First World War, 'not yet fifty'—just. I wondered if he guessed how effective it was, bringing Jane in. I'd often tried to imagine what would have happened if Jane and I had never separated, if *we* had been born as *I*. The idea was part of my fairy-tale world in which everything was all right; and now that world contained the image of a curious toad-like boy and his yellow toad-like mother coming to this bay so that she could teach him his letters in the sand. For some reason the mental picture, combined with B's real face in front of me now, made me see something I hadn't seen before.

'You've got Negro blood, haven't you?' I said.

He didn't answer for several seconds. I cursed myself for my stupidity. Then he said, 'Does it matter?'

'Not to me. Not a scrap, darling, honestly. It's just interesting.'

'The true reason why the other planters chose to have nothing to do with my grandfather was that he had married a quadroon. My mother is therefore an octoroon.'

'How lovely. That's a word I've never come across except in crossword puzzles.'

'It is a word which has ruined lives.'

'I suppose so. But it's nothing compared to the Halper side of you, is it? That must be fantastically strong. If we had a baby I wonder whose face it would have.'

'Mine, of course. That's why we're not going to.'

'I think we'd get a slightly yellow Millett. You can see this piggy nose in the Long Gallery, snuffling out under wigs and over ruffs for generations. Even old Lely couldn't do much about it.'

'The Halpers would win all the same.'

'Got you!'

'What do you mean?'

'Whatever you say you're secretly proud of your family.'

'My family is still alive, in me.'

'It won't be much longer unless you start doing something about the next generation.'

'Haven't you noticed? My grandfather did quite enough to let me off the obligation.'

'You're scared of losing to the Milletts. I bet you . . .'

'Don't be a fool.'

'I'm serious, I think. I mean . . . you see, I've been wondering why you let me bully you into coming out here. You've hated it, haven't you? I think it might be your way of telling me what you think about me and Cheadle. That it isn't worth it, I mean. I ought to get loose from it and do something else with my life. Like . . . Do take those beastly specs off. I can't see what you're thinking.'

'I am thinking that if you say anything more about babies I shall boot you out.'

Booting me out was a running joke, though the possibility of it being true always gave me a slight kick, and him too, I think, reminding us of the tricky balance we'd set up and the certainty that we were going to fall off the wire one day —though when it happened it was not going to be anything like this.

'I've thought of a new and thrilling revenge,' I said. 'I shall picket your bridge club and proclaim the story of my wrongs on a sandwich board.'

'The police will move you on.'

'Policemen eat out of my hand.'

This was part of the game. B enjoyed fending off imaginary attacks on his power-bases, though he was incapable of producing the mildest leap of fantasy in response to my flights. We might have gone on for some time if a car hadn't drawn up behind us and blared its hooter. B drove forward, found a turning-place and reversed into it. As the other car came by I saw that the driver was the boring property developer, Henry van Something, with whom I'd had to put up all through an endless dinner party a couple of evenings before. He waved to us and drove on.

'Are you selling it to him?' I said. 'I couldn't stand that.'

'There's a syndicate. It's quite a big deal.'

'Worse still.'

I woke in the middle of the night and knew without reaching out to feel that B wasn't there. Normally he willed himself asleep in two minutes and slept all night, turning once as if he was a chop being fried. I lay for a while, listening to the distant whisper of the sea, then got up and went out on to the balcony. He was leaning on the rail in his pyjamas, staring out towards America. There was no moon, but lots of stars above and fireflies in the garden. Apart from them sea and land were pitch black and it was nothing like as warm as you'd expect a tropic night to be. I slid my arm up under his pyjama top and ran my fingers over the knotty muscles below his shoulder-blades. He seemed not to notice.

'What's the matter?' I said. 'Just money?'

'No. There's enough of that. Or there would be. It's in the wrong place.'

'Can't you move it?'

'I thought I could. Been setting it up for years. But now . . .'

'Because of Mummy?'

'Partly.'

'Can't you just buy her off?'

'Why should I?'

'I had an idea. It came to me in my sleep. Would you mind if *I* bought her off?'

'A hundred and twenty thousand pounds?'

'But would you let me?'

'Up to you. But I'm not going to lend you the money.'

'I know. But I could sell my sapphires.'

He grunted.

'They're insured for two hundred and fifty thousand,' I said. 'I know you don't get as much as that, and just as sapphires they aren't worth it. It's Mary's stone makes the difference. But I thought if you helped me find someone to buy them we might get enough. We could make it a condition they didn't tell anyone for a couple of years. I can go on wearing the replica if I have to. Would it help? Would it make any difference?'

He was silent so long I thought he'd stopped listening.

'You're certain they're yours to sell?' he said.

'Daddy left them to me outright. They're not entailed or part of the Trust or anything.'

'Odd.'

'I've always thought he wanted me to feel I had something of my own which I could do what I liked with. I wasn't a complete slave to the house.'

'I suppose it's a possibility. I told you it was only part of the deal your mother proposed?'

'You don't have to explain. Jane told me. That's nonsense. We may look alike but we're not swaps. Jane thinks so too.'

'So do I.'

He said it without thinking, a casual comment on a side-issue to the main business, but it was a fantastic relief to hear. I put my head on his shoulder and leaned against him. Both our bodies were chilly with the night air, but as the warmth came back between us I persuaded myself I could feel him beginning to relax.

'It might be a possibility,' he said at last. 'I'll have to sort it out. Would your mother stay bought?'

'Oh, I think so. Provided she didn't find out where the money really came from. She isn't a complete crook.'

VIII

Sergeant Sawyer was scowling in his booth as usual, the lift juddered up in the same old way, and there was the regular pile of Monday manuscripts waiting to be read on my desk. Rather than face them I went off to the middle room to say hello. When Tom looked up to ask if I'd had a good holiday he sounded perfectly normal—only slightly guarded when I asked how things were going. We arranged to have luncheon at El Vino's and I assumed he would tell me then.

The first real sign that I got that things were different was from Nellie. I'd skimmed through a dozen manuscripts, even direr than usual because writers who'd stopped trying, convinced that Jack Todd had a personal vendetta against them, were having another go—many of them actually said so in their covering letters. Depression had already set in when Nellie came through the swing doors.

'The Editor would like to see you, Mabs,' she said.

She spoke as though she hardly knew me. She didn't ask about my holiday. She sounded as though she was struggling through a miserable dream.

'Oh, Nellie, I'm sorry,' I said.

'I dare say we shall get used to things.'

I had to give the door a shove to force it over the pile of the new carpet. Elephant grey, I saw. And yes, white walls, Swedish chairs, stainless steel floor-lamps; linen curtains. No Buffets on the walls, though, but cartoons, new ones, including several blondes-in-bed-with-rich-old-men. Mr Naylor was sitting behind a huge, flat-topped, fake-antique partner's desk, reading next Thursday's magazine.

'Sit down,' he said and went on reading. He kept me waiting five minutes, at least. Some pages he merely glanced at, others he read for a while before turning on with an impatient flick. I wondered if he'd asked me in to say he had no more use for me. He put the paper down as if he'd found what he was looking for and stared at me through his beady little spectacles.

'I'm told you come from a posh kind of home,' he said.

'I suppose . . . well, yes.'

'What do you make of this?'

He smacked the magazine with the back of his hand. I had to stand to see where he'd got it open. The Round, of course.

'It's surprising how many people read it,' I said.

'Your kind of people?'

'And ones who like to think they are. I used to, when I could. You're a bit ashamed, but it's sort of addictive.'

'You didn't find it totally balls-aching?'

'I'm not actually equipped . . .'

He slammed the desk with his palm to stop me.

'Having ink slung at me I can take,' he said. 'Being picked up on the way I talk I can't.'

'I'm sorry. I didn't mean . . .'

'This is *my* magazine. It has to be the way I want it. I've got to be able to tell my staff what I want in my own language, uncensored, right? If I start trying to mince along like you and Duggan I'll end up running a magazine full of masturbating little articles about getting the lawn-mower to start.'

'Yes, I see.'

'I'm glad you see, Margaret.'

That was the first time he'd used his flat stage voice. Till then he'd had a neutral sort of accent, with only a slight nasal whine in it, and had sounded lively in a rather aggressive way. He'd really let me see he was angry, when he was. I assumed that this was the real Brian Naylor and the stage voice and personality were a defensive system. His behaviour with Jane hadn't suggested that he really expected women to be attracted to him. And that business with the ink—he'd seemed quite likeable then, playing the butt and fall-guy.

'That's what I used to think about the paper before I came,' I said.

'And then you were converted? On your way to Damascus-on-Thames?'

'Only partly. When we get it wrong it can be dreary. And sometimes it's clever without being interesting.'

'All right. What would you do with *this*?'

99

He smacked his hand on the Round again.

'Have we got to keep it?'

'I have got to keep it. You look at the advertising pages sometimes, Margaret?'

'Yes.'

'Then you will have noticed that forty per cent of our income derives from selling various forms of kitsch, and snob-appeal tobacco and perfume and corsets and shoes to a pathetic bunch of social climbers. Until I can build up a less repulsive class of advertiser I have to stick with this shit. So?'

'I don't know,' I said. 'I've thought about it, of course. I used to think you could just do what Mrs Clarke does but write it rather better, but you couldn't. It's really only lists of names, with a few adjectives. You could think up new adjectives, but they'd get dreary too after a few weeks. You couldn't do what I've done with Petronella because that depends on the existence of this. The only other possibility I can see is to turn it into the other sort of gossip-column, lots of names still, but bitchy stories about them. That would be quite expensive. You'd need extra staff, and money to pay your informants. People don't give dirt away when they can sell it. Remember, even doing it the way she does, Mrs Clarke has spent years building up her filing system. Honestly, I don't see a solution.'

'You're going to have to see a solution, because you're taking it over.'

'Oh.'

'Oh, Margaret?'

'I mean no thank you, I suppose. I'd rather not, please.'

'Why?'

'I'd hate to do it the way it is. The reason why people do read it is that somehow they feel Mrs Clarke loves it, and that comes through in spite of everything. Besides, I want to do other things. And on top of that Dorothy—Mrs Clarke—has been terribly nice to me. She hates what I write, but she couldn't have been kinder.'

Mr Naylor sighed, tilted his chair back and gazed at the ceiling.

'Are you there, God?' he said. 'Dear God, sweet God in

heaven, couldn't you have sent me one teeny little professional to work with, instead of a load of whining amateurs? It's not asking much, God, is it?'

He hung balanced, listening for an answer, before letting the swing of the chair flip him forwards to stare at me through his silly little spectacles.

'If you can't do what I want, girlie, you're no use to me,' he said.

'Don't be stupid.'

'So I'm stupid.'

'If I tried to do what you want it would come out boring because I'd be bored with it. There are other reasons, but that's what matters. I dare say there are things I don't know I can do, but . . .'

'How old are you, Margaret?'

'Twenty-one, but . . .'

'Just twenty-one, and so clever!'

'Do you want me to resign?'

'Oh, crap! This is just conversation. What you're going to do now is sit down and get some ideas together about what to do with the Round. Give your manuscripts to Nellie and tell her to put rejection slips on the lot of them. Oh, and don't waste time trying to tell me how la Clarke could jazz up what she's doing. She's out. Finished. Got that?'

He snatched up the magazine and started to read another page. I left and went into the middle room. Ronnie was in, sorting through the review books. Tom looked up with raised eyebrows, somehow aware that I had news.

'I've just offered to resign,' I said.

I got it wrong. It was meant to come out dry and whimsical, but a shake crept in.

'Soon we'll be able to start a rival rag,' said Ronnie. 'You, Dorothy, me. All we need is a backer. Coming, Tom?'

'Ronnie, you're not . . .' I said.

'No option. You know, there is a certain stimulus about getting the sack. New opportunities shimmer. Mirages, no doubt, but it gives one the illusion of being young and starting out afresh.'

'But why on earth?'

'Political incompatibility. I am a red under the bed.'

'But we're not a political magazine!'

'My dear Mabs, *Knitwear Weekly* is a political magazine. And Mr Naylor appears to be something of a Cold Warrior. I should be very interested to know whether any of Mr Amos Brierley's funds come originally from Washington.'

'What an extraordinary idea! You mean the American secret service, whatever it's called, paying for Bruce to draw this week's blonde-in-bed?'

'With Ronnie under it,' said Tom. 'You haven't made it clear, Mabs, whether you are actually staying?'

'Are you?'

'I appear indeed to be chained to this rock.'

'So do I, I suppose.'

'You Andromeda, me Prometheus.'

'I don't think they were chained to the same rock.'

'Not as normally depicted. An opportunity missed, in my opinion. Andromeda, of course, was only required to expose her outer surface, with a wisp of gauze by way of parsley, whereas Prometheus displayed his inward parts, as if for haruspication. It gives a new meaning to the phrase "according to my lights".'

He was juggling with language as usual, but only from habit. He sounded desperately gloomy, whereas Ronnie, by contrast, had seemed decidedly cheerful. I would have liked to ask Ronnie more about his theory that B might be getting funds from the American government, but I always felt I had to be very careful about even mentioning B in the office in case I let something slip. It was funny that Mrs Clarke had said something a bit along the same lines, as though it was a mystery in the City where B's original money had come from. I wasn't looking forward to meeting her, though really I knew there was nothing to be afraid of.

In fact when I got back to my desk I found a note on it in Mrs Clarke's purple ink, asking me to come to her room. I found her standing at her commode with the top drawer open, walking her fingers along a row of filing-cards. She picked one out before turning to me and smiling as if nothing had changed.

'I hope you had a pleasant holiday,' she said.

'Beautiful, thanks.'

'I always enjoy Barbados, but I do not think I would choose to begin there.'

I hadn't told anyone I was going to Barbados. I'd let people think it was Bermuda.

'I was expecting something a bit junglier,' I said.

'I find the social life there a little peculiar. They have their own ideas about things.'

This was certainly true of Mrs Halper, though perhaps not in the way Mrs Clarke meant. I made an agreeing sort of mumble.

'I think I shall spend more time in the islands now,' she said. 'Have you been told that I am leaving the magazine?'

'Yes. I'm terribly sorry, Mrs Clarke . . .'

'My dear, I wish I could say that I do not blame you at all.'

'Honestly, I think everything would have happened exactly the way it has if I'd never set foot in this place.'

'In my opinion you have allowed yourself to become an instrument in the hands of a wicked and odious man.'

'I don't think he's odious right through,' I began. Then I realised she wasn't talking about Mr Naylor. She glanced down at the card she was holding. It was covered in her curious code of symbols on both sides. It had come from near the left-hand side of the top drawer of the commode, roughly where the 'B's must be.

'A man who is prepared to betray his country and to defraud his own mother . . .' she said.

'Please, Mrs Clarke,' I interrupted. 'I think you're wrong. I met . . . but that isn't the point. I just can't talk to you or to anyone here about it. It's a completely separate part of my life. I promise you I never talk to him about anything that happens in here. Never. So I'm afraid that if that's why you asked me to come and see you I shall have to go away.'

I was just managing not to shout. Mrs Clarke looked at me for a moment, turned and put the card away.

'I must tell you that I believe you to be very sadly deceived,' she said, 'and that you will live to regret it. But I will respect what you say. No, I wanted to talk to you about the future of the Social Round. I understand that you are to take it over from now on.'

'Well . . .' I said.

I couldn't really tell her I didn't regard the idea as an enormous honour and responsibility, so we discussed the technical problems of a hand-over. She was chiefly anxious about her filing system which she wanted to take with her because it was full of confidential material, but at the same time she was convinced it was impossible to produce the Round without it. That was what really mattered to her, that the Round should go on. So I had to agree to a kind of consultation system under which I could ring her up and check if I was in difficulty, though I didn't imagine I would ever want to use it, supposing I took the ghastly job on after all.

When we'd finished she sighed and looked round the room.

'So many memories,' she said. 'It will be strange to leave it. I shall take my photographs, of course. Oh, my dear, do you think by any chance we might try again to persuade your dear mother to autograph one, after all? I know it seems pushing of me, but, well, she's actually one of the seven countesses I haven't got.'

'Oh dear,' I said. 'Shall I take it and see what I can do? She can be terribly tiresome about this sort of thing.'

'Oh, would you? That would be most kind.'

She had it ready in a drawer of her desk. A peculiarly awful picture of Mummy and Jane and me at some dance the year before, posed under a vast Constance Spry arrangement, one of her white constructions. The Milletts at their grimmest, doing their duty by the photographer. I had been wearing the sapphires, for some reason.

'I'll do my best,' I said brightly.

'You are a very sweet child. I must confess I am a wee bit anxious for you.'

'Oh, I don't think you need worry. I'm as happy as a sandboy.'

'Oh, my dear, if happiness were everything! Do you remember when you first came here I told you a little story about a girl called Veronica Bracken?'

'Of course I do.'

'Veronica believed she was happy.'

'But she was an idiot. Honestly, Mrs Clarke, I'm doing what

I'm doing with my eyes wide open and I'm certain it's absolutely worth it.'

'Oh, yes, I know that, my dear. That's always true.'

As it was B's bridge night I'd asked Jane to supper. I felt it was specially important to be nice to her now, as she'd taken over bearing the brunt, so I bought a bottle of good burgundy and some lamb chops. (One of the advantages of living with B was that as we almost always ate out I had his meat ration to play with as well as my own.) I also got a few bronze chrysanthemums, which filled the little room with their powdery reek, and cleared my papers and typewriter into the bedroom.

Jane noticed at once. She stood inside the door, looking round and wrinkling her nostrils at the chrysanthemum smell.

'It still feels like a hotel room,' she said.

'You are a beast. I've done my best.'

She hadn't taken any trouble. She looked the grubbiest kind of art student, totally graceless. There was a filthy bandage round the two middle fingers of her left hand.

'What have you done to yourself?' I asked.

She looked down.

'Burnt it with my blow-lamp,' she said.

'Have you shown a doctor?'

'Course not. You're worse than Mummy.'

She flopped herself on to the sofa. She looked utterly haggard. I'd opened the bottle to let it breathe so I poured her a glass and gave it to her.

'Haven't you got any gin?' she said.

'Not up here. If you really want I'll go down and get some.'

'This'll do.'

'How is she?'

'Bloody.'

'Oh, darling, I'm sorry. It's all my fault.'

'Yes.'

'Why isn't she at Cheadle anyway? This time of year . . .'

'I don't know. Can't be so bloody at a distance, I suppose.'

'Look, I'll come round and let her be bloody at me for a change. We're supposed to be going to the ballet but I could tell B . . .'

'Don't bother. She'd only be sweet to you.'

'Oh, God. What can I do?'

'Nothing, short of coming home.'

'Why don't you come and live here? Really?'

'Let's talk about something else. How was the holiday?'

I told her about the beaches and the night clubs and learning to water-ski and seeing Alan Ladd in a restaurant but she wasn't really interested. She kept fiddling with the magazines on the table beside her chair, picking them up, glancing at a page and then tossing them down again. I ploughed on until she reached further over and took the manilla envelope with the photograph in it Mrs Clarke had given me. If Jane had been in a different mood I'd been going to ask her what she thought about tricking Mummy into signing it. The alternative would have been for Jane to forge her signature, which she could do easily. She pulled the picture out and stared.

'God!' she said. 'The wicked stepmother and the pig princesses! If I wanted to show someone an example of what I utterly detest about the life I've lived so far, it would be this. What on earth have you got it here for?'

I explained, playing it down. To my surprise Jane seemed to take to the idea with a sort of grim amusement.

'Might infuriate her in a new direction for a few minutes,' she said, stuffing the envelope into her canvas carrier. 'Is there anything to eat?'

She gobbled her supper without seeming to notice the trouble I'd taken. I could see from the way she held her fork that her hand must be really sore but she got angry when I tried to sympathise. Between mouthfuls she gabbled on about some internal feud at her art college, where one gang of teachers was still trying to insist on students learning to draw from the life and so on, while the other lot only wanted to help them follow their own creative impulses, which mustn't be clogged up with learning outmoded techniques. She went through the current rumpus in detail, with all the names of these people I didn't know from Adam, but I could sense that she wasn't actually interested. It was just a way of stopping me asking about Mummy. After supper she jumped up and rushed off to the sink with the dirty plates.

'Oh, for God's sake!' I said. 'Can't you be a bit restful?'

'In this place? Sitting around like actors pretending we live here? Nobody lives here.'

'You might at least wait till I've made the coffee. Hell! Coffee! Look, there's some downstairs. I'll just . . .'

'Let's go and have it down there. I might feel more real down there.'

'Oh, well, I don't . . .'

'Honestly, Mabs! He isn't Bluebeard! Is he?'

'Of course not. But . . .'

'I don't want to hang on here. I think I'll go home.'

'Please, darling . . . Oh, I suppose it'll be all right. Provided you let me bandage your hand.'

'Have you got one?'

'That's the point. He's never ill, but he's a maniac about health. He's a frightful coward. The slightest scratch and you have to rush for antiseptics and plasters.'

'And if he comes home and catches us you can tell him . . Oh, Mabs, he is Bluebeard!'

She sounded much more cheerful now she'd got her way. When we got down she wandered round looking at everything while I made the coffee. I came back and found her holding a little ivory statue of a saint B had brought back from his last trip to Germany.

'This is perfect,' she said. 'The Brancusi's a dream, too, but this . . . He must have been in Italy.'

'No. Hamburg, actually.'

'Of course it's German, you idiot. Rather early. But he must have been looking at Italian . . .'

'Who must?'

'The artist, for heaven's sake. Are you blind? Look.'

She poised the carving in her damaged hand and ran her right forefinger down the line of the arm to the hand, which held a sort of flail. The face was an old man's, contorted with pain. B I knew loved it, as Jane did, but I preferred not to look. In my mind's ear I could hear the screams.

'They probably beat him to death with that thing,' I said.

'It doesn't matter. You know, I'm almost sure I've seen this in a book somewhere. Or its spit image . . .'

'Your coffee'll get cold.'

'Oh, all right. I've found some terrific chocs.'

'You haven't!'

'I've only eaten two so far, darling.'

When we'd had our coffee I went off to B's exercise-room and found a bandage, lint, and some antibiotic ointment he'd brought back from America. We settled side by side on the sofa so that I could get at Jane's hand. Her whole mood seemed to have changed, becoming sleek and purring.

'Does he love you, Mabs?' she said.

'I don't know. He wouldn't say. I'm fairly sure he likes me. I love him.'

'Really? I mean it would be easy to persuade yourself, in the circs.'

'Oh, I know. I'm having fun. And I like being told and shown. That was extra good wine I gave you, did you realise? I can tell now. Would you like some proper brandy?'

'Don't twist the knife, darling.'

'Luxury is lovely.'

'Is he really stupendously rich?'

'Oh, no. It's other people's money mostly. I get the impression he's had a pretty good year, but there's never enough for what he wants to do. He gets very frustrated sometimes about not being able to move it around as fast as he wants. You know, exchange controls and things. He thought the Conservatives were going to sweep all that away when they got in.'

'I thought that was only to stop you getting money out of England. You can be as rich as you like here. Some of these things must have set him back, Mabs. Brancusis aren't cheap. And that little *Pietà* . . .'

She pointed towards the dead grey face of Christ in the picture on the wall.

'He gets them in Germany,' I said. 'There's probably a lot of things just turning up still, and antique shops not knowing what they are.'

'I bet I can find out what that ivory is. Ouch!'

'Sorry. One more. There. Did you wash it before you put the bandage on?'

'Course I did.'

'It doesn't look very nice, darling. I hope this stuff is all right. It says burns and cuts.'

'Slap it on, Brown Owl. I wonder how you start getting rich.'

'In our case you become a master dyer and snap up a monastery.'

'But now? What about him?'

'I've no idea. Mrs Clarke once dropped some warning hints, though.'

'Sounds thrilling. Why don't you ask him?'

'Fatal.'

'I think he really must be Bluebeard, darling.'

'It was Sister Anne caused all the trouble, Sister Jane.'

'Don't you?'

'At least two of his exes are still alive.'

'That's a relief.'

'But you're right in a way. There is something dangerous about him. I realised that the first time I saw him, at Fenella's party, you remember, when we had that stupid fratch about Penny's dress. He's sort of wild. Not tame. And there's only one of him. Our rules don't apply. I'd better wrap this a bit tight so that it stays tidy. If it starts to hurt badly you've got to promise to show it to a doctor.'

'Promise. It's a pretty civilised sort of wild, Mabs. Brancusis and things. Stamping through the forest in his jewelled collar.'

'Spot on. That's him. And he's tame for me.'

'Lucky you.'

I wound the bandage slowly, partly to make sure of getting it neat and firm, but partly to prolong the process. The old magic of touching was having its effect, softening the scar where we had once been joined. In that mood it did seem possible, almost desirable, that Jane should move in, not upstairs but down here. B could take her to galleries, and to ballet which bored me almost as much. Nobody would know it wasn't the same girl. And when we were alone, three who were almost two . . .

I tied the knot and snipped the ends off but didn't let go of her hand.

'What shall we do now?' I said. 'Shall I wash your hair for

109

you? You can't do it with a bandage, and it's high time by the look of it.'

'Mummy's trying to make me go back to having it frizzed.'

'Don't stand any nonsense.'

She eased her hand out of mine and tucked herself into the far corner of the sofa.

'You aren't there now,' she said.

I had been, for more than twenty years, but there was no point in saying so.

'Anyway, shan't I wash it for you?'

'No thanks. I don't feel like it.'

'All right. How's the roof?'

'Nothing happening. She's sacked the architect again.'

I asked B about the ivory statuette next evening.

'South German,' he said. 'Early. A bit unusual. Got an Italian feel about it.'

'Jane thought it was dreamy. I brought her down here to bandage her hand. She'd burnt it with a blow-lamp. I'm afraid she ate some of your chocs.'

(He was bound to notice so it was sense to warn him.)

'Tell her it's only a copy,' he said.

'Is it?'

'If I say so. What did you put on her hand?'

I had to explain in detail. He seemed much more interested in that.

IX

He came in with a brown paper parcel under his arm and put it on the corner of his desk.

'Something's come up,' he said. 'I've got to go abroad.'

'Oh. When?'

'Tonight.'

'Germany?'

He shook his head.

'Barbados?'

'That general direction.'

'Can I . . .'

'No.'

'Is your mother all right?'

'As far as I know.'

'What about the theatre?'

'You go. The tickets are in the telephone drawer. Take your sister.'

'I'd rather be with you.'

I'd been waiting for him in a new dress, flame-coloured silk, which I thought I looked specially good in. We were going to the first night of something called *The Boy Friend*.

'How long will you be away?'

'Can't be sure. Few days. I've got a present for you.'

He passed me the parcel. I'd assumed it was just another exercise gadget of the sort he was always experimenting with. I took it from him with a feeling of doubt. He'd sometimes brought me things like scent, and often chocolates so that he could eat them himself, but never anything unusual. The parcel was just a box in a brown paper bag, which rattled as I turned it over. I pulled the bag off and sat looking at a picture of a tapestry, a white unicorn sitting in a fenced enclosure, the dark green ground peppered with tiny flowers, a tree in the middle to which the unicorn was chained. 'The Thousand-piece Jigsaw,' it said.

I put the box on the floor and stood up.

'Is something wrong?' I said.

'Not too good.'

'And you want to say goodbye.'

'It may come to that.'

'Can't I come with you?'

'No.'

'When's your aeroplane?'

'Half-past ten.'

'I could come with you that far.'

'You'd better go to this play. I hear it might transfer.'

'I could sit quietly here in the corner and do your jigsaw.'

'Please, Margaret.'

He never said 'please'. I couldn't remember once.

'All right,' I said. 'Do you want me out of the way now?'

'Let's have a drink.'

He gave himself a scotch twice his usual size. I put some gin in my vermouth and sat on the arm of his chair. I wanted to be close to him. Vaguely, I suppose, I was still hoping I might be able to coax him into letting me come too.

'Do you remember,' I said, 'you told me you liked knowing there was one person in the world who trusted you?'

'Yes.'

'It's still true.'

'So is the reverse.'

It took me a moment to work it out.

'Of course you can,' I said.

'I meant more than that.'

This time I didn't understand at all, but when he was in one of his cryptic moods it just irritated him to be asked what he meant. I tried to relax. The drink wasn't being any help. I could sense his tension, like that feeling you sometimes get when you know something is humming near by though you can't actually hear it.

'Is it very bad?' I said.

'Moderately. The odds aren't as friendly as I'd like. It could very well turn out all right.'

'I wish I could help.'

He stroked the back of my hand where it lay on his forearm.

'It's been a pretty good year,' he said.

'Best in my life.'

'I'm glad of that.'

Obviously he didn't want a big fuss. We finished our drinks in silence. I went and changed into another dress—I'd been wearing the new one for him, and as I hung it up it struck me that I might never wear it at all. He didn't come and watch me changing or seem to notice the difference when I came back. I switched the telephone through and picked up the jigsaw.

'You needn't go yet,' he said.

'I thought it would be less of a nuisance if I did my telephoning upstairs,' I said. 'I've got to find someone to go to this play with.'

'Oh, yes. Leave that thing here. I don't want you starting it till I've gone. The idea is to keep you out of trouble while I'm away.'

It was absolutely the wrong thing for him to be saying, common, ordinary, inept. I longed to hug him, to comfort him, to cradle his worries away.

'All right,' I said.

I kissed his forehead and went upstairs.

I didn't actually try to find anyone to go to the theatre with. The last thing I felt like was watching a new musical, but I went because I'd told him I would. My taxi had one of those journeys you sometimes get, slishing through the April drizzle with all the lights green and magical gaps opening in the traffic to let you through, so I reached the theatre far too early. It was the Players, friendly and shabby. B preferred that sort of event to big Shaftesbury Avenue first nights. He liked to feel he might be in at the start of something interesting. At least it meant I didn't feel quite so conspicuous unescorted and with an empty seat beside me.

I was pretending to read the programme and wondering whether I would see him again when the rest of my row filled up with a dozen people arriving together. A large man settled beside me.

'Hello, Mabs,' he said. 'Alone?'

It was Mark Babington.

He sounded cheerful, relaxed, friendly. He told me that he'd put one per cent of the backing into the play and had brought some friends along to see that it got off to a good start. Afterwards he insisted on my joining the celebration party.

I let myself in at about one in the morning. There was always the faint, faint chance that B had had to cancel his flight or something, and in any case I wanted to sleep in our bed. No luck. His travelling case was gone, and his shaving things, and his light overcoat. The jigsaw had been picked up from the floor and placed in the middle of the table. My heart went small and cold as I looked at it. The mild alleviation of misery that had come from drink and company and the infectious euphoria of what was obviously going to be an enormously successful show slid away. There would be a message inside the box. Business arrangements, the rent for my flat and so on. He might say 'Thank you' but not 'I love you'. He did not think like that.

It was better to get it over. It always is.

The box felt heavier now, its rattle muffled. When I opened it I saw the jigsaw pieces were still there, but all huddled into one end. I noticed one printed with a milk-white hoof. The other end of the box was wedged tight with tissue paper. I picked it out and dropped it wad by wad on the carpet. Didn't he see I'd much rather not have anything, least of all some expensive gewgaw? He might not love me, but I loved him. I didn't need paying off, for God's sake! By the time I came to the central package I'd worked myself into a muddled frenzy. On the surface, rage. Beneath, panic. With a swoop of relief I saw the envelope with his gift in it.

It was an ordinary long white envelope, the sort he used for his business letters. It had my name on it in his writing, and a short sentence heavily inked out. It had been sealed, opened again, and re-sealed with stamp paper. That was the point. If he'd been paying me off he might have bought the jigsaw and put his present in an unglamorous white envelope inside, but it would have been a new envelope. This was incredibly not like B. Messy. Dithering. Wrong. I forced my fingers to pull the envelope open.

It was the sapphires, of course. Somehow I knew they were the real ones, although until that instant I had assumed that he had sold them for me, and I should never see them again. I

114

slid them through my hands until I found Mary's stone and turned it over. The little double cross was there, just below the point of the setting. I had to squint through my tears to see it. But he'd given me that enormous cheque for them, and I'd immediately paid it back for him to send to Mummy. I stood for ages, running the jewels from hand to hand like a rosary, filled to the brim with doom. At last I came part of the way back to my senses. I'd have to do something with the vile object. I refused to sleep with it under my pillow, not that near.

The obvious place was the wall safe, where he let me keep the replica and my other bits of jewellery. It was hidden behind a row of encyclopaedias in the bookshelf. I knelt and lugged the volumes out. The wheels were already set at the combination and the door opened when I pulled it. It was almost empty, only my own various little boxes. Usually it was stuffed with documents, and a wad of five-pound notes, and a wash-leather bag full of sovereigns. My hands thought for me, automatically taking out the replica case. They were aware that if there was only one case then the real necklace must have it. But it was empty. This did not seem strange in the general daze of strangeness. My hands arranged the necklace into the velvet pits and grooves, put the case back in the safe, closed the door, spun the dials and shoved the volumes on to their shelf. I rose and returned to the table where I stood staring down at the muddle of pieces in the jigsaw box.

He was sending me home. He had given me back the sapphires. He did not need my love.

I went up to my own flat to try and sleep in that bed where I'd never slept before, strange, narrow, cold.

They gunned him down in Rio. * It was thirty-six hours before I knew. He had flown off on the Wednesday evening. He was killed late on Friday afternoon, the small hours of Saturday

---

* This tawdry phrase is still my only means of thinking of the event. If I had been there at his side perhaps I could think of it (if I could think of it at all) in terms of the sudden clatter, the bewilderment, my own throat numb with screaming, the smashed body bleeding on to my dress. As it is, my contact is through a newspaper headline. I would rather have that than nothing at all.

morning our time. I was presumably asleep, or more likely lying awake and wondering whether I would get back to sleep and trying not to start again on the useless chain of thoughts trudging round and round in my head like prisoners in an exercise yard, about going home, and coping with Mummy, and Cheadle, and what was left of my life.

Saturday morning I spent moving my things out of his flat, as far as possible wiping out any traces of my ever having lived there. I found the replica of my necklace, loose, among my nylons. This was as strange as anything in the whole business. I almost felt that somebody quite different must have been in the flat after he'd left, doing things he would never have done. Dithering, panicking, changing his mind. Not having the nerve to say a proper goodbye to me, to my face. He'd been going to take the replica with him, but then, while he'd been packing . . . And before that he'd been going to take the real necklace. It hadn't been in the box when he gave it me. Only a message.

I went and got the envelope out of the waste-paper basket and for the umpteenth time tried to read the scratched-out sentence. No use. He didn't mean me to. . . . *one person in the world who trusted you? It's still true. So is the reverse.* My doped mind jiggled the words to and fro. *You trusted one person in the world. Who?*

Me.

B had left me a message because I was the only person in the world he trusted. He had told me so. And then he had changed his mind and left me the sapphires instead. And gone off in a panic.

I gave up thinking about it. There wasn't any point any longer.

In the middle of Saturday afternoon I spilt the jigsaw pieces out on to my desk upstairs and began. It had to be done. Then I could give it away to a hospital or something. It was a fiend, all muddy shades of green with little flowers, the paler tree, and a fair amount of brown fence. I kept the unicorn pieces to the end. It was a sort of magic, I suppose, as though the unicorn stood for him and when I pieced it together, whole, in its proper place, that would bring him back safe. Though not to me. I'd got about half done when I went to bed on Saturday,

116

after midnight. Pieces of jigsaw floated to and fro under my closed eyelids, but then for some reason I slept solidly till morning. It was noon on Sunday and I had almost finished when the telephone rang.

Jane.

'Do you . . . Have you . . . Mabs, do you know?'

'Know what?'

'Oh, darling!'

'For God's sake!'

'Oh, it's my . . . I can't . . . Didn't you get the papers?'

'The newspapers?'

'Yes, of course. The *Sunday Times*. Page One.'

I had no idea what she was talking about. It crossed my mind that Mummy might have gone mad and assaulted the architect. Something to do with Cheadle anyway. Something right outside me.

'They're downstairs, I suppose. I'll go and look now. I take it it's bad.'

'Yes. Oh, Mabs!'

I rang off and hurried out, too tired and drained for worry. One of the Dolphin Square porters used to come round leaving the papers on tenants' doormats, but naturally none were ordered for me upstairs and the other people on my floor had already taken theirs in. I took the lift down to B's. He liked several. They lay folded in a thick wad, but with the *Times* outermost, its main headline showing. PEACE MOVE IN KOREA. I opened the wad out and saw it at once, two-thirds of the way down the page. BRITON GUNNED DOWN IN RIO. There was a photograph. Photographs always made him look hideous.

The world closed right in. It became a tight little cell holding nothing but me and the paper in my hands. The words joggled about as if I'd been trying to read them in a dream. It must be someone else with the same name and they'd got the wrong photograph. He wasn't in Rio, he was in . . . 'That general direction'. Of course he'd got enemies, but not the shooting kind, surely. Only when we'd said goodbye he hadn't just been worried—he'd been frightened. Coming out of his hotel. Three men in a car. Sub-machine-guns. Stayed with us before, said the hotel manager, Sr Luis . . . No,

117

he hadn't. Not for a year, anyway. It *must* be someone else.

A man was asking me a question. I turned away but a hand gripped my elbow. Two men. Some sort of visiting card.

'I don't want anything. Can't you see? Not now.'

He asked again. The question had B's name in it.

'He's dead.'

They had a key. They took me into the flat and went on asking me questions. I stared at them and shook my head. They didn't seem real. Then one of them asked me my name. I told them, without thinking. They looked at each other.

You get used to it with policemen and people like that. It's a special sort of look when they find they're dealing with somebody who might have friends or relations who could get them into trouble with their superiors if they aren't careful. That look, and saying my own name, made a sort of crack in my cell wall. I was still alone, closed tight in, but I could hear the voices from outside now, and get a whisper back through.

'I'm sorry,' I mumbled.

'It must be a shock.'

'Yes. I'll try . . .'

They let me make a pot of tea and then I sat down in the chair where I used to wait for B to come home. I could understand what they were saying now. I told them the answers but not anything else. They didn't ask about the sapphires. While we were talking there was a ring at the door and one of them answered it. He came back as if nothing had happened and they went on with their questions. There was something about them not like ordinary policemen. They were quite old, solemn and fatherly. What they wanted to know about was B's foreign trips. I told them he usually went to Germany and sometimes to Barbados. Once to New York. They were interested in the ivory statue and the other things like that but I could only tell them he'd brought them back from Germany. When they'd finished the senior one said, 'Our caller was a journalist, Lady Margaret. For your own sake you'd better not talk to journalists. We'd prefer you not to in any case. My colleague will see that the coast is clear and then I think you'd better go up to your own flat and not come down here again.'

'It's bound to come out. We've been about together a lot.'

'We'll do our best to see that you don't have any problems. Since you have been so frank with us I will tell you that this is not a normal criminal investigation.'

'What do you mean?'

He shook his head.

I never finished the jigsaw. I rang Jane at Cheadle to tell her I was coming home. She was different now. She sounded cold and angry. She said she mightn't be there, although it was the art-school vac. I had to beg her. My cell was closing in again.

I packed a few clothes, took the jigsaw to bits and put it back in its box. I left my case at the porter's lodge while I walked down to the river with the box under my arm. A bright spring afternoon, the tide just past full, the dirty water sweeping seaward below the Embankment wall. I put the box on the wall, opened the lid and took out a handful of pieces, but before I could throw them someone gripped my wrist and forced it back over the open box.

It was a man, not one of the pair I'd talked to in B's flat but another of the same sort, only younger. He let me spill the pieces back in the box and took it from me.

'It was a goodbye present,' I said. 'It isn't anything else.'

He poked among the pieces, took some out one by one, held them up to the light and looked at them closely, back and front.

'It's the only thing I can do, you see,' I said. 'I haven't got anything else. Nothing that means anything.'

He closed the box, turned it over, looked carefully at the underneath.

'Please,' I said.

He handed it back to me and watched while I opened it again. I took the pieces and threw them in handfuls on to the river. They seemed to vanish as they touched the surface. The water was their colour, dark green or cardboard. The few white bits of unicorn might have been flecks of foam.

PART TWO
1982–1983

I

Maxine was out of the office so I answered the telephone, using my old secretary-voice.

'Cheadle Enterprises.'

'Mabs?' said the man after a slight pause. Nobody apart from my mother and sisters had called me that for twenty years.

'Who is speaking?'

'Ronald Smith.'

'Would you mind telling me . . . Ronnie?'

'Ah, it is you. Yes, Ronnie.'

'How nice to hear from you after all these years. What can I do for you?'

Maxine came in and I signalled to her to get ready to interrupt with the urgent-call-on-other-line routine. This was more excusable than it may sound. Ronnie had been something of a public figure in the Sixties as a television journalist specialising in Eastern Bloc politics but with a lucrative sideline in British traitors, most of whom he had known well. Then he had dropped rather suddenly out of sight, after a series of drunk-on-screen episodes.

'May I come and talk to you, Mabs?'

'Is it about money?'

'Am I hoping to touch you, you mean?'

'I'm afraid so. Most people seem to be.'

'In my case, no. But I'm told you make a charge for interviews.'

'Sometimes. If people are trying to use me and my name for their own profit I don't see why I shouldn't get a percentage.'

'Ah. This may be one of those times, then. The thing is, *Night and Day* is coming up to its fiftieth anniversary and I've been commissioned to write the official history to celebrate the event. I leave it to you, with your extensive knowledge of the publishing industry, to decide how much profit there is likely to be in that.'

One should never lift one's eyes from the treadmill, never. His voice had aged, blurred, but the old hoot was still very marked and the half self-mocking pomposity of phrase. Also, I persuaded myself, the old eager inquisitiveness, the school-boy's delight in secret knowledge.

'A bottle of champagne,' I said. 'Special price for you, Ronnie.'

'Right. You'll have to drink my share. I'm on the wagon.'

Of course. The world does not stay the same.

'A bottle of Perrier, then,' I said. 'Can you come here? My London visits are always crammed. Mondays are best. We're open the rest of the week. Not this Monday. Not next, not . . . hell! I suppose I could cancel . . . What about Monday March the 15th? Come to luncheon, one sharp, and I'll clear the afternoon till three. That ought to be enough. I was only on the paper ten months, remember.'

'Months of some significance.'

'I suppose so. It seems ages now. Give me your address and telephone number in case there's a crisis. One o'clock Monday the 15th. I'll send you a pass for the gate and a map about parking and finding the garden-room door.'

When I put the telephone down I saw Maxine watching me with a frown on her flat, plain face.

'Sorry,' I said. 'You never know where you are with long-lost friends. I didn't need rescuing after all.'

'You sounded sort of different. Not you.'

'Did I? Tell Pellegrini luncheon for two in the Satin Room on the 15th. No wine—a cup of some sort. Do a pass for Mr Ronald Smith and tell the gate to expect him. Ring Burroughs and tell them I can't see that man . . .'

'It'll be the third time you've put him off.'

'Sure? What am I doing before luncheon that day? All right, don't ring Burroughs—it won't hurt the man to wait ten minutes. Ring Mr Smith and ask him to make it 12.30. Warn him I may be a bit late even so. Oh, and check if he's got any diet requirements. He must be nearer seventy than sixty . . . Good Lord!'

And I had heard nothing of Tom for twenty years. I seldom looked at *Night and Day* but I knew Brian Naylor was still in charge—he'd got an OBE two years back, and he popped up on some television or wireless programme most weeks, the professional deflater, that flat voice still setting my teeth on edge. What on earth had made me think I wanted to see Ronnie?

'Have you decided on a name for this new girl yet, Lady Margaret?'

'No. Must I?'

'I can always put it in later.'

'I suppose I'd better or I shan't start thinking about her properly. Let's have a look at the file.'

'I've got them all on the processor now.'

'I knew I shouldn't have bought that bloody thing.'

It was what they call a mini-computer, in fact. Its chief function was supposed to be to keep track of the Cheadle accounts, if ever I and the accountants succeeded in agreeing how we wanted them kept. Meanwhile Maxine had taken it over. I went and stood behind her shoulder and watched the names ladder up the screen.

'Tara Faithfull,' I said. 'Nobody's called Tara Faithfull, even in a romantic novel. Or Prudence Hastie.'

'I think Tara Faithfull's lovely. I can sort of see her already.'

'Long raven hair with highlights like dark fire? Smoky voice? Slender fingers?'

'Sort of.'

'Not on your life, Maxine. I'm not that sort of writer. Almost, but not quite. I see this one as an Isobel, I think.'

'You had an Isobel Grandison in *Dark Pinnacles*, only three back.'

'I thought she sounded familiar. What've I called the last few hussies, do you remember?'

'I've got them too. Just a sec.'

She poked at the keyboard. The screen blanked. New names appeared. They were accompanied this time by columns of attributes, height, hair-colour and so on. She'd really been playing with her toy while she had it. I seemed to have been alternating talls with shorts. No redheads, I was glad to see.

'What does "Chuckles" mean, for heaven's sake?' I said.

'Deep soft chuckles, like a man's.'

'*Three* of them?'

'Yes. Didn't you know?'

'Of course not. Dear God! I seem to be that sort of writer after all.'

'You don't have to decide about a name if you don't want to. It's so easy now. You can call her Ann Brown and when you've made up your mind I can just tell the machine to go through and change it. No sweat, honest.'

'The trouble, my dear Maxine, is that I shall write differently about a girl called Ann Brown from a girl ... one moment! Do you mean to say that suppose I'd made the current hussy a chuckler and then you pointed out I was getting into a rut I could tell you to give her a silvery gurgle and hey presto, she gurgles?'

'Oh. Well, not quite like that. I mean you might have made a footman chuckle, or someone. I could tell it to find *all* the chuckles, though, and then tell it which ones to change.'

'Really? This opens ... No, don't let's let it open. I invariably get sick of a girl around Chapter Ten. I start happily off with some flaxen-haired romp of a Gibson Girl but by then I'm yearning for a lissom and consumptive brunette. Would your toy do that for me?'

'You're joking, aren't you, Lady Margaret?'

Maxine is perhaps my most dedicated reader, against stiff competition. She sometimes seems to me to know all my books by heart. She came to Cheadle in a coach-party in the hope of meeting me and asking me for a job. When she didn't she camped, metaphorically, on my doorstep, like some Indian would-be servant, until in an emergency I took her on for a fortnight, thinking that at least I'd be able to pay her less than an agency girl. She's stayed two years now. Her devotion seems entirely uncritical. No book is better or worse than another, because the question does not arise, any more than it arises with episodes of real life.

'Joking?' I said. 'Please God, yes.'

One's personality is laid down in layers, like a landscape. Placid lives are like old lake-beds, sedimentary stratifications each scarcely different from the one below. Others, if one dug down, would show evidence of the long-ago upheavals that cause the rumplings of the surface under today's thin turf.

And in most lives there are outcrops, barely changed beyond a little weathering, persisting through all the sediments, still there.

For thirty years, winter and summer, I have risen at six and gone upstairs to write until breakfast. These words are leaping into existence letter by letter at twelve minutes past seven on a yellow September morning in what used to be the housekeeper's bedroom in the top passage of the West Wing. The house at this hour is almost empty, and seems emptier since all Mark's clothes went from his cupboard, though Simon and Terry are still here after the summer. Sally is in Sri Lanka. Maxine is in her own room, very likely with John Nightingale, the assistant gardener. I no longer try to keep track of Maxine's affairs, but am still amazed by her ability to attract presentable young men and later get rid of them with, as far as I can see, no fuss at all. She seems to run her love-life with the same down-to-earth practicality with which she runs my office. This room, by the way, is not my office. It is the place where I write. I do not remember choosing it deliberately for being the same size as my living-room in Dolphin Square and for looking out over a well of the building; it is not in other ways very like, nor can I smell the Thames. But it is now necessary, just as this hour is necessary. Now as then I am too busy at other times of the day. Necessary in another sense too. I cannot imagine this part of me functioning anywhere else. Granite protruding through the strata.

The morning after Ronnie's telephone call was a peculiarly bad one. Naturally I have bad days, not only when I have influenza coming on, but I have trained myself to slog through them. I imagine that on a real treadmill rhythm is vital, the work is only tolerable if you and your fellow-slaves keep it groaning round at an even pace. I do not like to write rubbish but I would sooner do that than let the treadmill stop. That morning I wrote nothing at all. Superficially I spent it trying to decide whether the new girl was tall or short, plump or skinny, quick-tempered or placid. Usually these things accrete and stick to a few early and almost random decisions, building up to a coherent character, but one has to make the random decisions and then stick to them. I couldn't.

It was not as though it yet mattered. The important thing was to get the girl on to a boat for South Africa, where she was going to hire a laconic and embittered white hunter and start looking for her brother, missing since the Boer War. There was also the business of the cousin, apparently in love with the girl and doing everything to help her, but in fact using his connections in the Colonial Office to thwart her efforts so that he could inherit. It had all seemed reasonably promising in a run-of-the-treadmill way, quite interesting enough in its own right to publish under my name and not as a Mary Mason, for which I would have had to hot up the affair with the hunter. There was almost no research to do—after thirty years I know the surface details of my period better than most professional scholars. Six months should see it through, one more step on the groaning wheel that helps to keep this house in being.

The wheel stuck. Jammed tight. No give at all.

Interviewers, patronising to varying degrees, tend to ask whether I actually believe in the people I invent. Usually I open my eyes very wide and speak with practised sweetness about how real they seem to me. Occasionally with an interviewer both intelligent and understanding (not at all the same thing) I feel impelled to greater candour. I write much better than average romantic novels, I say, with a big and loyal readership, and that means that readers must be aware that I am not simply exploiting them. They find my characters real because I, while writing, hypnotise myself into a similar belief. There are passages—the hot bits in the Mary Masons, for example—which are written with little enthusiasm. The reason this does not show is that similar parts of books by my competitors are, I'm sure, also inserted without any real gusto in response to a publishing fashion as tiresome (and let us hope as transient) as the hideous beehive hats at the end of my period. When I consider the difficulty of writing about something like Maxine's actual love-life I am thankful for the set of wooden conventions that have evolved to cope with the problem in books like mine.

But mostly I have to believe. It may be easier for me because I can start by believing in the world I write about. In some ways the twenty years before the First World War have become more real to me than the period in which I find myself living. I am mentally at home there, relaxed and happy. By comparison my life in the last thirty years has been one of almost constant struggle, a long defensive war for a cause that must be doomed in the end but not, thanks to my efforts, in my lifetime. The giants of my childhood—my great-great-uncle, Nanny Bassett, my mother—behaved and thought as though they still inhabited that earlier world, as though Cheadle could be maintained as a fortress loyal to the past while the present raged and ruined outside its walls. Wheatstone, who died less than three years ago, had come to Cheadle as an underfootman on getting his discharge from the Boer War. (He was invaluable to me to the end. My 'Historical Consultant'. I got his funeral as a tax-allowable expense by hiring black-plumed horses and having it filmed for publicity purposes.) In fact my heroines are seldom born into houses like Cheadle, but I am convinced that my emotional grasp of what Cheadle was like towards the end of its heyday allows me an imaginative entrée into the reality of other possible lives of the period. My heroines are not fantasy versions of myself. You could say that my heroes are more likely to be that.

It happened that this new girl, because of the plot about the cousin and the inheritance, needed to come from a family of some wealth. Still, she was not going to be any possible version of myself. She had to be a horsewoman for a start, which I have never been. Or . . . yes, almost as I'd said yesterday, she could start as consumptive, doomed by the doctors. I'd never had a consumptive as a main character, surely, though I'd killed a few minor characters off with the scourge. Yes, she determines to spend her last few months finding her brother, but then the good sun, the open-air life on the veldt . . . really, it was extremely promising.

In desperation I began to rewrite yesterday morning's stint, replacing horses with physicians. The wheel would not move. The day-bed was there, the view through the shaded windows to the croquet lawn, the telegraph boy bicycling up the curve of the drive, but no one lay on the stupid bed. No name was on the buff envelope. It was all Maxine's fault. I would have to get rid of that stupid machine.

Or was it Ronnie's?

I was not aware of having thought about his call, though I had a vague idea that I might have dreamed of something to do with *Night and Day*. I seldom remember dreams, unless they are nightmares that wake me in mid-story. Perhaps it would be wiser to put Ronnie off. I did not wish to think in detail about thirty years ago. I could manage two lives, one in the period of my books and one in the here and now. A third might be a disaster. The extreme, unrepeatable happiness of those ten months in 1952 and 1953 was better left down among the sediments. I was too busy in my other lives for that kind of day-dreaming. It was safer for it to stay where it belonged, in the night-dreams. But I had said I would see Ronnie and somehow the way in which I had agreed had seemed to involve a different level of promise from, say, the appointments with the man from Burroughs. I would think less of myself if I cancelled.

Having determined not to day-dream, inevitably I began. I was actually on my feet, standing by the window, running my fingertips vaguely down the bobbly old wallpaper and thinking about the room in Dolphin Square where I began my real writing, when I heard a faint but definite movement from the corridor. I stood still. At first I thought it was the East Wing Ghost. You never see him. He just moves around, muttering in what we think is Old Dutch, and opening and closing doors. There is something comic about him. I mean this literally. Strangers who have chanced on him have never been frightened but have often mentioned a sudden impulse to laugh. What was he doing over here? And comedy was far from what I felt at the sound. Footsteps and a slithering, trailing whisper.

I crossed the room and opened the door slowly.

My mother was shuffling towards me. She had contrived to get one arm into her dressing-gown and then had given up, so that it was trailing along behind her. As usual since her stroke her head was tilted sideways, but her mouth was not hanging open. She held in front of her, as though it was the purpose of her visit, one of the small towels we use for wiping the dribbles from her face. I was appalled to see her. How on earth had she managed the stairs? Was she going to start wandering round the house at odd hours? She might have slipped and broken her neck. Oh, but if only she had!

'Mummy, darling,' I said in the calm, amused voice I have trained myself to use, 'what *are* you up to? It's not breakfast for an hour yet.'

She looked at me with her old sharp arrogance, but with no apparent recognition, and came shambling on. I moved to meet her, intending to turn her gently in her tracks and lead her back to bed, but she tugged her arm determinedly free of my grip and pushed on into the room. I dare say I could have had my way with a struggle, though she is still surprisingly strong—the apparent feebleness of her movements is misleading, the result, according to Dr Jackson, of lack of confidence in her own motor control. I followed her in, mysteriously relieved to have a tangible reason for not being able to do my work.

'I just came up to make sure you were all right, Mabs, darling,' she said.

It was her old voice, perfectly clear, but slowed. She had not spoken to me but to the room. Now she faltered, apparently perceiving that it was empty. She shuffled to my desk, pushed at the chair, patted my typewriter. Being electric it responded by printing a few meaningless letters. She nodded approvingly, then turned and looked at me.

'Where is . . . ?' she began.

Her eyes dulled. Her mouth dragged open.

'Urrh? . . . Urrh?' she mumbled.

It was the same question. Where was Mabs? Where was the child she had borne and trained, and fought for, to take Cheadle over and keep it going, and to bear and train and fight for another child to do the same in its turn?

I guessed what had happened. Long ago, when I had first come back to Cheadle to live, and get ready to take up the responsibilities of my inheritance, my mother had deeply resented the two early-morning hours in which I lived a life beyond her grasp. Her attack had not of course been direct, but had consisted of excuses for interruptions, getting up earlier than she ever used to, for instance, and losing some essential article of clothing and then coming up to try and make me help her find it. My first permanent victory over her had been to make her stop, to keep my two hours mine, untouchable.

Over the years her attitude changed, partly because like many strong-willed people she was capable of thinking her defeats into victories, of altering the past so that what had happened became what she had decided would happen; partly also because she began to realise how my books were contributing to Cheadle; also because she read and enjoyed them, though she can hardly have read a book before in her life. (Mark used to say that the real reason for my success in my genre is that I have all the time been unconsciously striving to win her affection and approval. This may be true. I hope there is more to it than that.) Over the years too she must have grown used to the sound of my typewriter, as regular as the birds' dawn chorus. Her room is not directly below my writing room, but only the opposite side of the corridor on the floor below, and the machine is 'silent', not silent. She may never have heard it more than subliminally, but this morning she must have missed it. The erratic connections of her brain had functioned after their fashion—indeed the momentary clarity of her speech showed that something remarkable of that kind must have happened. She had come to see why the noise was not there. What was wrong? Where was Mabs, her Mabs? Once, almost, Mabs had escaped, ceased to be hers. Had it happened again? Was she going to have to track her down, bring her home, all over again?

She stared at me like somebody trying to make out the features of another person in a dim-lit hallway. I moved towards her. My mind was numb with the horror of her visit, but my dutiful body knew what to do—get hold of her, prevent her falling, put the dressing-gown round her shoulders, lead her back to bed. Her face changed as though the movement had brought me into the light. Recognition flooded into her eyes.

'Darling Janey,' she said. 'You're the one I can trust.'

'Of course you can, darling,' I said.

Her mouth drooped open. She let me cover her up and lead her back downstairs.

II

Mark had not been home for the weekend before my appointment with Ronnie—Saturday had been his fortnightly constituency visit and presumably he'd spent Sunday in Wiltshire with his Julia. I knew what his letter would say before I opened it, but it still came as a shock. Not of betrayal, not—or so I persuaded myself—of sexual jealousy, but of passing a milestone, a whole stage in one's life officially being declared over. Knowing that he would screw himself up to a divorce fairly soon, now that his political career was at best in abeyance for the next few years, I had already decided to make things as simple as possible, though there would be no getting out of the public fuss over the divorce of an ex-minister and a best-selling novelist, with Cheadle itself as the stage. It is in my nature to prefer to get unpleasant things dealt with as quickly as possible, so the letter should have come as a relief. I was not mentally prepared for the feeling of a great door swinging shut, its key grinding in the lock, of the corridor still stretching in front of me but opening into rooms that might in themselves look pleasant enough but would become steadily smaller and barer, and be imbued with a sense of having already been abandoned by the inhabitants I should have liked to meet in them.

I read Mark's letter twice and put it in the pile for immediate answer. The rest of the envelopes looked routine, but one contained an enormous goody, also vaguely expected but still a surprise when it actually happened. Then, Monday being the day to which everything gets put off because in theory I shall have time for it then, I was too busy to pine or rejoice and certainly had no leisure to fret about Ronnie's visit.

He was waiting for me in the Satin Room, a stooped and somehow wavery silhouette standing at the window. He turned as I closed the door and came towards me with uncertain steps. The lenses of his spectacles were as thick as bottle-glass and his walking-stick was painted white. In other respects he had aged heavily too. I imagined he was a bit over sixty-five but he looked nearer eighty. Despite that, I felt an extraordinary flush of delight at meeting him. Nervousness too, not about what he was going to ask me or anything rational, more a superstitious knowledge that I was doomed to say or do something that would burst the bubble. He took my hand and held it like a long-forsaken lover. He peered.

'Less changed than you sound on the telephone,' he said.

'I have to be a dragon in working hours, but this is time off. Sorry I'm late. Did you have any trouble getting here?'

'Fred drove me. I have a sort of arrangement with him so that I can get about at all. He's gone on to visit some cousins in Nottingham.'

'Nottingham seems to be entirely inhabited by Indians these days.'

'Exactly.'

'Oh, Ronnie, you've brought the champagne after all! I should have realised . . . you see, if you aren't having any and I've got to work this afternoon . . .'

With a trembling hand he took from his pocket a brass gadget on which a rubber washer nestled between two flanges.

'June suns, you cannot store them to warm December's cold,' he said. 'But Cyril Ray tells me that with this device you can.'

'What's happened to Tom?' I said, following a natural train of thought from the quotation. 'He wasn't on the mast-head last time I saw a copy.'

Ronnie put the bottle on the table and answered in jerks as he unwired it. I could see that he was already used to doing such tasks by feel rather than eyesight.

'Not very good. Stuck Naylor for twenty years. Does the odd piece still. Bit of book-reviewing here and there. Lives with a sister in Kent. Goes around wearing an old tweed coat and skirt of hers. A peculiarly dislikable woman. Shouts at him as if he were deaf. But she sees he doesn't starve.'

'How dreadful. And Naylor is still editor. Who could have believed it, that evening we first met him?'

Ronnie grunted, working his thumbs round the cork to ease it up. I knew it wouldn't do to offer to help. The pop came at last. I held my glass for him as he poured with a quivering hand. He took only a mouthful for himself, then clipped his gadget on to the bottle to seal the pressure in.

'Cyril tells me it will keep a fortnight in the refrigerator,' he said. 'You can have a glass whenever the necessity strikes you.'

It was Krug, and somehow he had managed to keep it cold on the journey. I was absurdly moved that he should have understood that it would have such meaning for me.

'Sealed in blood,' I said as I lowered my glass.

'You will have to explain.'

'I nearly put you off at least three times. I'm not sure what it's going to do to me, bringing up those old days. But I couldn't. So much of me was longing to see you.'

'My dear Mabs . . .'

'I'm a bit hysterical this morning. I got a letter from my husband saying he wanted a divorce.'

'Did you now?'

He managed to make his voice condole, but the near-blind eyes were still able to gleam.

'No nice scandal, I'm afraid,' I said. 'He's just found a pleasanter woman to live with. I've known it was coming for ages. But that's not all, Ronnie. I've had a piece of terrific financial news.'

'Enough to cure heartache, by the sound of it.'

'Almost. You won't have read a book of mine called *The Gamekeeper's Daughter*.'

'I don't think so. But I assure you I have read some of the others. You must give a lot of people pleasure, Mabs.'

'A tactful way to put it.'

'Not intended as such. I count myself among them. But that one, I take it, came just after the Chatterley trial.'

'Palest of pale blue by today's standards. It's being made into a film.'

'Congratulations. But I was under the impression you'd had several.'

'Five. This one is going to be a big one. Top stars and so on. But that isn't the point. I've been fighting for years to get some of the running expenses of Cheadle allowed against my income from writing for tax purposes. The tax people have always said they were two separate businesses, but I maintain that they aren't. They depend on each other. I integrate them as much as possible. I keep Cheadle exactly in the period I write about. Visitors who come to see it see a great Edwardian house being got ready for a big house party, and so on, but the tax people have always said I can only claim the proportion I actually use for writing, which is a couple of rooms. They think they're being generous allowing me two per cent. My own accountants have been perfectly infuriating too. They keep saying I'll never get away with it.'

'I can imagine. Where does the film come in?'

'I put a clause in the contract that it had to be shot here. I did it for the publicity, mainly, but just on the off chance I forced my accountants to argue with the tax people that it showed the two businesses weren't separate, and believe it or not they've given in at last. Just like men. It wasn't a real argument, but they'd got tired of fighting me and they only wanted an excuse for saying yes without losing face.'

'Well done. A lesson to us all.'

'But that's not the best of it. I'm going to be able to claim back tax for years and years. I've got a huge bonanza coming. When I took over here, you see, it was absolute touch and go. If it hadn't been for my turning out best sellers Cheadle would have gone bankrupt. I made a lot of money those days, even after tax, and the house hadn't really begun to bring the visitors in. It still runs at a loss, of course, and these have been bad times for writers . . .'

'Don't I know it! I hadn't thought of you, Mabs, as the Walter Scott of our era.'

'Oh, but I am. "This good right hand shall do it." And all before breakfast, too, like him. Do you know, Ronnie, it looks as though I shall be able to take a whole year off and not turn out a single word!'

'Dangerous.'

'But exciting. Let's eat. I've got somebody coming at 2.15 but I propose to keep him hanging around for a bit.'

Pellegrini is an inconceivable nuisance in many ways, a quarreller, liar and cheat with no apparent sense of shame. It is as though all his capacity for honour has been absorbed by his cooking. He would not dream of producing even the simplest snack for some unimportant visitor without making it look and taste and smell as good as it was possible with those ingredients. My mother notices at once and complains when her meals have been prepared by someone else. I couldn't remember Ronnie's attitude to food. Most of my meals with him and Tom had consisted of burgundy or champagne, with a few dry and savourless sandwiches. As I put the food on to his plate it struck me that I had been babbling away about my private concerns to a man whom I really hardly knew at all. Even in the old days I had seen only one aspect of his complex existence. Tom and I had talked, and he had responded, as though his membership of the Communist Party had been an aberration of youth, retained as little more than a convenient stance from which to view the British political scene as an outsider. I only learnt from his later television appearances that his involvement at the very time I knew him had been a good deal stronger and more intricate. I had also gathered that he had been married but was separated from his wife and living with someone else. I had never met her. He had once, I remembered, asked my advice about a birthday present for his daughter, then around seventeen.

The sense of ancient intimacy renewed was an illusion. The intimacy had never been there. What had been there was a girl who was prepared to take the world on trust, and she no longer existed.

Ronnie ate with slow relish. It was I who had to suggest that we had better start talking about the purpose of the visit. He sighed. I could sense a mental squaring of shoulders.

'I have to tell you that I am here, not exactly on false pretences,' he said, 'but at least on a somewhat different basis from that which seemed to be the case when I telephoned you.'

'Yes?'

'I have learned in the interim that you were, shall we say, somewhat better acquainted with Amos Brierley than I, at least, at the time realised.'

'I see.'

'What is your attitude to this? I should point out that I need not have told you that I knew.'

'In that case I will point out that you could quite well have told me beforehand that you were going to want to talk about this.'

'I could have. I thought you might refuse to see me.'

'I certainly should have.'

'Well?'

'Oh dear . . . Just tell me one thing before I answer. When did you decide to bring the champagne? Before or after you learnt about me and Mr B, I mean?'

'Before, Mabs.'

'All right. In that case my attitude is that I'll tell you anything I can about my time on *Night and Day*. I always kept that absolutely separate from the other thing. He would have been furious if I'd done anything else. We never talked about it at all. I don't see that you need to know a single thing about my life outside the office. Put it like this: I'm prepared to walk round my private garden with you. I'm not prepared to let you bring a spade and start digging for bones.'

'I'm afraid there's . . .'

'And if you are intending to mention the relationship, or even to hint at it, in your book, I completely withdraw my co-operation. I won't even talk about *Night and Day*.'

'The problem is this, Mabs. Brierley is of crucial importance to the book. He introduced Naylor, who, whatever we may think of him, has been a very successful editor. Without some such change the paper was doomed. I may as well tell you that the line I had expected to take when I first spoke to you was that you were, so to speak, the first swallow, a sign of Brierley's flair that he was able to spot someone who was going to turn out a hugely successful writer at such an early stage. This was then going to be evidence that his choice of the not immediately obvious Naylor was more than a fluke.'

'There's no reason why you shouldn't still take that line. I met him at a dance for about five minutes. To extricate me from a ludicrous little social embarrassment he told me to tell the other person concerned that we had been discussing the possibility of my working at *Night and Day*. I didn't see him again until Jack Todd had taken me on and let me start writing my Petronella pieces. And I'm almost certain it wasn't because Mr B had told him to.'

'Your arrival appeared to us at the time to be a mechanism for beginning to prise Dorothy out. When he met you at the dance Brierley could well have been on the look-out for a girl of unimpeachable social authority and with some pretensions to be a writer.'

'Oh. I suppose so. I hadn't thought of that. You were extraordinarily nice to me in the circumstances.'

'You were a fetching child, Mabs. I wish I could see you more clearly. My impression is that it's still there.'

'Bless your bad eyesight. What are we going to do, Ronnie? I'd genuinely love to help, but I've got to get this cleared up before we go on.'

'I will continue to put my cards on the table. Histories of weekly magazines do not command a wide sale—the larger libraries and other institutions, and a few honest citizens whose names occur in the index. The publishers would not have taken the project on in these hard times if they had not thought they could do better than that. I need hardly tell you, Mabs, that they are pinning their hopes on Amos Brierley.'

'Typical.'

'His death—is it painful if I talk about that?'

'Not after all these years, but I can tell you absolutely and categorically that I know nothing about it. Nothing whatever.'

'Has anyone ever asked you before?'

'Not since . . . No.'

'Does not that in itself strike you as peculiar?'

'Not specially. There wouldn't be any point. I don't know anything.'

'It strikes me as very peculiar indeed. How is anyone to know what you know? Brierley's death, being a matter of mystery, still retains considerable interest. It is in fact two mysteries: first, why was he killed; and second why the authorities both here and in Brazil made so little effort to answer that question. Journalists have told me that investigations by them were actively discouraged. I happen to have a lead of a sort which I've not been able to pursue, but I now see that it might well tie in with this singular failure of anyone to ask you whether you have anything to contribute. If I'm right, then your closeness to Brierley is of definite moment.'

'In a history of *Night and Day*? Really, Ronnie!'

'This is an imperfect world, in which books need to be sold by often spurious means. My publishers expect me to devote a disproportionate amount of space to Brierley. My excuse is that though he controlled the paper for barely a year, that year was a turning-point. His reorganisation of the managerial side, which had been more than moderately chaotic, was described to me as masterly. And he brought Naylor in, of course.'

'Well, Ronnie, for old times' sake . . . let me put it like this: I'm prepared to talk to you, in this room, for this hour, as though I may have been what you call close to Mr B, but I must make it clear that if the slightest hint about this appears in the book I shall sue. No, let me go on. You may think you could do it in such a way that I wouldn't have a case, but I promise you I'd sue all the same. The kind of publisher who would do a history of *Night and Day* is much too stuffy and timid to risk it, I promise you. I've won three libel cases in the last fifteen years, all settled out of court. They'd be scared stiff of me.'

Ronnie grunted, peered about the table, reached for the champagne bottle and unclipped his gadget. I put my hand over my glass.

'I shall have to think about that,' he said. 'Meanwhile let's talk about something else.'

I took my hand away and let him pour me another glass. We both did our best but the mood would not come back. There was one brief moment when I'd been explaining how I organised my life these days.

'You take a lot on, Mabs,' he said.

'It has taken me. I try not to whinge, that's all.'

He shook his head.

'When you were on the paper you didn't exactly leave stones unturned or avenues unexplored. You came as Dorothy's assistant, but not a week had gone by before you had Tom's glue-pot in your hands.'

'Only as a defence against Bruce Fischer.'

'Momentarily. But you had your finger in every pie, and you were writing a book. I say nothing of your extra-curricular activities.'

'It was the best year in my life. I knew at the time I had to make the most of it. I breathed happiness all the time. Didn't you notice anything different? I don't mean because of me. Just in the air.'

'Morale in any organisation has its own mysterious ups and downs. My impression is that we were near the bottom of a trough when you arrived, which we then began to climb out of. But you know, Mabs, everybody has his own personal Golden Age. One of the weaknesses of the English is that for too many of them it is located in their early childhood. Mine ended when I was sent to prep school.'

'Is that why you became a Communist?'

'In part, no doubt.'

'What happened to Bruce, by the way.'

'Naylor gave him the boot after a couple of years. Row over who controlled the art side. Drove his car into a bridge a few years later. Deliberately, it was thought.'

I tut-tutted vaguely. Bruce Fischer. Blood all over the nylon shirting. The mood died.

I had said goodbye to Ronnie and was on my way to my appointment with the man from Burroughs—less than five minutes late after all—when it struck me that I should at least have asked him who had told him about my affair with B. He had seemed quite sure of his ground. Not Jane? No, of course not. Who else had known? . . . But *she* couldn't still be alive, surely.

I told Simon about the divorce at supper. I chose to do it because Terry was there and I felt a need for human contact. As far as I am concerned, although Simon is my son he might as well be an elf-child. I mean that I have no idea at all what it can be like to be him, though he has my eyes as well as the Millett nose (much more unfortunate, for some reason, on a man than a woman). He is not simply a stranger; I see plenty of strangers, doing the occasional stint of conducting a tour round the house; I make a point of studying faces, trying to imagine inner lives, and usually succeed in constructing a coherent personality, not necessarily the true one but credible to me. I cannot do the trick with Simon. He lived inside me for nine months and his birth was an immense satisfaction. A happy baby, smiling and active. A busy, inquisitive, pleasing child, enough trouble at times not to seem unnatural. And then, about seven, the first awareness on my part of this alien-ness, an only faintly worrying sense of oddness in him, a little patch, spreading in the next five years, inexorable as a disease, until the whole personality was absorbed. I suppose he was about fourteen when I gave up attempting to persuade myself that I loved him.

Now he opened his eyes wide and produced his charming but meaningless smile.

'Poor Mums, that's tough on you.'

'High time, if you want my opinion,' said Terry.

'For Mark or for me?'

'For the both of you. How long before you start feeling old? Ten, fifteen years, if you're lucky. Why waste it? Sir Mark can marry this Julia who seems to think he's the best thing since the Beatles, and that's something you've never been able to do for him. Now you can stop feeling guilty about it.'

'Is that all I get out of it?'

'You want me to find you a man, Marge?'

'Providing he's a roofing specialist.'

'An arsonist would be more to the point,' said Simon.

Terry shook his head, as usual treating the banter as if it were in earnest.

'Not after all the work she's put in,' he said. 'Trouble is, what kind of a man would take you on?'

'Thank you.'

'Come off it. You know what I mean. For looks you can still knock spots off most women, and you've got brains and guts with it, only you expect such a hell of a lot of anyone. My theory, if you want to know, is that you were spoilt for men by somebody way back. I don't think it was ever Sir Mark, though.'

He studied me, candid and serious. He wasn't being inquisitive, let alone prurient, but typically just wanting to check his ideas out. I have got used to Terry and now thoroughly approve of him. If only he were a woman he could have married Simon and I could have worked on the assumption that he would take over running Cheadle when the time came. The fact that Simon is at best only faintly interested in the house would not have mattered. Not that Terry is in love with Cheadle, any more than I was thirty years ago, but he (she) would have recognised the need.

Mark, of course, cannot stand him. He says that living with Terry is like living with a mental nudist—company acceptable in a nudist camp but not where everyone else walks around with their minds fully clothed. Though he speaks with a mid-Atlantic accent he is English, one of a large family whose parents run a bakery in Doncaster. He is eight years older than Simon, his curly dark hair thinning fast, and though he and Simon jog ritually round the park every morning his weight is getting out of hand. They act the parts of footmen when the house is open, but I shall soon have to promote Terry to butler, rather than go to the expense of new livery. They spend their spare time perfecting programmes for computer games, always ending up with something far too sophisticated for commercial exploitation. Another reason why I approve of Terry is that Simon seems not to be an alien to him, nor he to me, so I still have indirect contact.

'If it were true I wouldn't tell you,' I said. 'Let's change the subject. You might like to know that the financial outlook is suddenly a good deal rosier than it's been for ages. I can actually see a future.'

I explained about the tax repayments, speaking to Terry because Simon always shuts off when anything serious to do with Cheadle comes up. It took me by surprise when I discovered that this time he had actually been listening.

'Well done, Mums,' he said. 'You mean you could give up your smouldering heroines if you wanted, and the old place would still chug on?'

'For a few years, yes, I think so.'

'In that case it sounds like a good time to break it to you that I've decided to abdicate in favour of one of the Duncans.'

He was looking at me half-sideways. There is somebody there behind that pretty-pig mask. For an instant I experienced one of our rare occasions of almost-touching as he watched to see how I would take the suggestion—not, alas, with apprehension or eagerness, just curiosity.

'Is he serious?' I asked.

'I reckon,' said Terry.

He too was watching me. Clearly this was something they had discussed, more than once perhaps. My sister Jane is married to Angus Duncan, a Canadian insurance executive, and has three children, the eldest two years younger than Simon. Jane has always tended to find excuses not to visit us so I haven't seen a great deal of them, but Simon knew them better, having stayed six months in Canada when he left school. The possibility of transferring Cheadle to my nephew or one of my nieces had occurred to me often since Sally left, but it had always been something I had refused to think about, I suppose because it would mean accepting decisively that she would never come home. I yearn for my daughter with a passion that disgusts me when I allow it to happen. Last October I drove back from the annual jamboree of the Romantic Novelists' Association in Cheltenham, and because of something one of my colleagues had told me I made a detour to see the monuments in Crome d'Abitot church, but took a wrong turning and found myself winding down the drive to the house itself. There had been a board up at the gate—Something-ishi Foundation—but I was through before it registered. It was a heavy, hazy morning. The house, as large as Cheadle but much plainer, lay looking out over flat and almost treeless parkland below the ridge I had descended. On the grass a number of cattle were tethered. Near the spot where I began to turn my car a thin young man in a long coat and a sort of skull-cap was inspecting from a distance of a few feet a large fly-infested sore below the eye-socket of one of these animals. He carried a briefcase and looked Western enough in a mildly eccentric way until I realised that beneath the skull-cap his head was close-shaven and that the coat was in fact a robe. His thinness and stoop suggested under-nourishment, and he seemed to study the sore with a resignation indistinguishable from despair. Very likely I am doing him and his organisation a complete injustice and his bag was stuffed with fly-repellants and antibiotics which he was about to administer, but in the few seconds it took to get the car round I was gripped with a fit of the horrors. His hopelessness, and the hopeless patience of the animal, spread and filled the valley, drowning the splendid house like one of those villages lost under new-built reservoirs. I think anyone might have felt it, but to me with my preoccupation with Cheadle and my longing for my daughter apparently dead to me in her Sri Lankan *ashram* the scene was a particular hell.

Sally was born before Simon. I had always intended that she should inherit, though my mother and Mark tried to insist on Simon's right as first-born male. Sally, almost as soon as she was aware of the possibility, rejected it, continued to do so more and more firmly as she grew up, and on her eighteenth birthday gave me a document prepared by solicitors formally renouncing any claim. She writes long and friendly letters from her sanctuary, never with any hint of return. Suppose, I asked myself as I drove home from Crome d'Abitot, I offered her Cheadle; and suppose the money were available from rich converts to maintain it in however threadbare a fashion as an -ishi establishment; would I pay that price to have her back? It would be a life of a sort for the house, wouldn't it, arguably more genuine than that provided by the sightseers who now flood through it, so transient as to seem less material than its own old ghosts?

I sighed and looked at Simon.

'Have you thought what you would live on?' I asked. 'Every penny goes with the house. It has to.'

'We'd get by, Mums. That doesn't matter. Why don't you write to Aunt Jane? Don't let her push Gavin at you—he's an oaf. Fiona's the one to go for.'

'She can't be more than sixteen.'

'Eighteen more like. In fact, don't write to Aunt Jane. Write to Fiona direct. Invite her over. Offer her a job for the summer.'

'I'll think about it.'

I was in the kitchen making my hot Bovril before going to bed, when I realised Terry was in the doorway, watching me.

'Must be feeling kind of down about Sir Mark, Marge,' he said.

'A bit.'

'Would you like me to come along to your room tonight?'

I am still able to blush. On the other hand I didn't spill my Bovril. Nothing is surprising, coming from Terry.

'No, thank you. It's very kind of you . . .'

'Come off it. I wouldn't be suggesting it if I didn't fancy you.'

I wondered whether he had cleared the idea with Simon. Quite likely. He would have told me if I'd asked, too.

'I belong to a different time, Terry.'

'You belong now, Marge. You have to. There's no place else to belong.'

I shook my head.

III

Fiona was one of us. It was obvious the moment she came into the office. Jane had sent the occasional Christmas photograph but I hadn't seen my niece in the flesh for six years, and though family traits had then been apparent, these had been half-formed and tending to come and go, as they do with children, almost from day to day. I didn't remember the sense of kinship striking me with such force. Perhaps because she had grown away from the mould in some respects the remaining points of likeness stood out. Jane and I at Fiona's age had been tallish, big-boned, a bit gangling but not lumpy—promising in fact to become reasonably good lookers quite soon. The same could not be said of Fiona. She was not merely a chunky young woman. She was a chunk. Three or four inches shorter than I am but broad across the shoulders with a naturally high colour and tight-curling dark red hair. 'Young woman' is right. Any stages such as Jane and I had had still to go through before hardening into our final cast Fiona had already behind her.

But she was one of us all the same. It wasn't merely the forward-facing nostrils, broad-set eyes and wide mouth. Recognition leaped between us, in a way it never does between me and Simon, though he has those features too. Of course in her case she would already have been used to my looks in Jane. The same thought must have struck her.

'I can't help wanting to say "Hi, Mom",' she said. 'Only she does her hair different, uh.'

She had a little light voice, the modern girl's twitter, equivalent to the modern young man's mumble. The Canadian accent was quite marked.

'I do hope you'll feel at home here,' I said.

She laughed.

'Be like feeling at home in the Grand Canyon,' she said. 'I'd reckoned it might look smaller now I've grown up, but it's still big, big.'

'We came in by the portico,' said Simon. 'I thought Fiona ought to make a grand entrance.'

It being Monday that was possible, but I thought unwise. One didn't want to frighten the child.

'We live upstairs really,' I said. 'In ordinary little rooms. That's home. The rest of it . . . well, sometimes it seems more like a factory. This is the office. Places like the Banqueting Hall and the Long Gallery are what you might call plant. Sightseers are the raw material. We suck them in through the portico and extrude them through the brew-house.'

'Mums has a passionately romantic attitude towards Cheadle,' said Simon. 'You mustn't let her con you with the way she talks about it.'

'Mom warned me,' said Fiona.

'How is she?' I said.

'Fine. She got her pilot's licence. She's into a new form of art with a bunch of crazy kids who do abstract sky-writing.'

'I'll write and tell her you arrived intact,' I said.

'Right. I better warn you she and me had a fight about me coming here in the first place. Mom reckons you might be trying to take me over, uh?'

I was looking directly at her and saw, at the memory of the argument, a slight flaring of the nostrils, a patchiness in the pink of the cheeks. At the same time I experienced, not all that far down inside me, a quite irrational spurt of rage with my sister that she should attempt to thwart me. I looked quickly away.

'I'll mind my step,' I said.

It turned out to be less of a case of my taking over Fiona than of Fiona taking over Cheadle, and me with it. I cannot remember anyone in my generation, male or female, who had even the beginnings of her kind of assurance. Some, myself included, had been self-confident by our own standards, but these were not the same. Fiona's style seemed devoid of either brashness or naivety, without any pose of cynicism. Some of her views and arguments might be naive, but the mode in which she thought and felt was wholly mature, as far as I could see. Theoretically she was with us three and a half months, and my idea had been that she should spend ten weeks doing a series of jobs at Cheadle, ostensibly for the sake of variety but really so that she should learn as much as possible about the place and its workings. She would then have accumulated enough money to pay for a month in Europe. Some time in the following year, supposing I had made up my mind that she was the right person, I would find a way of suggesting that she should come to Cheadle on a permanent basis, and eventually inherit.

Fiona's timetable was far less leisurely. I dare say that whatever project she had joined for the vacation (she had in fact given up going with friends to continue the excavation of an old French fort in northern Quebec) she would have thrown herself into with the same energy, inquisitive, co-herent, unabashed, assertive. She had no hesitation in telling me what she wanted to do with her time, and this did not include either touring round Europe or dressing up in house-maid's uniform in order to stagger past each group of tourists on the back stairs with loaded coal-scuttles for two of the bedrooms. (The coal is of course blackened polystyrene and weighs nothing.)

'I'm not that keen on pretending,' she said.

'You want *real* coal?' said Terry, who had been gazing at her with his usual open interest almost throughout that first supper. Fiona took the question seriously—it is hard to tell with Terry.

'It would still be kind of sham. I guess if I was taking it up for a real fire which was going to get lit for someone to dress in front of, that would be OK.'

'But the whole place is sham, in that sense,' I said. 'Apart from the few rooms we live in it doesn't exist for any purpose except to be looked at. In one sense it never did. Nobody built the portico, for instance, to keep the rain off a visitor ringing the front doorbell. Sometimes I think of myself as the stage manager of a very, very slow play. Each act takes about a century. Cheadle itself is the star. We are now well into the last act, the old age of the hero. There's nothing I can do to alter the plot, but I am doing my best to see that the perfor-mance isn't a shambles.'

'See what I mean about Mums and the high romantic line?' said Simon. 'You've read some of her books, I take it.'

'Cheadle's much more important than my books,' I said. 'But it's an example of an art-form, just as they are. It's not any more real, in the sense Fiona was talking about.'

'I guess I read quite a few,' said Fiona.

'You don't have to like them,' I said quickly. I always say that. It has the advantage of being true. If I were a better writer—or at least someone who thought of herself as a "great" writer, I expect I should find it hard to sympathise with readers who didn't respond to my work. As it is, to assume that every intelligent person must enjoy what I write seems to me as vulgar an attitude as to assume that guests have something wrong with them if they don't enjoy zabaglione.

'I liked some of them all right,' said Fiona. 'Times when I want to give up and forget, they're great for that. Other times, though, I guess I get impatient. All those girls. Why's it always got to be some man who sorts our their problems for them?'

'Hear, hear,' said Simon.

'Why indeed?' I said. 'I suppose the only answer is that it's a convention of the art-form. I've tried to get away from it occasionally. There was a girl I made chuck over both men and go and be a nurse in Ethiopia.'

'I remember cheering,' said Simon.

'At least I didn't have her pegged out and eaten by ants,' I said. 'But my publishers were full of doom and gloom. I didn't mind, but the next book sold much worse, and that did matter.'

'Mums always talks about sales figures when she's near the romantic bone,' said Simon. 'Or roof repairs. It means she feels she's let you get too close to her secret garden.'

'Where would we be without sales figures?' I said. 'Secret gardens don't pay plumbers.'

'But they do,' said Simon. 'Your books don't sell because you've put exactly the right number of dots on the heroine's veil for 1911. They sell because somehow or other underneath all that there's this utterly romantic place which you're the only person's got the key to.'

'Oh, really!' I said. 'We're not here to try and analyse my

sources of inspiration. My sources of inspiration are the account books for Cheadle.'

'See what I mean, Fiona?' said Simon.

'I guess account books can be pretty romantic,' said Fiona. 'They must go back years and years, uh?'

'Lord, yes,' said Simon. 'If you want to know what a hundredweight of horse-shoe cleats cost in 1796, it's all there.'

'Can't I help with the accounts, Aunt Mabs?' said Fiona. 'I get pretty good grades in math and I'm aiming to major in economics.'

'I suppose you might,' I said. 'I hadn't thought . . . You see, the accounts are done by an outside firm called Burroughs and I've been having endless discussions with one of their men about getting it all on to Maxine's new computer. That's what I bought it for, after all. The trouble is it involves somebody sitting down and actually doing it. If I let Burroughs it will cost the earth and then they'll get it all wrong. There's no one here I can trust and spare. It's worse than that because my own mind goes blank. I'm frightened of ending up with a system I don't understand, which'll mean I'm in somebody else's hands. I'm not having that. Simon and Terry could do it, but they won't . . .'

'Dead boring,' said Simon. 'Nothing to it. Endless, endless entries. Stock control. Oh, God!'

'We could write you a basic programme, Marge,' said Terry. 'But after that . . .'

'The man from Burroughs keeps talking about basic programmes. They have this one they sell to farms which he thinks will work with a bit of adapting. I simply can't believe it's not going to turn out more trouble than it's worth.'

'Listen, Aunt Mabs,' said Fiona. 'Why don't Simon and Terry and me put our heads together? They write the programme, I do the entries. That kind of thing really turns me on, getting it all cleaned up and running. We did a lot of work with computers, tenth grade.'

Even Simon seemed interested, probably not in the task itself—he takes a very blasé attitude to the workaday uses of computers—but in making me see that Fiona was going to be an asset to Cheadle. I did not believe I had shown any hint of

151

the bond I felt between myself and the child, had felt from the moment Simon had brought her into the office that morning. I knew it was vital to keep all that side hidden, to pretend even to myself that Fiona was only in England for a vacation job, in exchange for Jane's hospitality to Simon a couple of years earlier, but I couldn't keep my eyes off her as the three of them started on micro-chat. Simon, sulkily, had helped me to choose Maxine's machine but had made it obvious that he wasn't going to let it become a means of sucking him into the digestive processes of the Cheadle-ogre. I wondered if he knew what he had paid for his escape. I'm not talking about his homosexuality, though I'm aware of what they say about too-dominant mothers. No, it was what I felt to be a kind of spiritual numbness, not merely to me, but to the world in general. You can imagine a small boy, growing up in the innards of the ogre and in his childishness treating it as no more than the place where he happened to live, but then, around the age of seven, beginning to realise from things that his father had said, and his grandmother, what his relationship with it was supposed to be and deciding with that mysterious inward astuteness children possess that somehow he was going to withdraw from a bargain he had never made. He would begin, wouldn't he, by building a fence between himself and the priestess of the ogre, me. He would make the facets of himself that turned towards me numb, numb to my demands or offers, to my anger, to my love.

Now, though, as he explained the technicalities of Maxine's toy—all Ks and bits and other barbarisms—he did not seem numb. Or perhaps he was merely reflecting the energy of Fiona's interest and enthusiasm. She leaned across the table, eating without noticing, her eyes brilliant, making piggy grunts of comprehension or wrinkling her snout at something she didn't follow (another Millett trait, frowning with the nose, Mark used to say). Hauling my stare away from her for about the tenth time I saw Terry watching me. He nodded.

On the strength of that I decided to give it a try. Burroughs were not going to like it, not at all. I would have to get them in to explain the accounting system in detail to the children, and the output from the computer they would need for

purposes of tax and audit. I would see how things stood after a
month. There'd still be time to go back to the adapted
farm-account system. Burroughs would try to make all
possible difficulties in their chilly, bureaucratic style. Never
mind. For the first time in ages I felt the old tingle of
anticipation at the prospect of a fight, of imposing my will on
some body of reluctant, hierarchical, narrow-minded males. I
was going to enjoy that. Why, all of a sudden, now? Because I
would be doing it—though she wouldn't know—to satisfy
Fiona. How extraordinary.

'When can I visit Gran?' she asked at breakfast.

'You don't have to, my dear. She'll never know. She hasn't
much idea what's happening or who anyone is, except me.'

'But I want to. And, too, I'll have to tell Mom I did.'

'Oh, all right. Let me finish my toast and I'll go and see if
she's still presentable. I cleaned her up before breakfast, so
she shouldn't be too bad.'

'Don't you have a nurse for her?'

'Only part-time. She's like a baby, you see, wanting its
mother and no one else. She throws a tantrum if it's anyone
but me for some things.'

'Wow, Aunt Mabs, you keep busy!'

'I've already done my two hours' writing this morning.'

I was ridiculously gratified when she looked impressed.
Simon and Terry never get up till ten so I had her to myself
and would have preferred not to introduce a third person, let
alone my mother, but I was ashamed to make excuses.
Obviously the visit would have to be paid. I was going to be
busy all day, and by evening my mother would be tired and
her company yet more painful.

She was sitting up in bed watching the breakfast television
(a real boon to me, in the few months since it started). She
ignored my presence as I straightened her coverlet and wiped
the spittle from her cheek.

'You've got a visitor, darling,' I said.

She paid no attention but continued to stare at the screen,
making impatient little movements if I got in her line of
sight. I was glad to have her so preoccupied, and not whining
or snivelling.

Fiona tapped at the door, came in and walked straight across to the bed.

'Hi, Gran,' she said, and without any sign of distaste kissed my mother on the mouth, then took her hand and held it.

'I'm Fiona,' she said. 'I'm Jane's daughter.'

She had slowed her twitter but otherwise might have been talking to any normal person. My mother had begun to make a waving gesture at not being able to see the screen, but slowly turned her head and stared.

'My dear,' she whispered. 'Oh, my dear.'

Tears welled in her rheumy eyes and I thought she was about to begin one of her bouts of silent weeping, but it didn't happen.

'Mom sends her love,' said Fiona.

'Jane?' said my mother. She can only have been trying to puzzle out who this girl with the Millett face could be, but Fiona took the question straight.

'Right,' she said. 'Jane's fine. She's learnt to fly. Happy as a squirrel all day long.'

She'd speeded up. My mother flicked her hand angrily towards the TV, a much more commanding gesture than her usual feeble fidgetings. I turned the sound down.

'What did you say, dear?' she said. 'I'm getting a little deaf.'

'Jane's very happy. She's learnt to fly. In an aeroplane.'

'How lovely. And your name is . . .'

'Fiona.'

'Fiona. That's Scottish. My daughter Jane married a Scot. He took her away. They always do.'

'Well, I'm Jane's daughter. And I've come back to see you, Gran.'

'Not Gran. That's ponsy, darling. I don't want to hear it again.'

Fiona glanced at me.

'Granny,' I mouthed.

'Right, Granny. I'll remember.'

'And you've come to stay for a long time? How lovely.'

Full of curiosity, astonishment, admiration and absurd wriggling little jealousies I watched and listened to the almost meaningless repetitions and retracings, a slurry of rotted-down memory from which now and then some new phrase would emerge to show that my mother had partially grasped something Fiona had said, perhaps several sentences ago. Fiona coped with this mode of conversation with perfect composure and sympathy, which was no doubt why she was able to elicit more intelligent responses than I would have been able to—or, I have to admit, would have wished to. In the end, though my mother showed little sign of tiring, I had to butt in.

'I've an appointment at nine,' I said, 'and I'll have to settle her down before that. So I'm afraid . . .'

The vague animation on my mother's face faded at the sound of my voice.

'I'll give you a hand, Aunt Mabs.'

'Oh, you don't want to. It's medicines and ointments for bedsores and other little unpleasantnesses.'

'You just show me how.'

'Well, if you're sure . . .'

So I heaved the old carcase around, and emptied the bag and so on, while Fiona watched. My mother hardly grumbled at all and seemed perfectly happy when we left her propped up and staring at an advertisement for cheap jeans.

Fiona took to visiting my mother daily. It was not a formality. I would have sympathised (could have understood better than I did) if these visits after the first few days had consisted of a quick peck on the cheek, a few ritual phrases about health and weather, and then leaving with the catharsis of duty done. But Fiona would stay for an hour on end because she wanted to. They conversed, not usually as coherently as on that first morning, but even on bad days with something being exchanged to and fro. For all her energy the child had a patience I found unbelievable. I had to assume that it came from the Lowland Scots ancestry of my brother-in-law.

'It's just like digging out our fort, Aunt Mabs. That's slow work, slow. You spend a morning and an afternoon on your knees, brushing away a half millimetre of dirt at a time, and if you strike lucky you find a chip of charred timber. I've been meaning to ask—what's "ponsy", Aunt Mabs?'

She didn't seem to find the explanation silly or unacceptably snobbish, merely a detail of the behaviour of our tribe and interesting for that reason.

'You got to listen hard,' she went on. 'Sure she gets things wrong and she doesn't know what she's saying part of the time, but you've got to take it all on board and run it through a kind of sieve, the way we did at the fort, and then you pick through what's left and sometimes there's a wee bit that isn't a pebble and isn't a clod and you turn it over and over and suddenly you see it might have been part of the handle of a jug. And then you find a few more bits and you begin to guess what kind of a jug, and then it gets easier because you know what you're looking for now. I've been taking up some of the old account books and reading through and asking her about things. Gee, they're fascinating. Mostly she doesn't remember but suddenly she'll come out with something about Mr Wheatstone trying to give notice or having the Americans in the Park—that must have been in the Hitler war, I guess —and I've got another piece of my jug.'

'I think you're a wonder. I'd never have the patience.'

'Mom warned me you and Granny didn't hit if off, uh?'

'I'm afraid not.'

'It's because you're so like her—much more than Mom is.'

'Be careful what you say, darling. It may be true, but you're on dangerous ground.'

'Right.'

I was confused in my own reactions to this growing relationship. Of course it was a great practical convenience. My mother became far easier to cope with. She was happier, whined and wept hardly at all, slept all night, seemed less feeble, made fewer demands on my time and emotions. I had to insist on doing my share of the nursing or Fiona would have taken it all on herself. And Fiona clearly got satisfaction from the relationship, so I was glad for her.

But there was no denying that I was also jealous. At a surface level I was simply jealous of Fiona's openly expressed fondness for my mother. I do not mean that I too wanted to be kissed at each meeting, or would have permitted it. With me she was open, friendly, interested, as she would have been with almost anyone; but for my mother she seemed to feel something particular, and I'm afraid I minded. Browning has long been my favourite poet, and the husband in *My Last Duchess* seemed to me, in these moods, marginally less of a monster.

At a different level I was also jealous *of* Fiona, of her ability to love my mother. For thirty years I have more than fulfilled my duty as a daughter. After my mother's stroke Mark tried to persuade me to put her in a home; from this disagreement, and from the extra demands on me which resulted from keeping her at Cheadle, I date the decline of our marriage, though given Mark's character and mine he was probably destined to turn to a Julia-figure around now—but there's no point in talking about what might have happened. I can fairly claim that in the world's eyes I have been an admirable daughter—but all without love, and what is the good of that? Irrational feelings of guilt I know are the lot of many women my age; I am lucky to have so much to take my mind off them. But to my disgust I became aware of a growing impatience with Fiona's ability to think of my mother as a worthwhile person and not, as she was in my eyes, an embarrassing and useless wreck, a monument to all my defeats in our long war, crumbling but still erect where it had always stood, in the heartland of my life. Once recognised I could control the impatience, but not get rid of it.

One evening about a fortnight after her arrival we gathered before supper. It had been a heavy but satisfactory day for me, a flood of summer visitors safely handled, a further step in the negotiations with the film company about *The Gamekeeper's Daughter*, a meeting—myself, Fiona, Simon and *two* men from Burroughs—at which the accountants had finally seemed to realise that we were going to computerise the accounts to suit our own needs and that if they didn't co-operate I would take the business elsewhere; and before all that, before anyone else was awake, a fulfilling couple of hours in which what had promised to be a no more than a linking scene between plot and sub-plot had, in that mysterious manner I suppose all writers are used to, become an episode of real interest with a life of its own, and with the prospect of sending unexpected currents of that life through scenes yet to come. I was tired but cheerful. An extra source of satisfaction had been the way in which Simon had coped with the accountants. Their computer man, though only a few years older than him, had started to patronise him as an amateur and Simon, for the first time ever in my presence, had, so to speak, made his true weight known. It gave me hope that he might indeed be able, as he had said, to get by on his own.

'It's been a good day,' I said. 'I thought we'd have some champagne.'

'Any excuse, Fiona,' said Simon. 'It's her Achilles heel. Good days we celebrate, and bad days we need cheering up.'

'It happens about once a month,' I said. 'Even with Ronnie's gadget. I think I've been fantastically abstemious.'

'Is there another glass?' said Fiona. 'So I can take some to Granny?'

'I've only put one bottle to chill.'

'Just a mouthful, Aunt Mabs.'

'Oh, all right.'

When she came back she said, 'There's something I wanted to ask you, Aunt Mabs. I don't get it. I was reading one of the old account books, 1952, all about repairing the roof on the Banqueting Hall. Gee, they did things cheap those days.'

'I was paid four pounds a week for my first job,' I said.

'On a joke mag,' explained Simon.

'No, I got ten pounds for that. This was selling lampshades for a frightful old harridan in Beauchamp Place. I haven't thought of her for years, thank heavens. What about the roof?'

'Where did the money come from?'

The question ambushed me.

'How much?' said Terry.

'Round a hundred and forty thousand pounds,' said Fiona. 'All it says in the book is "Cheque".'

'Christ!' said Simon. 'That wasn't cheap! That was money those days! We must have sold some Canalettos.'

'It would say in the books,' said Fiona. 'It doesn't.'

'Are you OK, Mums?' said Simon.

'Nose trick,' I said. 'Always worse with champagne. No, for God's sake don't slap me—I can't stand that. I'll be all right.'

I prolonged my recovery while Fiona prattled on about her

search through the account books. I had in fact no idea what transactions had taken place between B and my mother. I had got the necklace out of the bank and given it to him. A few days later he had presented me with a cheque for a hundred and forty-eight thousand pounds, signed by a man I had never heard of. I had paid this into my account—oh, blessed days before the Tax Inspectors thought my statements worth inspecting—and written B a cheque for the same amount. He had said nothing at all and I'd had no wish to talk or think about it. I had bought my freedom, or so I believed. Until I found the necklace in the jigsaw box I assumed that he had paid the money to my mother. Afterwards I deliberately refused to brood on any of the events surrounding his death. I wrote down what I knew and put it in a drawer. Since nothing could bring him back, nothing that had happened to take him away mattered any more. I put it out of my life. My mother never mentioned it either. It was evident that he had kept the necklace, perhaps always intending to give it back to me when the affair was over. It had, so I thought, cost him nothing, and he may merely have wished to gratify me by letting me believe I had made the sacrifice for him, and gratified himself by the knowledge that I had thought it worth it. He had presumably decided that my mother was not after all in a position to do him any damage, and it was certainly unlike him to allow himself to be blackmailed.

'Honestly I don't know,' I said. 'Mummy ran everything. I didn't inherit till I was twenty-five and I'd married Mark before that, and there was his career, and then Sally. I didn't really start taking an interest till you came along, Simon. I imagine we must have sold something. It wouldn't be Canalettos, because they're all still there and, besides, the art market didn't start exploding for another ten years or so. You'd have had to sell a couple of dozen to get anywhere near that.'

'Besides, that kind of thing would be in the books, uh?' said Fiona.

'Do you really want to know?' I said.

'Oh, I guess not. Only curiosity. I'm only looking through them to try to spot the odd-ball items that might crop up again and tie a knot in our programme, but I keep getting fascinated. I asked Granny and she just said, "That horrible man".'

'The architect I should think,' said Simon. 'She was always fratching with architects.'

'But you should have seen the way she smiled, Aunt Mabs. I guess she won the argument.'

A few days before Fiona left I chose a suitably vile morning and walked with her down the avenue between the statues of the Enemies of Zeus. I noticed some fiend of a visitor had climbed up and put a fruit-flavoured yoghurt pot into the upstretched hand of Tantalus. We rounded the fountain and stood looking up at the house while the wind thumped my umbrella. The sky was all fast-moving, sagging clouds and the squalls came and went unpredictably. The leaves of the limes had barely begun to yellow but even so the wind was stripping the first few away. The spray from the fountain whipped to and fro. At the far end of the avenue the portico stood unmoved.

'Take a good look,' I said. 'Pity it isn't November.'

Fiona stared earnestly. I had kept my inward vow and not once hinted at my intentions, but we had by then reached such a level of rapport that I was sure she knew.

'Looks kind of like it was waiting to eat someone,' she said.

'We used to call it the stone ogre look. Your mother and I, I mean. I can't see it any more. It just looks grim and enduring now. Remember to tell her I showed you, won't you, darling?'

'Right.'

IV

Fiona addressed her weekly letters to my mother, with a short covering note for me. They were several pages long and full of things my mother couldn't possibly grasp, about her own doings and those of all her friends, but they were an extraordinary help. At first I simply re-read the latest one to my mother morning after morning until the next arrived, but as soon as a stock built up I read the old ones, for variety. They were not in any normal sense good letters; the child could neither spell nor punctuate and had no literary talent whatever, no ability to give the feeling of a place or personality or event, and a rather limited vocabulary. She simply rattled unselfconsciously on, not writing down because she was addressing a senile mind, not trying to maintain a false cheerfulness. If she was bored or unhappy she said so. I was amused (and encouraged) to notice that she had stopped calling her frequent arguments with Jane 'fights' and had adopted the Millett word 'fratches'.

One week when no letter came—Fiona had had flu, it turned out—I thought of faking one but didn't, mainly because it wasn't worth the trouble, but also because I felt it would be a betrayal of Fiona to do so. Besides, I had an instinct that however accurately I did it my mother would somehow know. For the first time in my life I was feeling something that might be called fondness for my mother, beginning from our shared affection for my niece but existing, however vaguely, in its own right. Though she always complained and often wept at Fiona's continued absence, I found these manifestations more tolerable than I would have six months earlier, because I could sympathise with them. Moreover, my mother maintained the improvement in her grasp of the world which Fiona had produced while she was with us, and I felt it my duty to both of them to try and see that this was at least not let slip. It was still impossible to hold anything like a coherent conversation (would I have welcomed that, I wonder?) but she usually called me by my own name and understood that Wheatstone was dead, and so on. She was more selective about what she watched on television, prodding her remote-control switch and rocketing from channel to channel until something promising showed up. She enjoyed American serials most, not the shoot-outs but the emotional traumas, sometimes displaying a definite understanding of the causes of that week's row, and even remembering parts of what had happened the previous week. I forced myself to watch with her so that we should have something to talk about—duty or no duty I could not bring myself to chat, as Fiona did, about my own doings.

One evening I was reading proofs while we waited for *Dallas* to come on. I had turned the sound down so as to be able to concentrate while my mother fidgeted with her control switch. Suddenly she said in a strong, clear voice, 'Absolutely no dress sense. When I took my girls to dances . . .'

I glanced up and saw it was an advertisement for toffee, which the manufacturers were trying to invest with snob appeal. I'd seen it before. Dancers at an Ivor Novello-ish ball twirled past the camera. In a few seconds the lens would zoom in on an ambassadorial figure, all ribbons and orders, who would push aside a vast offering of caviare and then surreptitiously take a packet of the advertiser's toffee from his coat-tail pocket. As it is important to respond to my mother's remarks but there is no need to maintain coherence I said the first thing that came into my head.

'Do you know, I think Mrs Clarke may still be alive.'

'Nonsense. I wore one of her own hats at her funeral.'

We had all suffered mildly from my mother's conviction that the daughter of a previous Cheadle head-gardener could make us more becoming hats in her little shop in Bolsover than anything we could buy in Sloane Street, and at a tenth of the price.

'Not that one,' I said. 'I'm talking about the Mrs Clarke who used to write "The Social Round" in *Night and Day*. She signed herself Cynthia Darke.'

'Tiresome woman.'

Really she was alarmingly her old self this evening. Like many people of vehement opinions she had never had more

162

than a few words to express them. Condemnation ran a gamut from 'unreliable' through 'tiresome' to 'horrible'.

'She was extremely kind to me,' I said.

'Expected me to sign a photograph,' said my mother. 'Of all things!'

'You were almost the only countess she hadn't got.'

'Ridiculous. Useless woman. I admit she told me about that horrible man being up to no good on that island. Minnie was so interested. He got money from the Jews, you know.'

She turned directly towards me and gave me the old witch-smile. It was like a story-book illustration which used to give one nightmares as a child, why one can no longer perceive.

'Do you mean Amos Brierley?' I said.

Instantly she hid in the thickets of amnesia, letting her mouth sag open and her eyes blear, bringing senility deliberately on, though I could still sense a sharpness somewhere inside, watching me. Her fingers fumbled with the TV control and there were the towers of Dallas, cross-cut with the performers. I rose and turned the sound up, then went back to my chair. I found I was quivering, a faint, repulsive inward tremor. It happened that a few days before, looking for a container in which to pack some silver to send for repair, I had turned out a battered little cheap suitcase containing a jumble of Sally's possessions dating from when she was about nine, blurred snaps taken with her first camera, crayons, scribbled exercise books, a broken mascot and so on. The pang of nostalgia over these trivial things had been most unpleasant, a blurred physical ache filling my throat and upper chest. I imagine almost all parents know the feeling. Now, I realised, I was going to have to go back to my own life with B and experience those sensations deliberately, over weeks or months, and perhaps with more painful intensity. It was necesary to know what had actually happened about the money for the roof and the whole nexus of events surrounding it. Not for my own sake, but for Fiona's.

No secrets. I must hold nothing back. Whatever had happened thirty years ago might be irrelevant, but it might not.

Shortly before Wheatstone died he told me a secret that had been held back. The cause of the trouble in the Banqueting Hall roof had not been an accident or oversight, but a deliberate skimping on the part of the builders to save the price of new lead by re-using the old. My great-great-uncle's overseer had been too friendly with the builders' foreman and had allowed himself to be hoodwinked. If this had been realised in time the rafters and the elaborate plasterwork would have been saved, and the repairs of 1952 would have cost less than a twentieth of what they in the end did. Wheatstone had known something was wrong. He didn't say as much to me, but I deduce it from the manner in which he insisted on telling me the story and the importance he gave it. Owing to some unexplained feud with the overseer he had decided that it was 'not his place' to attempt to warn my great-great-uncle. What this means, I have come to believe, is that in 1924 it had seemed necessary to Wheatstone that his enemy's failure in duty should work itself out and be publicly demonstrated by the processes of decay. For the wrong to be then and there detected and put right, with no other damage done, would have been unsatisfying. Later, of course, his own failure must have troubled him, though still perversely mitigated by the general condemnation of his dead enemy. Telling me was a half-hearted attempt at confession.

I was not having any of that. No hidden rots handed on unbudgeted for. It seemed to me that B, despite not having sold the necklace, had paid my mother for the roof repairs, and then my mother had not, in his words, 'stayed bought'. She had learnt something from Mrs Clarke (how? when?) and had passed it on to Minnie Trenchard-Yates.

And Minnie was dead. So was Sir Drummond, of a heart-attack in a Kensington brothel. It had been hushed up but I knew about it because, indirectly, it had been important to Mark's career: two members of the government had been in the house at the same time and had resigned soon after 'for personal reasons', one of those minor tremors that foreshadowed the end of the Macmillan era. Mark had got his first ministerial job in the subsequent reshuffle. It had been the period of the first 'sick jokes'. I remember wondering whether Bruce Fischer had begun to play necrophilic variations on his single theme.

My mother had told Aunt Minnie something because she wanted it passed on to Sir Drummond. Aunt Minnie, shrewd as anyone behind her sugary manner, would have had her own reasons. She would have been aware of Sir Drummond's blondes and prepared to tolerate them, provided he changed them frequently. But the one I had actually met in his company had struck me as something of a sticker. Though Aunt Minnie would not have cared for that, a direct counter-attack would have been far from her style. She would have been more likely to embark on a series of gentle sappings, one of which could well have been to tell Sir Drummond something she had learnt about B, something which, as a representative of the City's financial probity, he would have to act on. It would not just be a case of Aunt Minnie using his public duty to remind him of his private duty; she would also have manoeuvred him into letting down a fellow-member of that vague club of men who kept women, breaking the sense of mutual support and thus undermining Sir Drummond's own confidence. It would all have been no more than a minor tunnelling in Aunt Minnie's whole campaign—a campaign in which, to judge by the circumstances of Sir Drummond's death, she had succeeded all too well. I wondered what had become of the blonde, poor thing.

For a moment my attention was caught by the screen, at which I had so far been gazing unseeing. Two of those mysteriously implausible beauties drawled hate-words at each other. My mother was rapt by the conflict, all on the surface, visible, explainable.

Mrs Clarke had told her something about B's doings on Barbados. (But when had they met again? Surely they couldn't have got that far at the *Uncle Tosh* party?) I had been aware from the first that B had been engaged in some kind of financial jugglery to do with the Halper's Corner estate and the hotel in the bay, and had guessed from his obsession with the subject that he was trying to use it to evade the currency control regulations. Mrs Clarke, keeping her ears open as she used to say, might well have picked up a rumour on one of her West Indian expeditions. Or she might have written directly to some contact and asked—her file-card on B had been crammed with her coded writing when I last saw it. It was peculiar how vividly that scene in her office suddenly came back to me, though I had barely thought of it for thirty years.

It was all written down in a manuscript somewhere, and locked away. I decided I'd better have a look through it and see whether there was anything in it I'd forgotten which might help me now . . .

And what did that mysterious sentence about B getting money from the Jews mean? It sounded more like something out of my period, or earlier—the lavish life-style, the increasing debts, the sudden dash abroad. But not that death. No. That was something else.

Besides, he had told me that he had plenty of money, only it was in the wrong place. And he seemed to have paid for the Banqueting Hall roof. Why on earth should he do that?

You could get into real trouble for fiddling exchange controls, I seemed to remember. There'd been that fuss about the Dockers, hadn't there? But B had done all his spending inside the sterling area. He'd kept complaining about having to. There'd been those knick-knacks he'd brought back from Germany, but apart from that . . . and it still wouldn't get you killed, would it? Ruined, perhaps, but not shot. Gunned down in broad daylight in Rio?

And why hadn't he sold the sapphires?

One moment. Ronnie had said something—he'd had a lead . . .

I had heard nothing from Ronnie for about eight months. After his visit to Cheadle he had sent me a formal note of thanks, adding that he would have to consult his publishers about my terms for co-operation. Suppose I were to offer to mitigate those terms . . .

'That girl is too clever by half,' snapped my mother, smacking mental lips at the prospect of the character in question coming to grief.

'They all strike me as complete numskulls,' I said.

'Her eyes are too blue. I expect she dyes them.'

'They probably use a special filter. I'll be seeing some film people next week. I'll ask.'

The dark one was in tears, in close-up. The camera tracked away and showed that she was by the swimming pool in the usual minimal swimsuit while beyond her one of the blonde ones was strutting away with a display of buttocks which would have done credit to an ape asserting its right to its territory.

That would all fit in rather neatly, I thought. I could go and see Ronnie the same day.

V

It was a tall, narrow, peeling house in a terrace well north of
Hyde Park. Ronnie had been resistant, even grudging, about
meeting me. He had hurt his foot in some way, he said, which
prevented him from getting out to keep appointments. When
I had said I would see him at home he had tried to marshal
secondary excuses, but I had over-ruled them. I assumed he
was ashamed of his domestic circumstances, perhaps com-
paring them notionally with mine.

It looked as though I'd been right. I picked my way down to
a basement area containing some reeking dustbins and a
rusty old motor-bike frame. The door opened before I could
ring and I was confronted by a stout middle-aged Indian in a
turban.

'Mr Ronald Smith?' I said.

'He has injured his foot. It is ironic that so distinguished an
intellectual should be susceptible to the frailties of fleshly
nature. He can see no one.'

'He is expecting me.'

'One should expect only the unpredictable.'

'I'm it. Are you going to let me in?'

'Very well. Be kind enough to tell Ronnie I made my best
endeavours.'

He led me down a narrow passage partly barricaded with
old gas cookers to the back basement room. He opened the
door without knocking and said, 'A bird of paradise has
alighted on our withered bough, Ronnie.'

'Mabs?' said Ronnie's voice.

'Yes,' I called. 'Sorry I'm late—they've found a new place to
dig up the M1.'

'Oh, well. Thanks, Fred. Push off, will you? Come in, Mabs.
You find me at a decided disadvantage.'

He was half lying in a low wicker chair which had itself
begun to subside laterally. His bandaged foot rested on a
cardboard carton full of what looked like loose sheets of

Keesing's Contemporary Archives. The room was a chaos of books, magazines, newspapers and jumbled objects, not apparently souvenirs or even knick-knacks but things which had washed up there—the handset of a telephone with no instrument attached, a child's football boot, garden shears, a road-mender's warning cone and so on, besides odd crockery, suitcases piled into a corner, plastic bags full of clothes. A roughly made bed lay against one wall. Beneath the window was a desk with modern electric typewriter and working papers neatly stacked, but all lightly powdered with dust. A pocket of civilisation, a city state of the intellect, but empty of its citizens. The hordes of disorder beyond its walls had only to find a ladder and it would be theirs. At eye-level through the window I could see the ruins of a garden half buried in junk. The room itself had that particular smell, musty, dank, slightly sweet, that hangs around the houses of old people who are losing their ability to cope. It wasn't too bad yet.

An enormous black cat rose from a basket and stumped across the room to inspect me.

'I'm sorry to force my way in,' I said. 'Your friend did his best. And I haven't even brought you any champagne.'

'Not exactly the occasion, though it has been in my mind I might as well go back on the bottle.'

'But I've brought you one of Pellegrini's cold pheasant pies.'

'Have you? Very thoughtful.'

'Is there a fridge?'

'Bust, like most other things. Let's have some now.'

'Not me. I'm just about to have a gross luncheon with a Chicago film executive.'

'I thought you were smelling somewhat glamorous.'

'I'm not looking bad, either. You have to live up to these people's expectations of you.'

'Live down it would be, in my case.'

I found a knife and plate and cut him a slice of pie. Almost from habit, because of dealing so often with my mother's food, I chopped it into smaller pieces for him. As soon as he took the plate from me he started to cram his mouth and chew as though he had been literally starving.

'This might amuse you,' he said, mumbling through

crumbs. 'I own this building. I inherited it from an aunt. You remember we're some kind of distant cousins—well, I did a bit of research, and believe it or not you are at this moment standing in part of the Millett inheritance, a little dribble of property come down to me through dowries and jointures. You are still in a sense at Cheadle. I hope the thought doesn't depress you.'

In fact he clearly hoped the opposite. The cat came to his elbow, clawed at the chair and mewed. He dropped a piece of pie for it. I sat on the edge of the bed.

'Do you still own the whole house?' I said.

'Yes. It's all let. I've become a slum landlord in my old age. I seem to attract a peculiarly hopeless class of tenant. They're almost all on supplementary and most of them owe me about six months' back rent, but I haven't the energy to go through the rigmarole of turning them out.'

'What about your friend Fred?'

'He does a few things for me in exchange for his rent.'

'It doesn't look to me as though he was worth it.'

'Oh, he's all right. You've caught me at a bad time. He's such a bore that I can't help being bloody to him, and now I'm stuck in here he can't get in to do anything. The trouble is he's read too much and tried to fit it all in. Marx, of course, Spengler, Toynbee, Webern, Levi-Strauss, Derrida, you name it. He's a natural polytheist, always looking for another niche to fit a god into. Can I have some more of that pie? And a glass of water? Turn right outside the door and you'll find a tap.'

I cut him another large slice, found a tumbler and filled it in a greasy little hell-hole of a kitchen. I felt in danger of getting emotionally side-tracked. Ronnie clearly needed taking care of. He was teetering on the brink of that pit of non-coping into which old people so suddenly can fall, and from which there is so little chance of recovery. It shouldn't be a long-term commitment. If the tenants were as badly behind with their rent as he said there should be no problem about getting them out. He could then sell the house well enough to buy a sizable annuity and could find a small modern flat somewhere . . . But that wasn't what I'd come for. Later, perhaps. Meanwhile I'd have to find someone to keep an eye on him. But he had a daughter, didn't he, damn it? Ask about her later. First things first. I was an hour behind schedule already, but still felt I couldn't afford to rush straight in.

'How's the book going?' I said as I sat again. 'It must hold things up not being able to get out and see people.'

'Doesn't make any bloody difference. The book's kaput.'

'Oh, Ronnie!'

'The editor I'd set it up with moved on to another publisher. The fellow who took over farted around for a bit looking for an excuse to cancel.'

'They can be swine, can't they? It happens again and again.'

'Yes.'

No wonder he was depressed. No wonder that the pit had opened for him, too. Even in the slight backwater of *Night and Day* Ronnie had given the impression of living in the rushing midstream, like one of those fish native to Alpine rivers. Events and people had been his element, much more so than we had at the time realised. I remembered his liveliness on his visit to Cheadle, his sense of excitement with the projected book, and realised now that that had been a chance —very likely a last chance—to get out not exactly into the main stream again, but at least into waters where some current flowed. Not this stagnant and decay-smelling mud-hole. Something about the dullness of his last reply—about his whole attitude to my visit—struck me.

'Was I the excuse, Ronnie?'

'As a matter of fact, yes.'

'Oh, God!'

'They took the line that the book wasn't worth publishing unless it contained important new material on Brierley, and they weren't prepared to risk that if you were likely to come down on them with a ton of writs.'

'But you needn't have mentioned me. I thought I'd made that clear.'

'They wouldn't see it. As a matter of fact there was a complication. Apparently the editor who'd taken me over had had a scrap with you in some previous firm. I gathered you'd given him a mauling. Name of Eric Martleby.'

I remembered the specimen only too well. Handsome in a lanky, strawy, drawly way, but with the soul of a little blue-chinned thug. What they used to call a whizz-kid, which seemed to mean whizzing from one firm to the next, leaving a trail of mess and breakage.

'Oh, Ronnie, I'm sorry. I suppose he wanted his pound of dirt, and if you couldn't give him that he wasn't taking anything.'

'Maybe. You couldn't have known. But they were looking for an excuse anyway. If it hadn't been you it would probably have been something else. It's not all loss. I got a third of the advance, and I can salvage two or three articles about the early days, Graham Greene and that gang. I could probably put together something on Brierley. Might even make a TV piece. Lots of shots of planes flying in and out of airports to pad it out. It's just that I haven't felt like starting.'

And wouldn't again, ever, if he didn't do something soon. Suddenly his needs and mine seemed to coincide.

'That's what I came to ask you about,' I said.

'Oh?'

'I want to know more about Mr B for reasons of my own. Nothing to do with writing or journalism. When you came to Cheadle you told me you had a lead which you'd never followed up. I would very much like to know what it was. In exchange, provided you promise not to involve me or my family, I'll tell you enough to get rid of your airport shots and replace them with something worthwhile.'

'Oh, God!' said Ronnie. The wickerwork squealed as he tried to slump even further. I seem to have spent a lot of my life coaxing or bullying men into doing what they don't feel like, so I paid no attention.

'I'll start,' I said.

Before I came I had made careful mental inventories of what I was and was not prepared to tell Ronnie. I found it remarkably difficult to keep to them. I had rummaged out my old manuscript a few days ago and had read it through with less distress than I had expected. It had even struck me that I could use it to help Fiona to see what sort of decision I was asking her to make, and that I understood the difficulty of the choice. But that had been about all I did understand. I had read with growing bewilderment, not simply at the events but at my own relationship to them. The words 'my own' beg the question. The gulf between myself now and the girl who had

172

experienced the events and then written about them seemed almost unbridgeable. My urge to tell Ronnie more than was sensible may be accounted for as an unconscious attempt to close the gulf, to assert the identity and value of my single life. Perhaps the squalid and imprisoning little room added to the impulse, with its sense of last chances almost lost. Certainly as I was speaking I discovered in myself a longing for the day when I would give Fiona the manuscript to read and then tell her as much as I knew of the rest of the story, uncensored.

Even with Ronnie I was more expansive than I'd meant to be, so that time was beginning to run short before my luncheon appointment. He listened with little sign of interest to the details of our stay in Barbados, which I'd thought might stimulate him with its potential for television. I said B had been very nervy. I explained in general terms about my mother's attempt to blackmail him, and how he'd taken it seriously although she didn't appear to have any special knowledge to threaten him with. I said he'd managed to get hold of a very valuable piece of jewellery, which I'd been under the impression he'd sold in order to pay her off, but just after he'd left on his trip to Rio I found that he'd never sold it after all. I'd assumed he hadn't paid her off either, but had recently discovered he had. Finally I told Ronnie about the men who had questioned me the Sunday morning when I'd first learnt that B was dead.

'Interesting,' said Ronnie when I'd finished, in something ghostily like his old voice. 'A currency swindle of some kind, evidently.'

'That's what I've always thought.'

'There was a lot of that going on. Remember the Dockers?'

'Oh, he wasn't like that at all. We once had a very stingy weekend in Paris. He hated not having money to spend, but he wouldn't risk breaking the rules.'

'Very sensible if you've got something big on. The Dockers got caught because Lady D was always in the gossip-columns, splashing it out in Monte Carlo. I gather there was a lot of money to be made if you could get round the rules. What he'd have been doing on Barbados would be selling a supposedly run-down estate so that he could show a low figure in his accounts of the transaction. But if he had it in good order it might have fetched a fair sum, with the Commonwealth Sugar Agreement due to operate soon. The sale of the estate would also have provided cover for whatever he was getting out of the transaction over the hotel. All that could have gone through on the side, in dollars. He'd have had a very good chance of getting away with it, provided nobody tipped them the wink at the Treasury.'

'If somebody happened to tell a Director of the Bank of England there was something fishy going on in Barbados, you mean?'

'That would have done. They couldn't stop the system leaking, they could only make things as risky as possible for the leakers. They operated largely on hunch and hearsay. Those chaps who came and asked you questions at the end sound like Treasury investigators to me. They went in for retired bobbies. Did you tell them about this piece of jewellery?'

'As a matter of fact, no.'

'Very handy, that might be. Small, easy to smuggle, not gone through the trade, and so on. Professional jewellers had to report all transactions over a certain value, so something like that . . . until anyone noticed it was missing, of course.'

'There was a very good replica.'

'Perfect.'

'But he left it behind.'

'Perhaps he wasn't ready to use it yet. But it raises an interesting point. We've been assuming that the deal on Barbados was set up for the general purpose of making a quick buck, but it sounds to me as though it was for something much more specific than that. He had a deadline to meet, and something extremely nasty was going to happen if he failed.'

'It certainly felt like that.'

'And the Barbados deal couldn't go ahead if there was a threat of investigation. Then this gewgaw turns up and he can use that instead, so he can make the Barbados deal legitimate, though I don't see why, if he does that, he's got any need to settle with his blackmailer.'

(Because it would have been cheating *me*, of course. Curi-

174

ous how you can suddenly be perfectly certain of something as apparently unknowable as that.)

'And as we are aware,' said Ronnie, 'a deadline was eventually met, in an unpleasantly literal sense.'

'He was a terrible coward. I mean, he didn't give a hoot what anyone said or thought, but the slightest scratch and he wanted trained nurses hovering over him with antiseptics. That's still one of the worst things about it for me, though I tell myself it must have been over in an instant.'

'Oh, I should think so,' said Ronnie, casually. He had probably never, even at his liveliest, been much interested in questions of pain and blood, but the more theoretical side of what had happened seemed genuinely to have caught his imagination now.

'One more point before I contribute my mite,' he said. 'These men who interviewed you in Brierley's flat, they more or less told you they were expecting to hush the whole thing up?'

'Oh no. All they said was they'd try and keep me out of it.'

'Very altruistic. Think of it the other way round. If they want to play it down, how enthusiastic do you think they're going to be about the newspapers learning that a glamorous and titled young lady has been the dead man's closest friend? I think I mentioned this when we met at Cheadle. Doesn't it strike you as extremely odd that nobody from that day to this, in spite of intense journalistic speculation at the time and continued interest ever since, has asked you whether you have any light to throw on the matter?'

'I've always taken it for granted. I shut that door, you see. It was all over. But I do see it's a bit odd.'

'More than a bit. Remember the fuss over the Dockers? In the papers for months on end. If there hadn't from the very first been a decision to hush things up, you'd have been there too. A decision from somewhere quite high up, what's more. Not because of the Barbados swindle, either. They'd have wanted all the publicity they could get for that, to discourage the others. One's conclusion is that Brierley had been up to something which if it became generally known would thoroughly embarrass the British Government.'

'But he wasn't remotely interested in politics.'

'One doesn't have to be. We are now moving into what you might call my territory. If I may say so, Mabs, you yourself did not at the time give much impression of political awareness.'

'Lord, no. I was totally self-absorbed. I've just been reading some stuff I wrote about it soon after. A mass of things must have been going on—Korea, the Cold War, the King dying, Eisenhower getting elected, all that business with Mossadeq in Persia—but you'd hardly know from what I wrote that it had been happening at all.'

'The Cold War is the element that concerns us. You may have since gathered, Mabs, that I was not quite the dilettante Party member I made myself out to be at the time. I was, in fact, quite a hard-line Stalinist and was very well in with King Street. My function was that of an *agent provocateur*, really. I posed, I am sorry to say, as the kind of civilised chap to whom Party members with doubts might turn for advice, and I could then warn King Street—or in certain cases, Moscow—that they were no longer to be relied on. I tell you this to some extent to show good faith. You have put yourself in my hands and I am offering a reciprocal hostage. I have not so far admitted it to anyone else.'

'You didn't have to.'

'Well, I've done it now. What are you up to?'

'Eating a crumb of pie. Like your champagne. Sealed in blood.'

'Don't tell Fred or he will smother you with Levi-Strauss. Yes, I was, you might say, the traitor's traitor. But when Brierley took over at *Night and Day* I got a message from my control demanding an emergency meeting. He gave me instructions that I was to do all I could to find out the source of Brierley's funds. I assumed at the time that he believed them to emanate from the CIA, and that the object was to use *Night and Day* for crypto-propaganda purposes, as with *Encounter*?'

'Oh yes, that's what they were doing, but no one had told Stephen Spender.'

'Something like that. You may be amused to know that Dorothy Clarke is convinced that Brierley got his funds from the Kremlin, for the sole purpose of manoeuvring her out of her position and thus undermining the self-confidence of the British ruling caste.'

'Mrs Clarke! It *was* her who told you about me and Mr B!'

'Not exactly told. She's stood the years pretty well, but she's stone deaf now, almost. She misheard something I said and took it that I knew already. What do you think about her suggestion?'

'It must be nonsense, surely.'

'I think so. What about the CIA?'

'I don't think it was anything like that. I mean he wasn't getting *funds* from anywhere. Not a steady flow. He'd made a bit of money somehow and started gambling with it in the City and done well enough to persuade other people to let him gamble with theirs. He told me once that he lived by surfing an ever-breaking wave. I don't think there was ever money coming in that he could rely on.'

'My view entirely, and I think also my masters'. When I reported Naylor's appointment as editor as evidence of an incipient pro-Washington line, my control was not remotely interested. Again I think we can assume that my side thought that Brierley had been up to something that might embarrass the British Government.'

'But he hadn't anything to do with the Government.'

'Not then, perhaps, but in an earlier stage he had been in their employment, like a great many other men of his age. He had been a soldier. He had been on the staff of the British Control Commission in Germany. The morsel I have to contribute is that he was in the department concerned with the confiscation of Nazi-owned property and its return, where possible, to its rightful owners.'

'Was he stationed in Hamburg?'

'Don't know. Why?'

'That's where he used to go.'

'Was it, indeed? It would certainly fit in. There would have been excellent opportunities for corrupt officials to acquire property in Hamburg, and also to arrange for the owners to disappear and not come back.'

'Oh, God. He got money from the Jews.'

'Uh?'

'Something somebody said about Mr B.'

'Did they now? Can you tell me more?'

'I'm afraid not.'

'You see where this might lead us? The Cold War in full swing, West German democracy just staggering to its feet, to the accompaniment of bellows from the East that the Allies were deliberately reviving the menace of National Socialism in order to attack Mother Russia once more. Suppose it is now made public that a British official had, while still in Government employ, used his position to help Nazis to conceal their ownership of property, to realise their assets and to transmit funds after them. Look at the fuss there's been about Klaus Barbie, thirty years later. From what I learnt from my control it appears that my side may already have had wind of this as an opportunity to embarrass the British Government, a view with which Whitehall apparently concurred, to judge by their treatment of you after the shooting. It also strikes me as significant that Brierley was killed in South America, admittedly in a country which had a fair record for not harbouring war criminals, but tolerably neutral ground for parties who may not have much trusted each other, one coming up from, say, the Argentine and the other down from Barbados. Does the theory distress you, Mabs?'

'I don't know. I haven't had time to get used to it, and I'm not going to this morning. I shall have to be off in ten minutes, Ronnie. I'll tell you one thing, though. I simply don't believe in Nazi art-hoards. People didn't realise what that sort of thing was going to be worth. I know, because we have a phrase in my family about selling the Canalettos. We say it whenever some hideous expense crops up and we've got to find money to meet it, so I know what that sort of thing used to fetch. Mr B sometimes brought little objects back from his trips to Germany, and I think he may have sold quite a few at Sotheby's and places, but we're talking about hundreds of pounds, or thousands, not hundreds of thousands.'

'Oh, I quite agree. You've got to remember that until the last year or so those people didn't think they were going to lose the war. They might have got hold of a few bearer bonds, by way of insurance, but a corrupt middle-rank official, say, would be much more concerned to conceal what he was doing from the German authorities. He would cover his tracks by bureaucratic means. His loot would be shops and factories and houses and so on, absolutely valueless in 1946, but beginning to be worth something by the Fifties. Do you know, I think one might be able to construct quite a reasonable documentary out of all this. I wonder whether I have the energy.'

'Of course you have. It would be terribly interesting.'

'It would be particularly interesting, my dear Mabs, if you were to appear on it and tell the world in the discreetest of possible ways some of what you have just told me.'

'Ronnie!'

'Brood on it, my dear. As one who has some experience of public soul-baring, I can tell you that it can be a therapeutic experience. But we have drunk from the same cup and eaten from the same cold pie and I will keep faith. Kipling, in spite of everything, is still the only British writer fit to stand in the same room as Shakespeare. Oh, my dear Mabs, I am glad you came. I did my best to fight you off, you know. I should have known Fred was not much use as a Maginot Line against the Millett blitzkrieg.'

'I'm glad to hear it. I'm going to put the fear of God into him on my way out. I am also going to arrange for regular meals to arrive for you for the next fortnight, and for a doctor to come and look at your foot.'

'This is all quite unnecessary.'

'It's absolutely no use your making a fuss, Ronnie. I invariably get my way over things like this. Ask your friend Eric Martleby. I may say he is the kind of creature who arouses the tigress in me—a man who is barely fit to sell detergent powder trying to tell someone like you what he may and may not write! I've got to go now and watch this American chewing his way across a vast slab of beef and drinking black coffee with it, but next time I come you will be able to tell me exciting things about how you are getting on with your script.'

'You make me feel like Boadicea's husband.'

'Don't say that. I do feel a bit manic at the moment, but it's only because I think you've told me what I wanted to know.'

'Don't put much trust in my lucubrations. Journalists have a notorious weakness for detecting non-existent conspiracies.'

'I'll bear it in mind,' I said. 'You sound a bit livelier too, if I may say so.'

'Oh, yes, I think so. I'm glad you came, Mabs. I think I might very well give this thing a go.'

'If you don't you really are going to find out how it felt to be Boadicea's husband. I'll come and see you again in about a fortnight. I'll give you a ring first.'

'Right. Take it easy with Fred, Mabs. He's not a bad chap.'

VI

I shall never get used to Americans. My mogul turned out to be one of the absurdly over-civilised sort. He had a Dutch-sounding name but ordered in easy Italian a very well-judged meal at a restaurant where he was obviously a valued customer, and so on. But still there was that sense of almost manic competitiveness about him, as though doing these things was a way of scoring points in an immensely elaborate game. I suppose we all do that more or less, but the difference is that in his culture they seem to regard the game as actually winnable, whereas in ours it is more in the nature of a ritual, whose function, if any, we've somehow forgotten.

I didn't mind. In fact, being of a competitive nature myself I took part with gusto and the meeting was going extremely well until, with no reference to anything we'd been talking about, something in my mind clicked. A silly little discrepancy. 'He got money from the Jews, you know.' But Mrs Clarke believed that B got his funds from the Kremlin. So how had my mother known? Oh, there were lots of possible explanations, but it would be nice to tidy it up and not leave it to nag away.

I smiled at my American, widening my eyes to acknowledge the elegance of his latest score, whatever it may have been, and returned to the arena with zest. I had to let him win in the end, of course, for business reasons. We were both perfectly aware of that, but he was a magnanimous victor.

After luncheon I telephoned Ronnie for Mrs Clarke's address, then my agent to report on my luncheon and cancel my appointment with her for that afternoon, then Cheadle to say I would miss supper and be late home. A traffic warden, pad at the ready, was approaching my car when I reached it, marvellous omen. In fact the whole day seemed to be going with a cohesive impetus in my favour, and the thing was to let it take me, to surf the wave of good fortune. I had turned out to be rather good at surfing, thirty years ago.

You do not have much time to meditate on a surf-board, but in the lull of driving down to Haywards Heath it struck me that my behaviour was quite uncharacteristic of the person I am now. My ostensible reason for not checking with Mrs Clarke to see whether she was in was that I didn't want to have to cope with a very deaf and elderly person on the telephone, or to seem to make too much of my visit. It was better to turn up and pretend to have been in the neighbourhood, then see how the land lay. I was at least partly aware that this was only a pretext to myself and that I was for some reason acting in a manner which would have been quite normal for the girl who worked thirty years before on *Night and Day*. Certainly I felt quite light-hearted as I drove, though I now wonder why I failed to perceive that the sense of urgency, of the wave rolling onwards, must, though it felt like something happening outside me, really indicate a subconscious compulsion, a foreknowledge of the shore-line I was riding towards on that slowly darkening afternoon.

I started to wonder about Ronnie's theory. Not whether it was true, but whether it mattered. Certainly it mattered that the money which he paid for the repairs to the Banqueting Hall seemed to have come from the sale of Halper's Corner, and so morally and legally had belonged to B. No doubt the plantation had had a lot of misery and wickedness in its past, but the filter-beds of the generations had washed it clean. There was no taint now. The same could not be said of B's other finances. Those horrors had happened well within my lifetime. What did I feel about that? If it had been anyone else, perhaps . . . But he was like a boy who has unearthed pirate gold. As he carries the jar of ducats home he isn't expected to think of the decks slopping with blood and the screams of the women in the cabins. There has been a break, and the coins belong to no one. So though that money may have paid for my year of happiness, and therefore in a sense helped to shape me into what I am now, the awareness of where it had ultimately come from didn't seem to tarnish the afterglow.

The house was one of a row lining a wide undulating road, neither town nor country. A dark brick bungalow with an over-imposing roof-line, which made it look as though a two-storey house had been bodily shoved into the ground, leaving only the upper floor visible. I rang the bell and was answered by a screaming klaxon. I remembered Ronnie had said she was very deaf. There was no answer. I rang two or three times and then started to peer through windows. I tried the side-door in a narrow alley. It opened into a kitchen which showed obvious signs of recent use. Encouraged, I went out again and on down the alley, hoping to be able to attract Mrs Clarke's attention at one of the windows that side.

She was working in her garden. Even in the grey November light it was an attractive place, despite measuring only a few yards in each direction. Raised beds, to eliminate bending. Pincushiony plants nestling among layered boulders and a scree of chippings. A slanting birch, almost bare. Everything extremely tidy. Mrs Clarke, her dumpy body supported by a walking-frame, was picking birch-leaves one by one out of a tussock of heather. She had her back to me so I walked on at an angle until my movement caught the corner of her eye. She straightened and turned slowly, thumping her frame round to do so. Her head went back to the old familiar angle.

'My dear Lady Margaret,' she said. 'It is you, isn't it? This is a quite unexpected pleasure.'

Ronnie was right. Apart from the hearing-aid and the frame she had scarcely aged. Her white hair was done in smooth, perfect waves, her face fully made up, her pale blue eyes unclouded. She was wearing a tweed jacket and skirt. Only her pink rubber gloves struck an odd note. She pulled one of them off in order to turn up the volume of her hearing-aid.

'I'm sorry to barge in on you like this,' I mouthed.

'Oh, but do come in. I have thought of you so often. You find me in a weeny bit of a mess. I was just tidying up my dear little garden for the winter.'

She thumped herself across the pavement and opened a French window for me.

'I do trust you will stay for tea,' she said. 'I was just thinking how pleasant a cup would be.'

'Only if you'll let me help.'

'I'm tiresomely deaf, you see. I used to depend so much on my ears.'

'I said . . .'

'Certainly not, Lady Margaret. I make a point of doing

things for myself. It is the only way not to become a helpless old woman.'

She closed the window and thumped herself across the room towards the kitchen, leaving me alone. I felt immensely relieved, almost exhilarated. Anyone my age must wonder at times what kind of old person they will become. The constant company of someone in my mother's condition gives these speculations a prurient intensity, though Dr Jackson assures me that there is no hereditary element in my mother's senility. To see Mrs Clarke so obviously unconquered was a moral tonic. The walking-frame and the deafness actually helped. They made the ageing process superficial, consisting of disabilities that could be coped with provided the will remained steadfast. She had recognised me at once—not quite the feat it might seem, because of my not infrequent appearances on television; she seemed to have taught herself to lip-read; she took getting a tea-tray together without help for granted; she did her own garden.

This sense of enduringness was confirmed by the room itself. It was just what one would have found her living in thirty years ago, lime green and ivory, frills and satins, framed photographs on every shelf, no books but neatly piled magazines. The enormous television was of course a modern note, but to balance it there were the well-remembered escritoire and commode.

The largest photograph, on the commode, showed an elderly man, the smooth baldness of his scalp contrasting with a many-wrinkled face, eyes hard and small, white moustache cut like a soldier's. Father or husband? The soft, society-portrait focus seemed inappropriate to the forbidding sitter. Mr Clarke, I decided, taken in the late Thirties, when *The Social Round* was still a separate magazine from *Night and Day* and Mrs Clarke might well have coaxed her husband into sitting for one of her regular photographers. In that case he must have been twenty or thirty years older than she was. He looked something of a pirate, and evidently understood how to make money. An utterly different creature from B, though, just as she was from me.

I nosed along the main shelf, looking at other photographs. These were the type I remembered, her famous collection, taken at parties, race-meetings, Henley, Lord's, with a central figure often vaguely familiar to me as the parent of a girl or young man I had once known. All the pictures were auto-graphed by their central figure. I had picked one out and was looking at it when Mrs Clarke came back, more silently because she was using the tea-trolley instead of her walking-frame to support herself.

'My little collection,' she said. 'I'm sure you remember. I haven't room for them all in this tiny house, so many are in albums. Which one have you there?'

'Um . . . One of those impossible signatures I dimly re-member the face. Actually I was looking at it because that's Veronica Bracken, isn't it?'

Names are presumably harder to lip-read than ordinary words. Mrs Clarke had clearly not taken in what I'd said. She pulled a lever at the side of the trolley to lock the wheels so that she could steady herself with one hand and use the other for her eye-glasses to inspect the picture as I held it for her.

'Dear Lady Trufitt,' she said. 'Her Mary must have been a year or two older than you.'

'But that's Veronica Bracken,' I said, pointing.

Unmistakable. Not just a very pretty girl, but still to me somehow an embodiment. The photograph had been taken out of doors in high summer at what looked like a wedding reception, to judge by the men's morning suits. Lady Trufitt occupied the centre, a tall, plain, weather-beaten woman wearing a pill-box hat and veil which looked as though they had been modified from her hunting gear. Veronica was in the picture by accident, in profile, wearing a simple hat with a wide gauze brim, talking to someone outside the frame—a man, to judge by the tilt of her head. The animation and buoyancy of her beauty flowed at me from the photograph, not simply nostalgia though that was there too, not the pathos of knowing what happened to her later, but existing independently of any history, like a statue unearthed in the desert.

'Oh, yes, Veronica Bracken,' said Mrs Clarke. 'Veronica Seago now. Her husband seems to have done very well in the Air Force. He must be about due for his knighthood, but I am very out of touch these days. Now, my dear—I hope you don't

185

mind an old woman calling you that, it seems so natural in the circumstances—if you will sit on the sofa and just wait while I organise myself a little—people will try to help when it's really quite unnecessary—I manage very well . . .'

Indeed she did. By the time I had put the photograph back in its place and sat down she had pushed the trolley a few feet further, locked its wheels again, and with careful but obviously practised movements was working her way round to an upright wooden chair with sturdy arms, which she used to lower herself to sit. If any part of the process hurt her, she gave no sign.

'There,' she said placidly. 'Now if you don't mind I will just turn this little light on. It makes it so much easier to understand what you are saying if I can see you clearly. I do hope that is not too bright for you.'

A good two hundred watts beamed straight at me. Mrs Clarke became a shadow beside the glare. I took my sunglasses from my handbag and put them on.

'How sensible,' she said.

'I didn't think I'd need them again this year. Haven't these last two weeks been foul?'

'Have they? I always think the weather you remember depends so much on how you have been feeling. And I am a long way south of Cheadle. How is your poor dear mother?'

The extra adjective showed that she was not so out of touch as she claimed. I answered briefly and went on to a noncommittal account of the doings and prospects of my children. Then Jane, and then my other sisters. Under that light it was like an interrogation. Mrs Clarke's talent for euphemism had not deserted her; she seemed to know a good deal about Selina's rackety adventures, but merely remarked that it was often a little difficult for younger sisters to settle down.

She continued to demonstrate her competence in coping with age. She needed to support her wrist with her left hand in order to pour from the teapot, but did so without splash or spill. The trolley was neatly laid with china all from one set, a variety of biscuits in a pattern on their plate, a fruit cake. The teaspoons and silver milk jug had been recently polished. The tea was hot.

The simplest course seemed to be to plunge straight in.

'I have been talking to Ronnie Smith . . .' I began.

'Who, my dear?'

I mouthed the name.

'Oh, Ronald Smith. He came to see me about his history of *Night and Day*. I must confess I was very doubtful about telling him anything. If I had known in the old days what we have since learned I would have done my best to see that he was locked up. Of course he claims to have had a change of heart, but you cannot ever tell with these people.'

'I think it's genuine,' I said. 'I saw him this morning. He's in rather a poor way, I'm sorry to say, but I'm going to try and get him looked after. And he's had trouble with his publisher about the history, which means it may not get written after all.'

'An excellent project, though I must confess I would have preferred to see it in other hands. I could have told him a great deal about my dear husband's doings, but he seemed to me much more interested in that dreadful man Brierley. My dear, I need not tell you how often I have given thanks that the scales fell from your eyes in time.'

'If they did, but don't let's worry about that. There's something I particularly want to ask you, Mrs Clarke. It's why I came. I'm afraid it's still about Amos Brierley. I know at one time you were trying to find out all you could about him. I wonder if you know where he got most of his money from.'

'From the Communists, of course.'

'I see. But you didn't tell anyone?'

'I did not realise in time. My late husband's friends had told me that there was something peculiar. Money doesn't come from nowhere, you know, and people in the City are very clever about that sort of thing. I did know of course about that business in Barbados of which I told you, but that had not then produced any funds. No, it was only after they had him shot . . .'

'Who had him shot?'

'The Communists, my dear.'

'Why on earth?'

'Because he was trying to cheat them. They gave him money to turn my magazine into a weapon on their side, and he pretended to be doing that, but all he wanted was to make

187

money, and when he appointed Mr Naylor . . . I do not care for Mr Naylor, but he is certainly not a friend of the Communists. You see, he gave himself away. They shot him, of course. They do not know the meaning of pity or forgiveness.'

I was not as disappointed as one might think. The theory might be absurd, but the fact that she had remembered a brief and trivial conversation with me showed that her grasp of the past was remarkably precise. I wouldn't have known what she was referring to if I had not recently read my old manuscript.

'So you didn't tell my mother about the Communists because you didn't know then?' I said.

'I beg your pardon.'

Perhaps, because she had been seeming to follow the conversation with such ease, I had allowed myself to speed up too much. I repeated the question slowly and clearly.

'I never told your mother anything, Lady Margaret,' she said.

'Oh, I'm sorry. I thought you told my mother about Amos Brierley trying to work a currency swindle in Barbados.'

'No, my dear. I told you. I didn't tell anyone else.'

'Yes, I know you did. Well, you hinted at it.'

'I told you very explicitly.'

'All right. Perhaps my memory's not as good as yours. But my mother certainly seems to think you told her.'

'I never met Lady Millett except the once, at that party when your little book was published. Of course, as you know, she was kind enough to sign my photograph for me.'

'She didn't!'

I don't know why I should have reacted with such vehement astonishment to this trivial bit of news. Not only astonishment, but also the amusement always aroused when somebody well known does something totally out of character. There was a long silence. Mrs Clarke, I remembered, was used to studying faces for information.

'If I may say so, Lady Margaret,' she said, 'this is all very extraordinary. I am beginning to wonder why you have troubled to pay me this visit.'

As she spoke I heard vague sounds of struggle in the blackness beside the glare. Craning sideways and shading my eyes I saw that she had heaved herself to her feet and was looking around in a frustrated way as though not sure what to do next. I rose too and, now able to see her properly, realised that she wanted to move, but her walking-frame was in the kitchen and the trolley encumbered with tea things no longer stacked for safe transport.

'Can I help?' I said.

She didn't hear, so I moved and took her arm

'Oh, if you would be so good,' she said. 'It must be a misunderstanding. Perhaps I didn't hear you aright. Oh dear, how strange.'

I steadied her across the room. Her movements were less purposeful than I had expected, nothing like as doubtful as my mother's but tinged with the same kind of uncertainty. We stopped at the inner wall by a shelf covered with yet more of the collection. Below it was a closed cupboard.

'In there,' she said.

I opened the doors and found a double shelf of albums. I ran my finger along the backs until Mrs Clarke stopped me.

'That one, I think,' she said.

I heaved it out, then helped her over to the escritoire where I laid it down. She opened it and leafed steadily through the pages. Faces flipped by. Long dresses and short. Tiaras, toques, pill-boxes. Organdie, cotton, furs, silk. And there we were.

The picture was in fact dominated not by any of us but by a flower-urn from which erupted a structure of white lilies and roses and gypsophila, with white delphiniums rocketing up above. Before it stood the Milletts, my mother severe and slim in the middle and on either side of her two girls, distinguishable only by their dresses and the fact that one was wearing a showy necklace. Something about the lighting had brought out the Millett look more strongly than usual. The pig princesses. My mother's emphatic scrawl spread across the bottom.

'There,' said Mrs Clarke. 'I knew it was there. I knew I wasn't dreaming. Sometimes when you get old you aren't quite sure. You brought it to me. You said you realised you had been wrong about Mr Brierley. You said it was because of a picture you had found in a book. A picture of a little statue.

You said it showed that he was a terrible man, and you asked me to explain what I had been trying to tell you before. I don't normally repeat secrets, but I have had a very soft spot for you almost since the day we met. I told you all I had heard about Mr Brierley cheating his mother, as well as our own government, over a plantation in Barbados. What was its name, now?'

'Halper's Corner,' I said.

She didn't hear. I left the album where it was and helped her back to her chair. She was extremely shaky now. I held her hand and knelt in the glare of the light. I took a deep breath.

'I'm terribly sorry,' I said. 'I'd quite forgotten about the photograph. Of course I remember now. It's just that my mother gets very muddled, and the other day she was perfectly convinced she'd met you and you'd told her all sorts of things you hadn't told me. I usually pay no attention because she gets so confused, but she did seem very on the spot that morning, and I really wanted to get it cleared up. Of course you're right. You haven't forgotten anything. It's all my stupid fault.'

I don't think she understood. I couldn't see whether she was looking at me, but she clutched my hand in a rubbery grip and sighed.

'It's all right,' I said. 'You haven't done anything wrong.'

'There was something funny about you. It's troubled me sometimes. I don't know what. Of course you were very distressed, finding out what sort of man he really was.'

'Of course I was. It was a fearful shock.'

'That must have been it.'

She seemed to be getting back her confidence, and understanding what I was saying. I imagine that deafness imposes a considerable strain on the will, to force oneself into continuous attention to the fragmentary signals that come from beyond the barrier. Any little tremor or weakening, and communication is lost.

'May I ask you one more thing?' I said. 'You'll think it's a bit odd of me not to remember, but really I can hardly have known what I was doing during those weeks. It's something my mother said again. Did you tell me—when I came and brought you the photograph, I mean—did you say anything about Mr Brierley getting some money from the Jews?'

A long pause, then a shaky whisper.

'No, my dear. Oh, no. That was what you told me.'

It was a drizzling November dusk by the time I started home, with five hours' driving before me. There was no avoiding London so I went to the flat in Charles Street and gave myself an omelette while I waited for the last of the rush hour to clear, then drove north. I remember nothing of the journey. I was thinking about Jane.

An episode that in some ways has shaped my life more than anything I have so far recounted was my return to Cheadle after B's death. My mother managed to conceal her triumph and behave in a subdued and reasonable way. I believe that if I had turned to her for comfort she would have done her best to give it. Instead I turned, naturally, to Jane, and Jane refused. Not in so many words, but in all her behaviour; by boredom and irritation and distress; by finding errands for herself that took her out of my company; by seeing that there was some third person present; above all by withdrawing into her art, absorbed and unreachable, as she constructed a thing like a metal pterodactyl in one of the old coach-houses. (I found it a few years ago and had it set up as a kind of guardian demon at the entrance to the grotto, but the effect was so depressing that we have allowed it to be almost engulfed with Old Man's Beard.)

I have always put Jane's behaviour down to unwillingness to let herself be involved in my raw misery, a sort of moral squeamishness, disappointing but not really blameworthy. I now saw that there was a different explanation. All the women in the chain of information—Mrs Clarke, Jane, my mother, Aunt Minnie—must have at least suspected that B's death was the result of their activities. I don't know about Aunt Minnie, but I'm sure my mother would scarcely have turned a hair. Any outcome which suited her purpose would by that alone have justified all she had done to achieve it. Mrs Clarke was in a different position. She was, in her own cranky way, a moral person. But believing that it was I who had been the intermediary, I who had made the choice and had thus consented, so to speak, to B's execution, she might well have felt herself absolved. What had so shaken her in our recent interview was the possibility that there was something mistaken about that belief, that in trying to help me she had in fact betrayed me. But Jane, of course, had known. Determined on her own freedom, she had decided to help my mother break up the affair, but had been totally appalled by the result and unable to face me alone, knowing what she knew.

So, instead of Jane or my mother or any human, I had in the end turned to stone and wood for comfort. I can remember the exact moment. It must have been eight months later because I had given up my job and was living at Cheadle. A December morning after a lonely breakfast – my mother always had hers in bed. A bright, illusory sunlight from the east, no warmth in it at all. Frost still in the shadow of the avenue, mist on the fields beyond. I stood by one of the pillars of the portico, my skin prickling in the barely perceptible warmth. I stroked my fingers down the fluting of the pillar. The stone was icy, but it was what I wanted. I stroked it again with the accepting caress of a bride.

As you drive up the M1 you see Cheadle on your left, a mile away on its hill. When the road was built various protesting groups expected me to add my outrage to theirs and were disgusted with me when I said I welcomed it. I was right, both practically and aesthetically. Seen from the house the sweeping line adds interest to a dullish middle distance. Seen from the road the house stands almost clear above the Avenue and looks truly magnificent. It is a splendid advertisement, and almost free. Almost, because I pay for the floodlighting. This is timer-controlled and switches itself off when there is no longer enough traffic on the motorway to justify it, but I get the bonus sometimes of driving home in the dark and seeing my house as even its builders could not have imagined it, theatrically sharp-shadowed, apparently floating against the dark, at first only the portico, but then as one climbs from the Saturn fountain the vista steadily widening to reveal the full proportion of the wings.

I may at moments have given the impression that I would have preferred to live my life without ever having known Cheadle, let alone owned and run it. This is, of course, far from the case. I may have bouts of depression or frustration such as occur in any marriage, but Simon is right—I am still deeply in love with the place. I am not merely proud of it and proud of what I have done for it. It feeds me, fuels me, gives me real exhilaration and happiness. I am not so sentimental as to believe that the house has feelings, but if it had I am confident that it would think well of me. It would know I had done my best.

You spoil things by brooding on them, so I seldom allow myself consciously to think along these lines. But the night I came home after seeing Mrs Clarke I was deliberately looking forward to that last half-mile to restore my own energies, self-confidence, balance. In some ways the shock of realising what Jane had done had been less than that of seeing how easily Mrs Clarke's apparent serenity could now be broken. Sturdily though she seemed to have withstood the passage of time, one tremor was enough to shake the tower. If not my visit, then something else, soon. A heroic old age is no more use than a feeble one. I am a battler (a battle-axe, perhaps) and have told myself I shall be one always. The only benefit is to my own self-respect, but normally I think that a gain worth having. On the motorway I found myself becoming less and less sure.

I rounded the basin of the fountain and slowed to a speed at which some ancestor might have cantered up the grass beside the gravel. The rain glittered in my headlights, spoiling the effect, so I switched them off. The wipers slished to and fro. The wind gusted and bustled among the tree-tops. Huddled in my warm steel egg I floated gently towards my floating palace. It too seemed serene, untouchable, safe from the storm of years. The wings began to widen before me.

Then the floodlights switched themselves off, the palace vanished and I was driving blindly into darkness.

VII

John Nightingale found me. He was bicycling down the
Avenue in the dawn after spending the night with Maxine. It
must have been the very early stages of that affair for him to
feel the need to conceal his comings and goings. I had driven
into the statue of Ixion and was unconscious at the wheel,
having been there about seven hours. I dare say doctors always
tell one it was touch and go, unconsciously emphasising the
drama of one's recovery and their own part in it, but it is a fact
that Sally came home and was by my bed when I recovered
my senses four days later. I remember nothing between the
floodlights going out and my waking up and seeing her.

Nothing external, that is. On the other hand I remember
with great vividness—no, that is the wrong word, because
there were elements I cannot put a shape to, in particular the
people I shall refer to as *They* or *Them*—with great vigour, as
episodes of crucial importance in my life, certain scenes I saw
in my delirium. I am now going to try and recount them. Of
course this is an unreal procedure. They came to me in
disorganised and recurring fragments, probably more chaotic
than I can now know because of the way the still-dreaming
mind tries to shape the pictures it makes into coherence. But
it is not unreal in the sense of being irrelevant because they
were only dreams. One's memories of the real past are only a
special kind of dreaming, in which one makes mental pictures and tries to explain them into a coherent sequence; and
in this case the visions of my delirium retained for me on
waking a cogency just as great as if someone had told me that
he had documents which showed that B, while working on
the Control Commission in Hamburg, had made contact
with a group of men who . . . and so on. I have *experienced* my
own explanation in a way that I could not have done if
somebody had presented me with second-hand facts. This is
the way in which I came to know it, and so the natural way in
which to present it here, though tidied up and ordered into

sequence so as to satisfy the waking mind. I fully accept that it may not be true.

I was in a shabby, bleak office. A man in uniform sat at a desk with his back to me. I thought it was my father till he half turned and I saw it was B. He rose, fetched a file from a green cabinet, leafed through it, picked out a sheet and began to compare it with one already on his desk. He sat very still, but I loved him so much I could feel his tension, his excitement. He reached for a telephone.

I was walking through smashed streets. I could smell the sea. One of *Them* was my guide. I didn't dare look at him, though he spoke and joked like an ordinary person. He showed me rows of shops, broken and shuttered, a block of offices, an empty factory. From the way he talked about them I knew that they all belonged to him. Then we were in a quiet suburb where a gaunt man was hiding in the porch of a large house. For a moment I was rigid with his nightmare. My guide muttered to someone behind us and suddenly the porch was empty. My guide took a huge key from under the doormat and opened the door. There was the little bronze head on the table in the hall, and the screaming ivory saint in a niche, and the grey dead Christ. My guide switched on a lamp. The lamp-shade looked like Mrs Darling. My guide opened a safe, took out some engraved certificates and put them in his pocket. He was in a hurry. Suddenly he noticed me watching him and showed me his machine-gun. He said that if I ever told anyone he would come and shoot me till the blood ran down my petticoat.

I was back in the street of shops. Some were still boarded up but others were lit and busy. Through the door at the back of a butcher's I saw B talking to the shopkeeper. The man gave B some money, then came into the shop and tried to sell me a Dior dress. Over his shoulder I saw B divide the money into two piles, then, moving his hands like a conjuror, take a lot of notes off one pile and add them to the other, which he slipped into his pocket. He put the first pile into an envelope with stamps on it.

*

We were children, playing on the beach. B wore knicker-bockers. He put some money in a bottle and tried to float it out to sea, but the wind kept pushing it back. Whenever the policeman came by he had to pretend to be building a sand-castle, so that he could hide the bottle in the sand. I felt sad for him. The bottle wasn't heavy enough. I went to look for something to weight it down with. Mummy was unpacking a picnic. She'd brought the Cheadle silver. My necklace spark-led among it. I dropped my handkerchief and picked it up with the necklace inside. I didn't think Mummy had noticed. On the way back to the water I saw B on the far side of the groyne. He was looking at a drawing of a machine-gun, scratched in the sand. *They* must have been there while we were playing. As I came up he scuffed the drawing out with his foot, but I knew he was afraid.

A board-game in the nursery at Cheadle. Myself, B, the people I'd met in Barbados, *Them* on the far side of the table. I didn't know the rules. The board was a map of a treasure island, but it was like Monopoly because you had to get hotels built. *They* were impatient and angry because we'd lost the dice, but at last B found them. He was getting ready to throw and we were all very quiet with excitement when there was Nanny Bassett in the doorway and we had to shut the box up and hide it because you weren't allowed to play that game on a Sunday and she was going to tell Mummy. She stared hard at B, using Mrs Clarke's eye-glasses.

Jane was lying on the floor drawing a picture of Wheatstone. She drew a thin line going up from his head and I was just thinking of something silly to put in the speech-balloon when she turned the line into a noose and a gallows. I was furious. She ran out of the room and I followed her, pig-faced and shrieking. She ran to a tiny door and waited. I knew we weren't allowed in there but she pushed me through and there was Wheatstone, white as bone, hanging from a clothes-rack, dead but still screaming. Jane stroked his arm and said it was lovely.

Mrs Clarke's office, only the make-up table had been moved in and she was Art Editor. Jane had come to show her a portfolio of drawings, but she was wearing my gold dress and pretending to be me. First Mrs Clarke showed her a David Low cartoon of B in a grocer's shop, standing behind the counter. There were only a few small sugar-bags on the bare shelves. The bags had signs on them. Under the counter was an enormous bag with a $ sign on it. Jane showed Mrs Clarke the picture of Wheatstone hanging, and then she showed her a book with a photograph she'd copied it from. She put a speech-balloon into the drawing. It said, 'He got it from the Jews.'

Sir Drummond was chatting with the policeman on the beach. He showed him the Low cartoon. The policeman was very interested, but when Sir Drummond showed him Jane's drawing of Wheatstone he looked worried and hid the draw-ings under a rock. He saw me watching him and told me to go straight up to my bedroom and not talk to anyone. When I looked back from the sea-wall I thought I saw someone I didn't know take something from under the rock and carry it round behind the groyne.

I was at a glorious party which B was giving to say thank you for my necklace. All my friends were there, loving it, and I was totally happy until I realised I hadn't seen B yet. I pushed my way among the guests, searching and searching, till I came to the little door I wasn't allowed through. Still, I opened it and went in. B was playing bridge so I sat in a corner to watch the television. It was closed-circuit and I could see my party still going on. Then I realised that the other three bridge-players were *Them*, and it was vital they shouldn't see what B was spending their money on, so I used the remote control to change the programme. It was an old black-and-white film, a long line of men, women and children, naked, skeletal, edging towards a big building with no windows. I recognised the old man I had seen hiding in the porch in the smashed city. B looked up and saw what I was watching, and made one of his small, strong gestures to tell me to turn it off. I prodded and prodded at the control, but nothing happened.

B and I were sitting under an awning in a foreign street. I was parched with thirst. B had ordered champagne. He was doodling cartoons of *Them* on a paper napkin, glancing sideways over my shoulder as he did so, so that I knew *They* must be there, sitting at another table behind me. At last the waiter came with our drinks, and slid the bill under B's glass. B glanced at it, and his hand started shaking so much that he couldn't pour from the bottle. It was only orange squash anyway. B looked at me. He said, 'You're the only person I can trust.' He folded the napkin he'd been drawing on and slipped it into my handbag. The chairs scraped at *Their* table. I thought I was going to faint and put out my hand to touch his arm. He'd been getting up to go, but it was as if my touch had given him an electric shock. He sat down and told me to shut my eyes. Through the fog of my eyelids I saw him pick up my handbag, take the napkin out and put something else in. He stood up and walked away. I needed my handkerchief to blow my nose and stop myself crying, but when I opened my handbag all there was in it was a pair of my old school knickers. There was something wrapped in them. My necklace. If I ran after him and gave it to him then everything would be all right, but the catch had got hooked into the felted grey wool of the knickers. I wrestled to get it free. My name-tape was on the knickers. Huge red letters. M. MIL-LETT. If *They* saw that . . . The cloth seemed to smother me, billowing like a blanket. Far down the street *They* stood and waited in the glaring sun. B had vanished. He was in the hotel. I heaved and fought with the grey cloth. Light glinted from the hotel front as the revolving door began to turn.

I was in a strange, soft bed in a medicine-smelling room. The air was full of fog. All my body ached. Something was fastened to my head to stop my neck moving. My right eye was gummed shut. In a clear patch in the fog I could see a young woman with a brown face under a sort of cowl. She was leaning over me and holding my hands to stop me tearing at my blanket, but she saw me looking at her and smiled.

'He couldn't do it, you see,' I said. 'Not with me. Anything else. He'd gamble with anything. Except me.'

'Hello, Mums,' said the woman. 'Are you awake now?'

She had a slightly chi-chi accent to go with her brown skin.

I thought she was some kind of nurse, but she had one of those faces you feel you know in dreams. She was there so that I could tell her what I had seen. It was all lucid in my mind, like a book just after you have written it, all the connections and mechanisms linked and sliding in their grooves. I had to get it out before I lost it. I began to gabble. The woman made shushing noises but she couldn't stop me.

'It began in Hamburg,' I said. 'He was on the Control Commission after the war, getting Jewish property back to its owners. He came across some property, quite a lot of it, which had been very cunningly stolen. I think it must have been a whole group of Nazi officials, covering up for each other. He was in their shoes now, and he saw that if he went on covering up he could have some of the loot. They'd gone to South America, but they'd left a contact behind so he was able to get in touch with them. The property wasn't worth much then, with everything smashed after the war, but they could afford to wait because they'd taken trouble to see that all the real owners were dead. He was going to sell it for them when it became valuable again, and take a commission. That was his side of the bargain. Their side was that if he cheated them they would send someone to kill him.'

'Take it easy, Mums,' said the woman.

'He did cheat them, of course,' I said. 'He took more than his share. He needed the money to help buy *Night and Day* and things like that, but he thought it would be all right provided he paid them back in time. That's why he had a deadline. It was always difficult with exchange control. You weren't allowed to send money out of the sterling area. But he thought he could get round that by selling Halper's Corner. Barbados was in the sterling area too, of course, but he was going to sell it in two parts. There'd be the sale of the plantation to show the Treasury. Plantations were cheap then. It wouldn't be much. But he could use it as a cover for what he was doing at the bay, selling the land and joining in a deal to build a holiday hotel. All that would be in dollars, which he could use to pay the people in South America. It was quite safe provided nobody told the Treasury there was something funny going on. They'd find out if they started to investigate, but they didn't usually. That's why he was so careful about not spending more than our travel allowance in Paris—he didn't want to draw attention to himself, the way the Dockers did.

'It was all going along fine until Mummy found out about him and me and threatened to blackmail him. Then, suddenly, it was more of a risk. It wasn't because of Mummy knowing anything—it was because of Aunt Minnie being her best friend and Sir Drummond being a Director of the Bank of England. He thought it was probably still all right, but he began to get worried. He was such a coward, you see. When we went to Barbados he was screwing himself up to take the risk . . .'

I saw the woman's eyes leave me and look with a query in them at somebody on the other side of the bed. I couldn't turn my head that way to see who it was, but I wasn't in any case interested. I waited impatiently till she was looking at me again.

'Then I offered to sell the necklace,' I said. 'B jumped at it. I don't suppose it was worth everything he owed them, but a hundred and fifty thousand pounds was a lot then, almost a million now. It would have been an instalment. The point was it was small, so he could smuggle it out, and the sale wasn't on anyone's books, so the Treasury wouldn't know, and I had the replica to wear, so no one need realise it had gone. He could do the whole Halper's Corner deal in sterling and use the money to buy the necklace by paying for the roof. He did that because if he hadn't he would have been cheating *me*. It wasn't because of Mummy blackmailing him. She didn't know anything, not then.

'Mrs Clarke did, though. She'd picked something up on one of her West Indies tours, keeping her ears open, the way she used to. Isn't it odd she's the one who's gone deaf, and Ronnie's the one who's gone blind? She tried to warn me, and I told Jane, and Jane went to see her pretending to be me. Jane said I'd found out about the screaming saint coming from a Jewish collection—he never sold it because he knew it could be traced, you see—and that was why I'd turned against him. So Mrs Clarke told Jane about Halper's Corner, and Jane told Mummy about both things and Mummy told Aunt Minnie, and so on. Of course there wasn't anything to find out abou'

Halper's Corner, not any longer, but now it was the screaming saint and what had happened in Hamburg—that was
what really mattered. Our people started to investigate. They
must have asked questions in Hamburg, and somebody there
guessed why they were asking and told the people in South
America, and they sent for B.

'I wish I knew what I said or did when we said goodbye. He
was going to take the sapphires, you see, and suddenly he
decided not to. He'd written a letter to me, telling me all
about them, in case they turned nasty. He was terribly
frightened. But he thought if they knew there was someone
he trusted in England who knew about them, they wouldn't
risk hurting him. The letter was in the jigsaw. And then, at
the last minute, he changed his mind. They were *my* sapphires, you see. They were valuable because of that, because
of the Mary stone. If he was going to persuade them to take
the sapphires as an instalment, he had to explain what they
were worth, and that would mean telling them about me.
And then they might guess who he'd left the letter with, and
send someone to get rid of me. I told you, he wasn't prepared
to risk it. He got in a sort of panic and dashed off, hoping he
could talk them into giving him more time.

'Of course they were going to kill him anyway, whether he
took the necklace or not.'

I closed my eyes and tried to sink back into the dark. A
fearsome, throbbing pain started at the side of my neck. I
wondered whether it hurt as much as that, being shot. Slowly
the pain slid away and I opened my eyes again.

'He wasn't used to it, you see,' I said. 'If you're going to be
that sort of creature and live that sort of life, love is too
dangerous. You daren't love anyone, because then there's a
hostage. You've got to stay wild, with the whole world your
enemy. You mustn't let yourself be tame for anybody. It was
all my fault, letting him love me. There was only one of him
in the whole world, ever. Only one in all the world.'

'Marge even dreams romantic,' said Terry's voice. He was
the person I couldn't see on the other side of the bed.

'It's all true,' I said. 'Ages ago, but all true.'

'I keep telling her she wants to stop living in the past,' he
said. 'The only time is now.'

The woman glanced towards him again. Something charac-
teristic about the slant of her face made me see that it was
Sally. My heart leapt.

'It's better not to live in time at all,' she said.

VIII

I have implied that I do my stint of conducting visitors round Cheadle. This is not strictly true, because I don't have the time. But the fact that I *may* be acting as guide does encourage more parties to book than otherwise would; members of Women's Institutes and similar bodies are among my most loyal readers; they come clutching copies of my books for me to sign, a problem I have solved to my satisfaction if not theirs by selling autographed Cheadle book-plates in the souvenir shop, where they can also buy my books. I always buy up remaindered editions and find it immensely satisfying to be taking ninety per cent of the published price instead of the usual minuscule royalty.

Of course, parties try to book me as their guide. Within the limits of my own commitments I play fair, taking pot luck, although my own preference is for working-class pensioners, women with the print of time on them, brave poverty-weathered faces. I like the way they think that because they have paid their fee they have a right to their money's worth. I like their sense of acceptance of transience, which in itself has the quality of endurance, and echoes what I feel about my house. Sometimes these parties include splendid old ladies who used to be in service themselves and reminisce about backstairs life, the appalling long hours, the incredible restrictions on their freedom, the tiny wages, but in no complaining tone, in fact with a scholar-like sense of reconstructing lost ways of life. I prefer such groups to middle-class women who drop quiet hints to each other that in childhood they were at home in surroundings like Cheadle.

When I could walk after my accident I took on a bit more of this work, to show my visitors and prove to myself that I was now up to it. One Wednesday afternoon I had an outing from Dorset. A mixed bag from a market town, no trouble but not very interesting. The tour ends in the kitchens so that visitors have to go out through the shop, which is in the old brew-house. I had said goodbye to them and was waiting to see that they did all in fact leave when a woman came up to me. I had noticed her during the tour, younger than most of the others, plump but trim, wearing a too-smart pale violet coat and bouffant blonde hair, a style that would have better suited someone twenty years younger. But she carried herself with confidence and did not at all look as though she had sat in a coach all morning, had a picnic luncheon and then trailed for an hour round a huge house. I had noticed too that the other women showed the usual unconscious signs of deference to her, so when she approached me I assumed she was the President of their WI and was about to say thank you on their behalf. Then I saw she was clutching a book.

I had already explained about not signing autographs because of the time it takes and the need to be fair to other parties, so I was irritated that this apparently educated woman had not got the point.

'You won't remember me, Lady Margaret,' she said. 'I was so hoping it might be you. You see, a million years ago I lined up next to you at Queen Charlotte's Ball.'

'You're not Veronica Bracken!'

'How clever of you. I haven't forgotten, of course, but I didn't dream you'd remember.'

'You're Mrs . . . Seago now, isn't it?'

'Lady Seago, actually. Paul got his K in the New Year Honours.'

'Congratulations. He's still in the Air Force then?'

'It's too brilliant of you to know all this. How on earth do you do it with everything else to think about?'

'Oh, I suppose it's just one of the things that stick. After all, you were easily the most beautiful girl in our year. Or in any year ever, as far as I'm concerned.'

She looked pleased, and younger now. I could sense rather than see it was the same woman. Handsome, certainly, but of course the unbelievable bloom had gone. Still, an innocence remained that had been part of it.

'I've read all your books,' she said. 'I think they're marvellous. But I'm afraid this is still my favourite.'

She had been carrying it clutched between two hands in such a way that I hadn't had a clear sight of it, beyond noticir that it was a hardback and well worn. Nowadays my books go straight into paperback. When she lifted her left hand from the cover I saw that she had needed to hold it like that because it was falling to bits. It was *Uncle Tosh*.

I took it from her and leafed delicately through. It was like a child's favourite book. The very paper seemed to have been worn soft with perusal. The pages were torn, taped, stained I understood that I was holding a talisman.

'It's been all over the world with me,' she said. 'That's why it's in such a state. I read it whenever I'm low and it cheers me up. She's so wonderful, isn't she? I can't spell, either.'

I found it difficult to say anything. The rest of her party were milling gently through the brew-house door, but a few were glancing back, inquisitive. It is so easy to give in to cheap emotion. After all, people who dislike the kind of book I write say that my stock-in-trade is to trigger such automatic easy responses, and there's some truth in the criticism. All I can answer is that at that moment and in those circumstances I felt I was in the presence of one of those simple, pure, totally unconsidered expressions of something essential to human nature, such as you get in certain movements of children, and to which you respond with an emotion that may be easy but cannot be called cheap. If someone else had put that book into my hand I would have been interested, might have been moved, but not in the same way.

'Tell me about your family,' I said. 'Have you got one, I mean?'

'Oh, yes. Three boys. Two in the Air Force and David at Theological College.'

'That sounds satisfactory.'

'Luckily they've got Paul's brains.'

I thought I could imagine the relationship. Four thoroughly male men, and this little woman whom they managed to treat as half way between a pet and a person, but adored on that basis. Good for her.

'Didn't you want a daughter?' I said.

She frowned. It was a most charming expression, suggesting both the difficulty of the question and the difficulty of the process of thought. I could see that if I had been a man it would instantly have aroused my protective warrior instincts, a response almost as automatic as that of insects or birds to particular innate stimuli.

'Paul longed for one,' she said. 'I was never sure. It isn't easy for girls. I've had a lovely life, but then I've been terribly lucky. I could so easily . . . But of course you're different, Lady Margaret.'

She reached out for the book.

'I'll sign it for you if you like,' I said. 'Nobody's looking.'

'Oh . . . I only brought it to show you.'

Obviously she didn't want me to. I guessed that I seemed less real to her than the girl who had stood beside her at Queen Charlotte's, and that that girl in turn was less real than the purely imaginary Petronella. The book had properties of personal magic, which might be exorcised by my attaching my name—the counter-magic of a formidable middle-aged woman—to her key to the unicorn's garden where only youth belongs. She gazed up at me, apparently perfectly content.

'I mustn't keep the others waiting,' she said.

Fiction

GENERAL

☐ The House of Women	Chaim Bermant	£1.95
☐ The Patriarch	Chaim Bermant	£2.25
☐ The Rat Race	Alfred Bester	£1.95
☐ Midwinter	John Buchan	£1.50
☐ A Prince of the Captivity	John Buchan	£1.50
☐ The Priestess of Henge	David Burnett	£2.50
☐ Tangled Dynasty	Jean Chapman	£1.75
☐ The Other Woman	Colette	£1.95
☐ Retreat From Love	Colette	£1.60
☐ An Infinity of Mirrors	Richard Condon	£1.95
☐ Arigato	Richard Condon	£1.95
☐ Prizzi's Honour	Richard Condon	£1.75
☐ A Trembling Upon Rome	Richard Condon	£1.95
☐ The Whisper of the Axe	Richard Condon	£1.75
☐ Love and Work	Gwyneth Cravens	£1.95
☐ King Hereafter	Dorothy Dunnett	£2.95
☐ Pope Joan	Lawrence Durrell	£1.35
☐ The Country of Her Dreams	Janice Elliott	£1.35
☐ Magic	Janice Elliot	£1.95
☐ Secret Places	Janice Elliott	£1.75
☐ Letter to a Child Never Born	Oriana Fallaci	£1.25
☐ A Man	Oriana Fallaci	£2.50
☐ Rich Little Poor Girl	Terence Feely	£1.75
☐ Marital Rites	Margaret Forster	£1.50
☐ The Seduction of Mrs Pendlebury	Margaret Forster	£1.95
☐ Abingdons	Michael French	£2.25
☐ Rhythms	Michael French	£2.25
☐ Who Was Sylvia?	Judy Gardiner	£1.50
☐ Grimalkin's Tales	Gardiner, Ronson, Whitelaw	£1.60
☐ Lost and Found	Julian Gloag	£1.95
☐ A Sea-Change	Lois Gould	£1.50
☐ La Presidenta	Lois Gould	£2.25
☐ A Kind of War	Pamela Haines	£1.95
☐ Tea at Gunters	Pamela Haines	£1.75
☐ Black Summer	Julian Hale	£1.75
☐ A Rustle in the Grass	Robin Hawdon	£1.95
☐ Riviera	Robert Sydney Hopkins	£1.95
☐ Duncton Wood	William Horwood	£2.75
☐ The Stonor Eagles	William Horwood	£2.50
☐ The Man Who Lived at the Ritz	A. E. Hotchner	£1.65
☐ A Bonfire	Pamela Hansford Johnson	£1.50
☐ The Good Listener	Pamela Hansford Johnson	£1.50
☐ The Honours Board	Pamela Hansford Johnson	£1.50
☐ The Unspeakable Skipton	Pamela Hansford Johnson	£1.50
☐ In the Heat of the Summer	John Katzenbach	£1.95
☐ Starrs	Warren Leslie	£2.50
☐ Kine	A. R. Lloyd	£1.50
☐ The Factory	Jack Lynn	£1.95
☐ Christmas Pudding	Nancy Mitford	£1.50
☐ Highland Fling	Nancy Mitford	£1.50
☐ Pigeon Pie	Nancy Mitford	£1.75
☐ The Sun Rises	Christopher Nicole	£2.50

Fiction

HORROR/OCCULT/NASTY

☐ Death Walkers	Gary Brandner	£1.75
☐ Hellborn	Gary Brandner	£1.75
☐ The Howling	Gary Brandner	£1.75
☐ Return of the Howling	Gary Brandner	£1.75
☐ Tribe of the Dead	Gary Brandner	£1.75
☐ The Sanctuary	Glenn Chandler	£1.50
☐ The Tribe	Glenn Chandler	£1.10
☐ The Black Castle	Leslie Daniels	£1.25
☐ The Big Goodnight	Judy Gardiner	£1.25
☐ Rattlers	Joseph L. Gilmore	£1.60
☐ The Nestling	Charles L. Grant	£1.95
☐ Night Songs	Charles L. Grant	£1.95
☐ Slime	John Halkin	£1.75
☐ Slither	John Halkin	£1.60
☐ The Unholy	John Halkin	£1.25
☐ The Skull	Shaun Hutson	£1.25
☐ Pestilence	Edward Jarvis	£1.60
☐ The Beast Within	Edward Levy	£1.25
☐ Night Killers	Richard Lewis	£1.25
☐ Spiders	Richard Lewis	£1.75
☐ The Web	Richard Lewis	£1.75
☐ Nightmare	Lewis Mallory	£1.75
☐ Bloodthirst	Mark Ronson	£1.60
☐ Ghoul	Mark Ronson	£1.75
☐ Ogre	Mark Ronson	£1.75
☐ Deathbell	Guy N. Smith	£1.75
☐ Doomflight	Guy N. Smith	£1.25
☐ Manitou Doll	Guy N. Smith	£1.25
☐ Satan's Snowdrop	Guy N. Smith	£1.00
☐ The Understudy	Margaret Tabor	£1.95
☐ The Beast of Kane	Cliff Twemlow	£1.50
☐ The Pike	Cliff Twemlow	£1.25